"Starr is such a polished writer that once you start reading it's painful to tear yourself away."
    —*Time Out*

"Suffice it to say that fans of Roddy Doyle, James Sallis, Samuel Beckett, Irvine Welsh, Frederick Exley, Patrick McCabe, George Pelecanos, Ian Rankin, and Chuck Palahniuk will all find something to like, love, or obsess over in this stiff shot of evil chased with heart-breaking irony. Highly recommended."
    —*Booklist (on Bruen)*

"From the first page of this noir thriller, you know things are only going to get worse, but you can't stop reading."
    —*Newsweek (on Starr)*

"A Celtic Dashiell Hammett."
    —*Philadelphia Inquirer (on Bruen)*

"A throwback to the spare, snappy writing of Jim Thompson and James M. Cain."
    —*Entertainment Weekly (on Starr)*

"Raw and fiercely funny."
    —*Seattle Times (on Bruen)*

"The King of Noir is back. It doesn't get any darker or funnier than this…The best novel of the year!"
    —*Bookends (on Starr)*

"[An] amazing writer, who can blend the darkest situation with a wisecrack that provides the perception that links life with death…The dialogue is priceless…If you haven't discovered Bruen, it's time you did."
    —*Crime Spree*

When he got back to his apartment, Bobby went right to the second bedroom, which he had turned into a darkroom, and started developing the film.

About twenty minutes later, Bobby called the lobby and asked the doorman to send a maintenance guy up to his apartment. When the little Jamaican guy arrived, Bobby asked him to take out a big box from the back of his hallway closet.

"I thought you had a problem with your shower?"

"Yeah, well I don't," Bobby said.

He was a strong little guy, but the box was so heavy it took all his strength to carry it a few feet. He was out of breath.

"What the fuck do you have in there?"

"Oh, just some old clothes," Bobby said, handing him a crisp twenty-dollar bill.

When the guy was gone, Bobby opened the box, tearing off the layers of masking tape. Finally, he got it open and removed the bubble wrap. He had three sawed-off shotguns, a couple of rifles, a MAC-11 submachine pistol, two Uzis, some smaller guns, and a gym bag filled with boxes of ammo.

Bobby was sweating. He wheeled into the bathroom and splashed cold water against his face, then he stared at himself in the mirror. This was happening a lot lately—looking in the mirror, expecting to see a young guy, but seeing an old man instead. Maybe forty-seven wasn't old for some people, but it was old for a guy who'd spent four-teen years in prison, one year in Iraq, and three years in a fucking wheelchair.

It was time to get back to work...

BUST

by **Ken Bruen**
and **Jason Starr**

A HARD CASE **CRIME NOVEL**

A HARD CASE CRIME BOOK
(HCC-020)
May 2006

Published by

Dorchester Publishing Co., Inc.
200 Madison Avenue
New York, NY 10016

in collaboration with Winterfall LLC

*This book is a work of fiction. Names, characters, places, and
incidents either are the products of the author's imagination or
are used fictitiously, and any resemblance to actual events or
persons, living or dead, is entirely coincidental.*

ISBN 0-8439-5591-0

The name "Hard Case Crime" and the Hard Case Crime logo
are trademarks of Winterfall LLC. Hard Case Crime books are
selected and edited by Charles Ardai.

Printed in the United States of America

Visit us on the web at www.HardCaseCrime.com

For Reed Farrel Coleman, La Weinman (Sarah), and Jon, Ruth, and Jennifer Jordan, ro-bust friends

BUST

Raves For KEN BRUEN and JASON STARR!

"Ken Bruen has become the crime novelist to read. He is…revolutionizing the art of crime fiction."
—*George Pelecanos*

"Jason Starr is the first writer of his generation to convincingly update the modern crime novel…It might be new-school noir but like the classics of the genre it has a brutal escalation of tension, pungent dialogue, a hardboiled simplicity and grace. It's also darkly funny and a pure pleasure to read. As you race through it you realize that Jim Thompson has just moved to Manhattan."
—*Bret Easton Ellis*

"[Bruen has written] the most startling and original crime novel of the decade."
—*GQ*

"Starr has plumbed the shallows of his brittle characters and their selfish lives, depicting them in a hard-edged style that is clean, cold and extremely chilling."
—*The New York Times*

"Bruen confirms his rightful place among the finest noir stylists of his generation. This is a remarkable book from a singular talent"
—*Publishers Weekly*

"Starr paints it blacker than black, putting his compelling characters through the wringer before hanging them out to dry."
—*Kirkus Reviews*

One

People with opinions just go around bothering one another.
THE BUDDHA

In the back of Famiglia Pizza on Fiftieth and Broadway, Max Fisher was dabbing his plain slice with a napkin, trying to soak up as much grease as he could, when a man sat down diagonally across from him with a large cupful of ice. The guy looked nothing like the big, strong-looking hit man Max was expecting—he looked more like a starving greyhound. He couldn't have weighed more than 130 pounds, had a medium build, startling blue eyes, a thin scar down his right cheek, and a blur of long gray hair. And something was very weird about his mouth. It looked like someone had put broken glass in there and mangled his lips.

The guy smiled, said, "You're wondering what happened to me mouth."

Max knew the guy would be Irish, but he didn't think he'd be *so* Irish, that talking to him would be like talking to one of those Irish bartenders at that place uptown who could never understand a fucking word he was saying. He'd ask for a Bud Light and they'd stare back at him with a dumb look, like something was wrong with the way *he* was talking, and he'd think, Who's the potato eater just off the boat, pal? Me or you?

Max was about to answer then thought, Fuck that, I'm the boss, and asked, "Are you…?"

The man put a finger to his messed-up lips, made the sound "Sh…sh," then added, "No names." He sucked on the ice, made a big production out of it, pushing his lips out with the cube so Max had to see them. Then, finally, he stuck the cube in his cheek like a chipmunk and asked, "You'll be Max?"

Max wondered what had happened to no names. He was going to say something about it, but then figured this guy was just trying to play head games with him so he just nodded.

The guy leaned over, whispered, "You can call me Popeye."

Before Max could say, You mean like the cartoon character? the guy laughed, startling Max, and then said, "Fook, call me anything except early in the morning." Popeye smiled again, then said, "I need the money up front."

Max felt better—negotiating was *his* thing—and asked, "It's eight, right? I mean, isn't that what Angela…?"

The guy's eyes widened and Max thought, Fuck, the no-name rule, and was about to say sorry when Popeye shot out his hand and grabbed Max's wrist. For such a bone-thin guy he had a grip like steel.

"Ten, it's ten," he hissed.

Max was still scared shitless but he was angry about the money too. He tried to free his wrist, couldn't, but managed to say, "Hey, a deal's a deal, you can't just change the terms."

He liked that, putting the skinny little mick in his place.

Finally Popeye let go, sat back and stared at Max, sucking on the ice some more, then in a very low voice he said, "You want me to kill your wife, I can do whatever the fook I want, I own your arse you suited prick."

Max felt a jolt in his chest, thought, Shit, the heart attack his fucking cardiologist told him could "happen at any time." He took a sip of his Diet Pepsi, wiped his forehead, then said, "Yeah, okay, whatever, I guess we can renegotiate. Five before and five after. How's that?"

Bottom line, he wanted Deirdre gone. It wasn't like he could hold interviews for hit men, tell each candidate, *Thank you for coming in, we'll get back to you.*

Then Popeye reached into his leather jacket—it had a hole in the shoulder and Max wondered, Bullet hole?—and took out a funny-looking green packet of cigarettes, with "Major" on the front, and placed a brass Zippo on top. Max thought that the guy had to know he couldn't actually light up in a restaurant, even if it was just a shitty pizzeria. Popeye took out a cigarette; it was small and stumpy, and he ran it along his bottom lip, like he was putting on lipstick.

Man, this guy was weird.

"Listen closely yah bollix," he said, "I'm the best there is and that means I don't come cheap, it also means I get the whole shebang up front and that's, lemme see, tomorrow."

Max didn't like that idea, but he wanted to get the deal done so he just nodded. Popeye put the cigarette behind his ear, sighed, then said, "Righty ho, I want small bills and noon Thursday, you bring them to Modell's on Forty-second Street. I'll be the one trying on tennis sneakers."

"I have a question," Max said. "How will you do it? I mean, I don't want her to suffer. I mean, will it be quick?"

Popeye stood up, used both hands to massage his right leg, as if he was ironing a kink out of it, then said, "Tomorrow…I'll need the code for the alarm and all the instructions and the keys to the flat. You make sure you're with somebody at six, don't go home till eight. If you come home early I'm gonna pop you too." He paused then said, "You think you can follow that, fellah?"

Suddenly Popeye sounded familiar. Max racked his brain then it came to him—Robert Shaw in *The Sting.*

Then Popeye said, "And me mouth, a gobshite tried to ram a broken bottle in me face, his aim was a little off, happened on the Falls Road, not a place you'd like to visit."

Max never could remember if the Falls were the Protestants or the Catholics, but he didn't feel it was the time to ask. He looked again at the hole in Popeye's leather jacket.

Popeye touched the jacket with his finger, said, "Caught it on a hook on me wardrobe. You think I should get it fixed?"

Two

To be nobody but yourself in a world which is doing its best to make you like everybody else, means to fight the hardest human battle ever and to never stop fighting.
E. E. CUMMINGS

Bobby Rosa sat in his Quickie wheelchair in the middle of Central Park's Sheep Meadow, checking out all the beautiful young babes. He had his headphones on, Motley Crue's "Girls, Girls, Girls" leaking out, thinking that his own crew would love all these great shots he was taking. Man, these chicks must've been starving themselves, probably doing all those Pilates, to look this good. Finally, he saw what he was looking for—three thin babes in bikinis lying on their stomachs in a nice even line. They were about thirty yards away—perfect shooting distance—so Bobby took out his Nikon with the wide-angle lens and zoomed in.

He snapped about ten pictures—some whole-body shots and some good rear shots. Then he wheeled toward the other end of the Sheep Meadow and spotted two blondes, lying on their backs. From about twenty yards away, he snapped a dozen boob shots, saying things to himself like, "Oh, yeah, I like that," "Yeah, that's right," "Yeah, right there baby." Then, right next to the blondes, he spotted a beautiful curvy black chick, lying alone on a blanket. She was on her stomach and the string on her bikini bottom was so thin it looked like she was naked. Bobby went in for a close-up, stopping about five yards behind her. He snapped the rest of the roll. He had another roll in the jacket of his windbreaker, but he was happy with the shots he'd gotten, so he pushed himself out of the Sheep Meadow, on to the park's west drive.

A panhandler came up to Bobby, with that annoying sad-eyed yet pissed-off look that all homeless fucks had. The guy looked strung out and the smell of piss, sweat and booze made Bobby want to puke.

"Got a few bucks, buddy?"

With the headphones on, Bobby couldn't hear him, but he could read the guy's lips. He gave him a long stare, thinking there was no way in hell some scumbag like this would have had the balls to come up to him back in the day. Just then, the Crue went dead, right in the middle of "Bad Boy Boogie," as the cassette got mangled—cheap rip-off piece of shit he bought on the street in Chinatown, what, ten years ago? He tore the crap out of his Walkman, thinking he had to go current, get one of those iPods. Then he flung the messed-up tape at the guy, spat, and said, "Here's some Crue. Broaden your fuckin' horizons, jackass...and take a fuckin' shower while you're at it."

The guy stared at the tape, stammered, "The fuck am I gonna do with this?"

Bobby smiled, not giving a shit, and said, "Stick it up your ass, loser."

And then he continued up the block, cursing to himself and at the people he passed. Nine ways to Sunday, Bobby Rosa had attitude, or in the current buzz jargon, he had *issues*.

When he got back to his apartment on Eighty-ninth and Columbus, Bobby went right to the second bedroom, which he had turned into a darkroom, and started developing the film. The three chicks in a row came out great, but the pictures of the black babe were Bobby's favorites. Somehow the woman reminded him of his old girlfriend, Tanya.

Bobby added the tit shots to the collection in his bedroom. He had three walls covered with Central Park boobs, taken during the past two springs and summers. He had all shapes and sizes—implants, flat chests, sagging old ladies, training-bra teenagers—it didn't matter to him. Then he had an idea, and said out loud, *"The Hot Chicks of Manhattan."* It had a nice ring to it; he could see it as a coffee table book. He could make a few bucks on the side and it was kind of classy too. Rich assholes would have it out right next to their champagne and caviar. Then, laughing to himself, he took the ass shots and added them to his collection in the bathroom. Next, he went to his shelf, grabbed another tape, *The Best of Poison*. Letting "Talk Dirty To Me" rip, he leaned back in his wheelchair, admiring his work. He bet, if he wanted to, he could sell his pictures to some classy art magazine, one of those big, thick mothers you have to hold with two hands.

After a few more minutes of staring at the walls, Bobby looked at his watch. It was 2:15. He realized it was past his usual time for his bowel routine. So he went into the bathroom and transferred himself onto the bowl. As he dug his index finger into the jar of Vaseline he laughed out loud, asked, "This suck or what?"

About twenty minutes later, Bobby called the lobby and asked the doorman to send a maintenance guy up to his apartment. When the little Jamaican guy arrived, Bobby asked him to take out a big box from the back of his hallway closet.

"I thought you had a problem with your shower?"

"Yeah, well I don't," Bobby said.

He was a strong little guy, but the box was so heavy it took all his strength to carry it a few feet. He was out of breath.

"What the fuck do you have in there?"

"Oh, just some old clothes," Bobby said, handing him a crisp twenty-dollar bill.

When the guy was gone, Bobby opened the box, tearing off the layers of masking tape. Finally, he got it open and removed the bubble wrap, getting a head rush when he saw his weapons. He had three sawed-off shotguns, a couple of rifles, a MAC-11 submachine pistol, two Uzis, some smaller guns, and a gym bag filled with boxes of ammo. No two ways about it—you got hardware, you got juice. Suddenly the world took on a whole other perspective: Now you called the fucking shots. Poison were into "Look What the Cat Dragged In" and he thought, Man, this is it, guns and rock 'n' roll.

He took one of his favorite handguns out of the box, a .40 millimeter Glock Model 27 compact pistol. The "pocket rocket" didn't pack the power of a shotgun or a Mag, but he loved the black finish. Holding a gun again gave Bobby the same buzz that it always did. The only thing better was firing one, feeling that explosion of power coming out of his body. He'd had a lot of women in his time, but given the choice between a woman and a gun he'd take the gun. It didn't talk back and it got the job done, plus, it made you feel like a player and you didn't have to reassure the motherfucker.

Aiming out the window, Bobby zeroed in on a pigeon that was sitting on the ledge of a building across the street. He felt the muscles in his index finger starting to twitch. He'd always been a great shot, practicing on the range down on Murray Street in between hold-ups. "Bang," he said out loud, imagining the bullet exploding through the bird's brain.

Bobby was sweating. He wheeled into the bathroom and splashed cold water against his face, then he stared at himself in the mirror. This was happening a lot lately—looking in the mirror, expecting to see a young guy, but seeing an old man instead.

He muttered, "How'd that happen?"

He used to have thick black hair, but lately his forehead seemed to be getting bigger and bigger, and he had more gray in his hair now than black. He'd grown a beard over the winter, hoping it would make him look younger, but no luck there—it had come in mostly gray too. He used to only get wrinkles around his mouth when he smiled, but now he had them all the time, and the circles under his eyes were getting so dark it looked like he was going around with two permanent shiners. Although his arms and shoulders had gotten big from pushing himself around, his legs had shriveled up to almost nothing and he had put on a gut. Fucking brews, man—they kept you trucking but blew you out.

"What're you gonna do?" he said.

Maybe forty-seven wasn't old for some people, but it was old for a guy who'd spent fourteen years in prison, one year in Iraq, and three years in a fucking wheelchair.

It was time to get back to work.

Three

Bust: A sculptured representation of the upper part of the body / to break or burst / to raid or arrest.

Angela Petrakos was raised in Ireland till she was seven and then her father packed them up, took her and her mother to America, saying, "Enough of this scraping and scrimping, we're going to live the American dream."

Yeah, right.

They wound up in Weehawken, New Jersey, living in what they call *genteel poverty*. "They" must be rich because Angela had never heard a poor person use words like that. Angela's mother was a pure Irish woman— mean, bitter and stubborn as all hell. She called herself a *displaced Irishwoman*. When she said this, Angela's father would whisper, "She means she hates dis place." Her father was born in Dublin, but his family was Greek, from Xios. Angela's Mom was from Belfast and constantly bitched about the huge mistake of marrying a Southerner with Greek longings. When Angela was a teenager, her mother went on and on about the glories of Ireland. All types of Irish music—jigs and reels, hornpipes and bodhrans—were shoved down Angela's throat, and a huge green harp hung on the kitchen wall. Angela's father, meanwhile, wasn't allowed to play Theodrakis or any of the music he loved, and Angela never even heard *Zorba's Dance* until she was twenty. When the micks lay down the rules, they're laid in granite—it was no wonder they'd coined the phrase *No surrender.*

All the songs of rebellion, the history of the IRA, were drilled into Angela's psyche. She was programmed to love the Irish and her plan was to go to the country and have an affair with Gerry Adams. Yeah, he was happily married, but that didn't ruin her fantasy; actually, it fueled it. Despite her years in America, she had a slight Irish accent. She liked the way she spoke, was told she sounded "hot" by the older guys who tried to pick her up—they often succeeded—when she was in junior high and high school. She went to technical college and learned Excel and PowerPoint, but she knew her real talent was seduction. By the time she was twenty, she'd learned all about the power of sex.

She worked her way through the crappy jobs and a string of asshole boyfriends. Angela wasn't pretty in the conventional sense but she knew how to use what she had and, by Jesus, she used it. She was medium height with brown eyes and brown hair, but she changed all that—went blond, went blue eyed, went wild. She got a boob job, contacts for her eyes and already had the attitude. Then her mother died and they cremated her—her father said he wanted her burned, "lest she return." Angela got the ashes, kept them in an urn on her bookcase. When *Angela's Ashes* came out she rushed out and bought the book, thinking it had to be some kind of sign or something. She didn't bother reading it, but liked having it on her shelf. Other books she bought but never read included *'Tis* and *A Monk Swimming*. She also had some DVDs like *Angela's Ashes*, *Far and Away*, and *The Commitments*. When it came to music, only the Irish stuff really did it for her—Enya, Moya Brennan and, of course, U2. She would've stepped on Gerry Adams to get to Bono.

Most of her money went on clothes. The most basic lesson she learned was that if you wore a short skirt, killer

heels and a tight top, guys went ape. Her legs were good
and she knew how to hike a skirt to really get the heads
turning. She saved her money and went online to book a
week in Belfast, brought the urn with her—which caused
some commotion with Homeland Security, but in the end
she was allowed to bring her Mom if she stashed her in
freight, which she did. She stayed at the Europa, the
most bombed hotel in Europe—that's what Frommer
said anyway—and the customers were pretty bombed
themselves. The city was a shithole—drab, grey, depressing—and the Sterling, what was the deal with that?
And people kept getting on her about Iraq, like she had
any freakin' say about it. She did all the sightseeing
crap—maybe seeing blown up buildings did it for some
people, but it bored the hell out of her. When she threw
her Mom's ashes into the Foyle there was a wind, of
course, and most of her mother flew back into her hair.
When she told the old guy at the hotel desk what had
happened he said, "Tis proof, darling, that the dead are
always with us."

Evenings, she ate at the hotel and had drinks at the
bar. She didn't want to go out, not because she was
afraid but because she couldn't understand a goddamn
word anyone was saying. The bartender hit on her and if
his teeth hadn't been so yellow she might have been into
it. For the first time in her life, she felt American and
that Ireland was the foreign country. The blended
accent that got her so far in New York seemed useless
here.

Her second-to-last night, she was sitting at the bar and
a drunk began to hassle her. The bartender, of course,
didn't help. The drunk had a combat jacket, sewage
breath, and was going, "Ah come on, you want to suck me
dick, you know yah do."

It took her a while to actually figure out what he was

saying because of the accent; it sounded like, "Orr...kom on...yer want to truck meh duck."

Finally, she put it all together. Before she could react, a man appeared out of nowhere, grabbed the guy by the front of the neck and had him out of there in no time. Shaking, she tried to put a Virginia Slim into her mouth, and the bartender raced over, flicked a bic, and said, "There you go."

She accepted the light as she wanted that hit of nicotine then blew a cloud of smoke in Yellow Teeth's face, said, "And there *you* go you spineless prick."

Unfazed, the bartender said, "I love it when you talk dirty."

The other man had returned and now stared at the bartender, and said "Leg it shithead." Then he turned to her, asked, "You okay missus?"

She could understand him, because he was from the Irish Republic and had soft vowels, sounding kind of like her Dad. He had a scar on his face, long grey hair and was as thin as the guys on Christopher Street. His lips were mangled but, hey, he was the first guy in the whole damn province she saw with good teeth. And the lips were kind of sexy anyway. They'd be strange to kiss, but they'd be great for other things. Maybe it was the near violence but she felt a raw sexuality oozing off of him that was so freaking irresistible. One thing that got Angela hot was danger and this guy reeked of it.

She felt a burning rise up her neck, spread to her face, and said, "Wow, I'm so, like, grateful. Can I buy you a drink?"

He smiled then said, "Jameson." He said it like a Hollywood tough guy, no bullshit with *please* or *ice*. No, just the one word, with a slight hard edge, the implication being, bring me the drink *now* and don't even think about fucking with me.

She asked, "Are you, like, for real?"

He parked his ass on the stool next to her, said, "The heart wants what it cannot hold."

Jesus, she thought, poetry and violence, how could a girl resist? The Irish might know shit about cool but they sure as hell knew how to talk.

And she loved his voice, deep, devilish, and, yeah, sexy.

With a little of the same flirty tone, she said, "You want that on the rocks?"

He gave her the look she would get to know and not always love, and said, "I take everything…neat."

He put his hand in his jacket, took out a slim book and she saw the title, *The Wisdom of Zen*. She was impressed that a guy like him was carrying around a deep book like that.

He asked her, "You like The Pogues?"

She thought, Screw them, I like you.

Four

Never do evil, always do good, keep your mind pure—
thus all the Buddhas taught.
THE DHAMMAPADA

Max screamed, "To hell with you, you crackpot!" and slammed the phone as he hard as he could and banged the desk with his fist. A moment later, he felt a jolt in his chest. Thinking, *Fuck, I'm dying*, he searched his jacket pockets for his Mevacor. Then he remembered he'd already taken his pills today but now feared that the Mevacor was interacting with his Viagra, causing some kind of reaction.

He was about to call Dr. Cohen, that jerk-off, back but he decided, What's the point? So far nothing that schmuck suggested had worked. Max took all the goddamn drugs he was supposed to, had even hired an Indian named Kamal to come over to his house a few days a week to cook macrobiotic meals. But his HDL-to-LDL ratio was eight-to-one, up from seven-to-one at his last check-up, putting him in the super-high-risk group for heart disease. Right now, he could feel his heart working on overtime, the pump already on its last legs.

To help relax, Max did a yoga breathing exercise that Kamal had taught him, inhaling and exhaling through alternate nostrils, but it didn't do crap. He made a mental note—fire Kamal, that Indian bastard, as soon as he comes back from his vacation. *Taj Mahal that, you little prick*.

There was a knock on Max's door.

Max yelled, "What?"

The door opened slowly and Harold Lipman, Max's new Networking Salesman, came into the office.

Lipman said, "Esc—" and Max said, "Not now."

"I just wanted to ask—"

"I said not now!"

Lipman left and Max went right to his office bar and made a vodka tonic. Ah, Max loved his office, the only part of NetWorld that he'd remodeled. Besides the mahogany bar, he'd paneled the walls, installed brand-new carpeting, and bought the most expensive desk and swivel chair available in the Office Depot catalogue. He figured it made a statement, that here was a hip guy, not showy, but with refined taste and a serious edge. You saw the office, you saw a guy who probably had drinks with the Donald, though not often because Max was "too busy." The office had no view, but elegant beige curtains concealed the windows. Behind his desk hung a custom-made picture of a blonde with Pam Anderson-size breasts sitting on a red Porsche. Inscribed on the car was the company motto, NETWORLD OR BUST.

The booze soothed Max enough so that he was able to concentrate on the important stuff again, like money. Over the past two days, Max had put away ten grand in his private safe. He had made small withdrawals from all of his bank accounts—corporate and private—and from his brokerage accounts where he had cash balances. But the bulk of the money, about seven grand, had come from the office's petty cash. Max thought this was a great idea because if the police investigated there would be no withdrawal slips or any other way to prove he'd hired a hit man. And fuck that crazy mick's demand for small bills—the money was mostly fifties and hundreds. What was he going to do, turn it down? Yeah, like that was going to happen.

As Max poured his second vodka tonic, there was a soft knock on the door, a pause, followed by a louder knock.

Max recognized the signal and said in his sexiest voice, "Come in, baby."

As usual, Angela looked dynamite. She was wearing shiny black boots, a short red skirt tight enough to see her butt-cheeks, and a lacy camisole. She had big blow-dried hair and was wearing the diamond stud earrings that Max had bought her at Tiffany's last Christmas.

"You had two messages while you were on the phone," Angela said, the soft Irish vowels driving him crazy.

"Fuck the messages. How about you put those magic little hands of yours to work?"

Angela locked the door and came up behind Max at his desk. Max breathed deeply, moaning, "Oh, yeah, that feels so good," as Angela worked the muscles in his neck and shoulders.

"You have a lot of knots today," Angela said.

"I bet my blood pressure's shooting through the roof too."

"Was that Dr. Cohen you were screaming at?"

"Who else? I swear, I don't know how that jerk-off got a license. You know what that asshole told me? That I should start eating brown rice. Like the bacon, the fried chicken, the shrimp, the pizza—that's not killing me. It's the fuckin' white rice."

"Calm down," Angela said. "You have to learn how to relax, not let the stress get to you. In Ireland we say, *Na bac leat.*"

The fuck was she talking about? He asked, "The fuck're you talking about?"

She said calmly, "In American...*No biggie.*"

Max exhaled, then took a long, steady breath. Angela was wearing some of that perfume called Joy he had bought her last month at Bloomingdale's. Max couldn't tell whether it smelled nice or not, but it had cost five hundred bucks an ounce so he figured it must be pretty good.

"You should be careful," Angela said, "screaming in the office like that. Everyone could hear you."

"So? If they don't like it they don't have to work here."

"Yeah, but I don't think it's a good idea to, like, yell like that. I mean people could remember. They'll tell the police 'Come to think of it, Max was kind of acting crazy lately.' "

"But I act crazy all the time, I'm a crazy kind of guy, it's part of my appeal."

"I'm just saying—it's probably not a good idea."

"Eh, you're probably right," Max said. "You know what else Cohen told me? He said I'm fat."

"I love your belly."

"Yeah, well, Cohen says it's unhealthy. He showed me some chart that said I'm obese for a man my height and age. Meanwhile, you should see the size of that asshole's gut."

"How does that feel?"

"Nice. Real nice."

Angela spun Max around in his chair, kissed him on the lips, then Max whispered, "I just want all this shit to be over with already. Last night I had a dream she was dead. The ambulances were there and they were carrying her out of our house, covered by a white sheet, and you know what? It was the best dream I've ever had."

"You shouldn't talk about her that way," Angela said. She had her hands behind Max's head, gently rubbing her fingers through his thinning hair. He was glad she was touching the back of his head, where he still had some hair left. "You know what they say—if you say things about your first wife you'll say them about your second wife too."

"You and Deirdre have nothing in common, sweetheart."

"That's what you say now, but in twenty years you might be paying to have me killed."

"I'd be lucky if I lived another twenty years."

"You're not denying it."

Holding her head steady and looking right into those fucking beautiful light blue eyes, Max said, "I love you. You think I ever went around telling Deirdre that I loved her?"

"You still didn't deny it."

"I deny it, I deny it," Max said. "Jesus Christ."

Angela smiled. Max kissed her then said, "You know, the only thing I'm worried about is this Popeye character."

"Why?" Angela asked.

"First of all, I don't like his name."

"What's wrong with his name?"

"Come on, it's a fucking cartoon character. It's like I'm hiring Donald Duck to kill my wife."

"You can't expect him to use his real name. I mean, he has to protect himself, doesn't he?"

"Yeah, but couldn't he come up with something better, more hitman-like. I don't know, like, Skull, or Bones, or something like that."

"You can't judge somebody by their name."

"Eh, I guess you're right. And I guess we've gotta assume he's good at what he does or your cousin wouldn't have recommended him, right? God knows the guy's crazy enough to kill somebody. You should've seen the way he grabbed my arm."

"So what're you worried about?"

"I don't know, it's just a vibe. I just got a feeling the guy's fucking around with me somehow. And I don't like the way he changed the terms. It was supposed to be eight, then he made it ten. That's no way to do business with somebody."

Angela held Max's hand, said, "Don't worry. I mean, it's only another two thousand. It's not like he asked for twenty thousand."

"Yet," Max said. "I got a feeling this guy thinks he's got me by the balls or something. That's how he comes off, like he thinks he's in control. You know what he called me? He called me a 'suited prick.' Asshole. And I couldn't stand looking at him, either. Those disgusting lips."

While he spoke, Max was massaging Angela's breasts. He loved her breasts—they were the main reason he'd hired her. He'd always been a breast man. Even Deirdre had big breasts, although they were starting to sag below her stomach.

"This is probably a bad idea," Max said as Angela started to kiss his neck. "Tonight has to be our last time for a while."

"I can't wait till we can be together all the time," Angela said.

"Ditto," Max said. "But until then, let's just try to keep things as quiet as possible around here."

For the rest of the day, Max and Angela went about their business. Amazingly, they'd managed to keep their affair a secret from everyone in the office. Around other people, Max was always very formal, asking Angela to send faxes, take messages, bring him coffee, order in lunch and other crap that presidents of companies ask their executive assistants to do. They never went out to lunch together or left the office together at night. If they were planning to meet for dinner, Angela would always leave first and then Max would meet her at a specified location. As for the times they fooled around in Max's office during business hours, it wasn't unusual for an executive assistant and her boss to be in the boss's office together with the door locked.

At eleven o'clock, Max had his weekly meeting with Alan Henderson, his CFO, and Diane Faustino, the Payroll Director. They went over the company's payroll and budget and talked about expanding the company website and the need to hire two more Senior Networking Technicians. Max also told Alan that he wanted to reward his employees with a ten-percent raise next year, and sent out a memo about this pronto, thinking at least no one could say he wasn't in a good mood a couple of days before his wife was murdered. Besides, he loved giving raises, the surge of power it gave him, that he could make or break these assholes.

That evening, when the last person had left for the day, Angela locked the front door, and came into Max's office. Max was already naked, lying on his back on his office couch, doing Kamal's breathing exercise. She turned down the lights. It was almost dark, the only light coming through the window curtains. She took off her clothes slowly, moving the way Max liked, like she was a dancer at Legz Diamond's, the strip club on Forty-seventh Street where he took his clients. Finally, she took off her bra, climbed on top of Max and gave him some nice warm kisses. Then she slid down and ran her tongue over his thick gray chest hair. As she dipped further, Max grinned, thinking, Who the fuck needs breathing exercises?

Afterwards, holding her tightly, feeling especially close, Max said, "Let's get married."

"We're going to get married."

"I mean right away."

"But we'll have to wait *some* time. I mean it would look suspicious if we did it too soon, wouldn't it?"

"What difference does it make? Just because my wife is murdered I have to spend my whole life in mourning?"

Angela thought about this for a moment, then said, "Yeah, I guess that's true."

"There's another thing I want to talk about—kids. I've always wanted a little Max Jr., just not with Deirdre. What do you think about being a full-time mommy?"

"I'd love it."

"Well, I want to do that right away too—while I still have some good seed inside me."

Later, while they were getting dressed, Max interrupted whatever the hell Angela was saying, said, "Ange, there's something I wanted to ask you. I don't really know how to say this. I mean I don't want you to get offended or anything. I don't think you will but—"

"What is it?"

"It's stupid, really, but…"

"What?"

"It's just…have you ever thought about adding another cup size to your tits?"

Looking down at her implants, she said, "Why? You think they're not big enough?"

Max said, "I didn't say that. I just asked you if you ever thought about it before, that's all."

"They're already thirty-eight D's. Why, you're serious? You really don't like them?"

"I didn't say *that*. I just didn't want you to think there was something you couldn't have if you wanted it."

"That's really nice of you…I guess."

"I'm not saying that bigger tits are something that you necessarily need." Max wound on his tie, trying to come up with perfect way to explain it. He came up with, "I mean, I want you to have everything you want in life, whether it's a gold necklace, a beautiful dress, a trip around the world, or great tits."

Strapping on her bra, Angela said, "You really think it would make me look better, huh?"

"Not necessarily *better*, but I don't think it could hurt. Anyway, sleep on it. Although I don't mean that literally." He laughed to himself, then said, "By the way, did you make that dinner appointment for me tomorrow night?"

"Yes. With Jack Haywood."

"Good. I'll have to take him out to some busy restaurant,

maybe some Italian place on the Upper East Side. They have all those little restaurants around Second Avenue."

"There're a lot of bars up there, too."

"I don't know, I'd look pretty stupid—an old guy like me in some singles bar."

"You're not old."

"I'm only not old when I'm with you."

When Max finished getting dressed, Angela came over to him and said, "So this is it. The last time we'll be together—for a while anyway."

Hugging Angela made Max think about breasts again. He said, "You know, I don't think a restaurant is public enough. We should be someplace more visible. I know, I'll take Jack to a strip club."

Five

If my grandmother had balls she'd be my grandfather.
YIDDISH SAYING

"So I'm riding on the bus, coming downtown, when this chick gets on," Bobby Rosa said. "I got Cinderella going, feeling nice and pumped, so I figure, Why not? She's like, I don't know, thirty years old, blonde hair, nice little shape. So I start staring at her, you know, trying to get her to look at me. Make the bitch's day, right? They always say how chicks are hot for guys in wheelchairs—I wanted to see if that was bullshit or not."

Victor Gianetti, sitting across from Bobby at a table in the back of Lindy's diner in the Hotel Pennsylvania, said, "So what happened next?" Trying to sound like he gave a fuck.

"The girl starts to smile," Bobby said. "But it wasn't just a smile, like 'Have a nice day.' This was the smile of a girl who wants to get laid. So I'm thinking, This is it, my lucky day, when, all of a sudden, my legs start to spasm. I mean it's like somebody stuck an electric prong up my ass. My legs are shaking, the chair's bouncing up and down, people're coming over trying to help me. Finally, I stop shaking and I look up at the chick and her mouth's hanging open, looking at me like I'm some kind of freak."

"You are a freak, buddy," Victor said straight-faced. Then he said, "I'm kidding, I'm kidding. Jesus, where's your sense of humor?"

"I think you're missing my whole point." Bobby wondered why Victor never seemed to understand what the fuck he was talking about. "It wasn't like I gave a shit what some chick thought of me—it's just the way it is when you're in a fucking wheelchair, you start buying into this whole being a cripple shit, know what I mean? I mean when it comes right down to it, what does anybody do with their lives? You eat, you shit, you go to sleep—I can still do all those things. I can even screw. They have medicine, all these devices. It probably would be a big pain in the ass, but I could do it. I ride the bus, I can go anywhere anybody else can go. There's a word for what I'm talking about but I don't know what it is."

"You feel like people are putting you down."

"I said a word, not a sentence." Bobby thought, Is this guy a freaking moron or what? "It sounds like erection. Perception. It's like everybody's got this *perception* of me right off the bat. They see a big guy, late forties, wheelchair—they either feel sorry for me or they think I'm a fuckin' freak. Kids, Jesus, they're the fucking worst. Last winter, I go out to get a bottle of Coke when these three little kids start throwing snowballs at me. Not snow—ice. You know, like we used to throw at buses in the old days, now they throw them at people—what's the fuckin' world coming to? I swear to God, I was ready to go get my shotgun and blow the little fucks away. What happened to getting a little respect? The old days I'd walk down the street nobody'd come near me, but now the *perception*'s changed. I'm the same guy—I can still beat the shit out of somebody if I had to—but nobody else sees it that way. You see what I'm saying?"

"I guess so," Victor said and took a sip of milk.

Man, Bobby couldn't get over how shitty Victor looked in that bellhop uniform. Was this really the same guy who used to dress in style, wearing snazzy pinstriped suits and shiny shoes? Yeah, he'd always had thin hair, but now he was completely bald and he looked like he might've lost twenty or thirty pounds since the last time Bobby had seen him, what, six years ago? There was something wrong with his voice too—it sounded hoarse and scratchy, like an old man. Bobby might not've even recognized him at all if he didn't still have his dark skin and his big bent-out-of-shape nose that he'd probably broken dozens of times as a kid. Bobby could understand how a guy could lose some pounds and pack on the years, but he couldn't see how anybody could go from armed robbery to carrying people's luggage. Bobby might have lost his legs, but this asswipe had lost his balls.

Bobby slurped his coffee, said, "Remember the Bowery jobs?"

Victor smiling, suddenly looking young again, going back in time, said, "Those were real beauts, huh?"

"You plan a job, just the way you want it all to work out, and then boom—it goes that way, without one fucking hitch."

"Except when that little Chink pulled the alarm and started shooting at us."

"That wasn't a hitch. You gotta expect shit to happen when you're stealing jewelry. I'm talking about everything else. Getting to the car, getting on the bridge, getting to Brooklyn, switching cars in Brooklyn, getting to Queens, switching cars in Queens, and then boom—we're on the Island, counting the fuckin' take. Like clockwork. We did it, what, three times? All that fucking gold. Man, that was it."

He felt a rush, just seeing it replay in his head. It was like he was there again—ten years younger, looking sharp and in shape. When he saw himself standing in the jewelry store, holding his Uzi, and then running out to the street, he could feel his legs, like in those dreams when it all seemed so real, then he'd wake up and still be a fucking cripple.

"I should never'a gone out on my own," Victor said.

"That's exactly what I was talking about," Bobby said,

"you can't second-guess your life. So you fucked up, you took a fall, you're still what, fifty, fifty-five?"

"Forty-four," Victor said.

Thinking, *Jeez, the fucking sad sack looks sixty*, Bobby said, "See? Forty-four is like what twenty-four used to be. With vitamins, all the new shit with doctors, everybody's gonna be living to a hundred soon."

Victor, looking at his watch, said, "Fuck, I gotta get back to work. So what brings you around here anyway? You just wanted to shoot the shit or what?"

"No, it's a little more important than that." Bobby leaned forward, making sure the young guy reading the *Daily News* at the next table wasn't listening. "I got a job to discuss."

"A job we did?"

"No, a job we're gonna do."

Victor stared at Bobby for a few seconds, like he was trying not to laugh, then said, "Come on you're joking, right?"

"Does this face look like it's joking?

"What's this, April fools? Come on, Bobby, give me a fuckin' break, all right?"

"I'm serious, man. I came to you first because I know you're good and I know I can trust you. But if you don't want to hear me out I'll go talk to somebody else."

Bobby wanted to reach across the table and slap him, get him focused.

"All right, so tell me," Victor said, trying not to crack up. "What's this *job*?"

"I wanna knock over a liquor store," Bobby said.

Now Victor couldn't hold back. He started laughing, but it quickly turned into a cigarette smoker's hack. Finally, he recovered enough to say, "A liquor store? Jesus, you're too much, Bobby."

Bobby still wasn't laughing, or even smiling.

"Come on, Bobby," Victor said in that scratchy voice. "A liquor store?"

"What's wrong with that?" Bobby said. "That time we were shooting pool downtown what, seven, eight years ago, you said you wanted to work together again someday, right? Well, this is fuckin' someday."

Victor was staring at Bobby like he felt sorry for him. Bobby had seen this look a lot from strangers on the street, usually old ladies. One time an old lady asked Bobby if she could help him carry his bags home from the supermarket. Bobby wanted to fuckin' belt her.

"You can't walk," Victor said. "You know that, right?"

The waitress came over with Bobby's cherry cheese-cake. Bobby took four full bites of cake then said, "So? Are you with me or not?"

"Come on, man," Victor said. "Weren't you just listening to me?"

"You know," Bobby said, chewing, "the old days you would've jumped if I told you I had a job to pull."

"The old days was a long fuckin' time ago. You're in a wheelchair and the doctor took some cancer out of my throat last year. They found a couple of spots on my liver they're watching—they said if it spreads down there, that's it—I'm a goner."

Bobby stared right into Victor's yellowish eyes. The cancer didn't surprise him—he knew there was *some-thing* wrong with the guy. He said, "You know what I do every day now? When I'm not watching the fucking line-up on TV, I'm out in Central Park, shooting pictures of the broads in bikinis. I've got hundreds of pictures of boobs and asses, lined up on my walls like a fucking porno museum. Now you know that's not me, right? You know that's not what I do."

Bobby realized that he was talking too loud. People at other tables were looking over at him like he was crazy.

Then Victor, looking at Bobby like maybe he thought he was crazy, too, said, "What's this? You a photographer now or something?"

"Why? You want me to take some pictures of your girl-friend? I'll make her look so good they'll put her in *Penthouse*."

"You couldn't make *my* girlfriend look good," Victor said. "To make her look good you'd have to shoot her with the fuckin' lights out."

Bobby and Victor stared at each other seriously for a few seconds then they both started to laugh. After a while they stopped laughing, but when they looked at each other they started again. Finally, they got control of themselves. Bobby felt like it was old times again, like he and Victor were twenty-five years old, shooting the shit in some Hell's Kitchen diner.

Victor, still smiling, said, "If you want to see some good-looking ass you should check out the whores they got workin' in this hotel."

Bobby knew Victor was just trying to change the sub-ject but played along anyway, saying, "What? They got some good-looking hookers here?"

"You kiddin' me? These chicks ain't the needle whores they got dancin' on the stages on Queens Boulevard, you know what I'm saying? These are some high-class models they bring in here for the insurance faggots. You know what I'm talking about—call girls, escorts."

"Escorts, huh?" Bobby was getting a new idea. "They come here a lot?"

"Every fucking night."

"Yeah? And you're the bellhop here, right? I guess that means you take people up to their rooms."

"Why?" Victor asked.

Bobby smiled, said, "Tell me something else. Can you get me some room keys?"

Six

She's a looker, yeah, probably. Jimmy's not known to pass on a piece. It's what got him into a fix more'n once, a looker. If you're asking because you're interested, remember what she's doing with you before you fall in love.
CHARLIE STELLA, *Cheapskates*

Max was in the Modell's sneaker section, trying on a pair of Nike running shoes. He liked the way they fit, but there was no way he was buying them. They were on sale for seventy-nine bucks, but Max never paid discount for anything. Nah, he'd rather go to some classy store on Madison Avenue to get them, even if it cost him double.

As he was trying on another pair, Max sensed movement next to him. He noticed that the briefcase he had put down next to him—with the ten thousand dollars, the extra set of keys to the apartment, and the code to the alarm with instructions—was gone. Looking back over his shoulder, he saw Popeye, wearing the leather jacket with the hole in it, walking away down the aisle at a normal pace, heading toward the stairs.

Suddenly, Max realized that Deirdre was dead—there was no turning back. Even if he wanted to call off the murder, he couldn't. He still had the phone number where he'd reached Popeye, but there had been a lot of background noise, and he'd had a feeling Popeye was at a pay phone somewhere. No, it was definitely over. By six P.M. Deirdre would be gone forever.

Max doubted that he'd miss her very much, but this

wasn't his fault. Deirdre was the one who'd changed, not him.

Max had met Deirdre in 1982 at a Jewish singles weekend at the Concord hotel in the Catskill Mountains. Back then, Deirdre was an upbeat, outgoing, friendly, big-chested girl from Huntington, Long Island. Max was living alone in a studio apartment on the Upper West Side, working as a twenty-four-thousand-dollar-a-year mainframe computer technician, and he decided that Deirdre was the best thing that had ever happened to him. After a few months of dating, he took her out for drinks at the bar at the Mansfield Hotel on Forty-fourth Street. It was a classy place, lots of books in the lounge, made Max feel well-read. Paula, the little blond barmaid, brought him his third screwdriver. He could see Paula understood he was a guy of wealth and fame, like the Stones song, what the hell was the title? Then Max, feeling nice and lit, thought, What the fuck? and popped the question to Deirdre. Six months later he was kissing her under the *huppa* at a synagogue in Huntington. They had a few happy years together—reasonably happy, anyway—living in a one-bedroom walk-up on West Seventy-seventh Street. Then Max left his job to start his own company. As his business started to take off, their relationship went downhill. They moved out of the walk-up, into a doorman building on the Upper East Side, and Deirdre slowly turned into the wife from hell.

She was constantly critical, angry, and depressed, and spent his money faster than it came in. But it wasn't the money that bothered Max so much as her personality. So, okay, it was the money too but, hey, that wasn't the main thing. It got to the point where Max couldn't stand spending more than a few minutes with her at a time. She was always starting arguments, telling Max that he was the cause of all her misery, that if she hadn't married him she would have been happy. Yadda, yadda, yadda. Then she started having mental problems. Manic-depressive, they called it, but Max had a simpler name—nasty bitch. Sometimes she was depressed, staying in bed all day, which Max actually didn't mind so much. But other times she was hyper—on the phone all the time or out shopping with his credit cards or picking fights with him. Max paid thousands of dollars for her to see the best shrinks in the city. They put her on lithium, which helped, but sometimes she stopped taking her medication. Max was convinced that on some sick level Deirdre enjoyed the torture she was putting him through. She was actually happy when she made him feel like shit.

Max tried to work things out peacefully. He went with Deirdre to a marriage counselor, but spending an entire hour cursing at each other didn't exactly help.

Finally, Max suggested divorce, but Deirdre said, "You know I'll never divorce you. I'm religious."

Max nearly laughed out loud, thinking, Yeah, if religion means tormenting a good man for eternity—wasn't that a Catholic thing? Deirdre was raised Orthodox Jewish, but she never went to temple or celebrated holidays—she didn't even fast on Yom Kippur, for Christ's sake. She was more atheist than Jewish and, besides, Orthodox Jews got divorces all the time. This was obviously just more bullshit Deirdre was using to try to prolong his agony.

When things got so bad Max couldn't stand living in the same house with Deirdre anymore, he considered moving out, separating. But he didn't see why he had to be the one to go. It was his house, he'd busted his balls to pay for it. If anyone went it should be her.

The situation seemed hopeless. Max knew that even if he could convince her to get a divorce, he'd be fucked. They had no pre-nup and Deirdre would take him to town in a settlement. She'd never worked a day in her life and they didn't have kids; Max didn't see why she deserved a cent of his money. But he knew a judge, especially a female judge, wouldn't see it that way. Deirdre would get away with the townhouse, the Porsche, and at least half the money, and Max was ready to stick out the rest of his life being miserable before he let that happen. He'd worked too hard for what he had and there was no way in hell he was gonna let some lazy cow steal it out from under him.

Then Max went on Viagra and everything changed.

Max had thought he was starting to lose interest in sex, maybe even becoming impotent, but then he took Viagra and it worked miracles. Like a horny teenager, he started thinking about sex constantly. Whenever he passed a good-looking woman on the street he found himself imagining what she looked like naked. He bought sex magazines and ripped out the centerfolds, taking them into the bathroom at work and at home. He rented porn videos and nights and weekends he locked himself in the den of his townhouse and watched them. It was like he couldn't get enough of breasts. It got so bad he never saw women's faces because he couldn't raise his eyes past their chests.

Around this time Angela interviewed for a job at the company. As soon as Max saw her, he knew he had to have her. She was young, she had that whole Irish accent thing going on, and holy shit, the tits on her.

What surprised him was, entirely apart from what her body did for him, he liked being with her. She'd come out with some Irish-ism like, *Where's me coffee,* and he felt something swell up inside him. They never fought. She always laughed at his jokes and never bitched at him about the way he dressed or whatever. Max couldn't help dreaming about how great it would be if Deirdre was gone and Angela took her place. He could listen to that lilt his whole goddamn life. Hell, things worked out right, he'd bring her on a honeymoon to Ireland, maybe take her to a U2 concert. She seemed to like that Bono. Max was more into the classical-type stuff. He'd worked at it anyway, bought the whole package of *Teach Yourself the Classics*. He still didn't understand what the hell it was all about, didn't even know the difference between an alto and a concerto, but he could fake it. He loved to bore the losers at the office, going on about his favorite arias.

When the murder idea came up, it seemed like a big joke. At first anyway. But the more Max and Angela talked about it the more it seemed like the only logical solution. He had offered Deirdre ways out, but she didn't want to take them, so what was the alternative? He was proud of himself, actually, for holding out for so long. A lot of guys who went through all the bullshit that he'd gone through wouldn't have had half his patience—they would have hired someone to knock Deirdre off a long time ago.

Outside Modell's, Max decided to walk back to his office instead of taking a cab. It was a great day—sunny, about seventy—and Forty-second Street near Grand Central Station was jammed with shoppers and businesspeople on their lunch breaks. Max felt cool, strutting along Fifth Avenue with his suit jacket slung over his shoulder, calling clients on his Blackberry.

When he arrived back at the office, Angela was sitting at her desk outside Max's door, eating a salad out of a plastic container.

Like it was any other normal afternoon, Max said, "Any messages?" and Angela said, "Not a one. How'd your meeting go?"

"Hard to say," Max said. "You confirmed that appointment for me with Jack Haywood tonight, though, didn't you?"

"Sure did."

"Terrific."

He felt his voice had the right mix of boss and mellow. Like he'd once heard a young temp say about some guy, *He had it going on*.

Max went into his office and closed the door behind him. He had a stiff vodka and grapefruit juice, thinking, This shit is good. At two o'clock, he met with Alan Sorenson, his Senior Networking Manager. There had been an emergency at a client's Newark office in the morning and Max wanted to make sure the situation was under control and that the company's network didn't experience any downtime. At three, Max met with Harold Lipman to discuss a quote Lipman was preparing for a new branch of a Japanese bank that was opening on Park Avenue. Harold had used a graphics program to design a full-color picture of what the bank's new Local and Wide Area Networks would look like. Max told Harold that the designs for the three-server network looked pretty and all, but it wasn't going to get him the sale.

The vodka hitting his stomach, Max said, "Take Takahashi to a strip joint or, better yet, call one of the escort agencies in my rolodex and buy him a whore or two. Trust me—that's the only way you'll close this thing."

Harold smiled, like he was embarrassed or thought Max was joking. Harold was thirty-six, tall and pale with thinning, graying hair, and he always seemed to wear the same wrinkled blue suit. Now *there* was a cheapskate who bought discount even if he could afford better. Before working for Max, Harold had worked as a retail computer salesman. He lived in Hackensack, for Christ's sake, with his wife and six-year-old daughter.

"I think I'll just take him out to lunch," Harold said.

"Guys don't want lunch, they want tits," Max said seriously.

Harold started to smile and Max cut him off with, "Hey, I'm not joking. If you want to start closing sales you'll have to learn this sooner or later. You want to be a big kahuna, get some money to buy yourself some new goddamn suits?" He was going to add, *And not at Today's Man,* but it was hard enough to educate the guy about table dances, he wasn't going to start fashion policing the poor slob.

"I don't think he's that kind of guy," Harold said uncomfortably.

"Is he a fudgepacker? If he is, I know a couple of guys who'd love to screw him."

"No," Harold said. "I mean, he wears a wedding ring and he didn't seem gay."

"Then I don't know what the problem is—take him to a strip joint. Believe me, as soon as he has some tits bouncing in his face you'll close the sale." Max waited then said, "In this business, it's make or break, and you gotta go for bust."

He let the joke linger, waiting to see if the schmuck got it.

Finally, Harold laughed uncomfortably, said, "I'm going to go to his office and present the proposal in person and see what happens."

Max said, "Is it your wife?"

"Is what my wife?"

"The ball and chain, the guilt trips, because if it is, don't tell her about it, that's all. You think I tell my wife every time I go to a strip club? But your wife'll be happy when you start bringing home the big commission checks. Trust me, I know this stuff and I certainly know women."

"It's not my wife."

"Then what is it, your kid? You?"

Harold, his face turning pink, said, "No."

"Look, you don't have to enjoy it, I mean if that's what you're worried about. You're not there to get off, you're there for the *client* to get off. He's Japanese right? Jesus Christ, the Japs love table dances. Trust me on this one. It's a cultural thing. Maybe it's because Japanese women, as a whole, have very small breasts. Why're you smiling? I'm serious. But whatever you do, don't, do not, buy him a Japanese dancer. Even if she has the big old-style silicone knockers, they don't like that. It gets them angry because it reminds them of what they don't have at home."

Harold stood up, took a few steps back toward the door, said, "Well, thanks for the advice, but I think I'll just stick to my own sales techniques."

"Listen, you putz, I don't want to have to let you go. I mean, I think you're a smart guy. When you started here you knew more about hardware than you did about networking, but you're catching up on your technical knowledge and I think in a month or two you'll be right where you need to be. That said, I hope you understand, I can't keep paying you your draw if you're not making any commish. I just can't run my business that way. Now I'm giving you some good, solid advice here. When I hired you I told you I'd give you all the training you needed, well this is part of your training."

Max was happy with this speech, his rally-the-troops schpiel. He knew he was great at motivation—that's why he was the head honcho and everyone else wasn't.

"I came here to sell networks," Harold said, "not table dances."

"Then maybe this is the wrong product for you," Max said. "Maybe you should sell bibles or something. Now go take Takahashi to a strip joint and close this goddamn sale, or else."

o

Toward five o'clock, Angela paid a visit. She locked the door and gave Max a few wet kisses and a neck massage and wished him good luck. Max said, "The funny thing is, I'm not even nervous."

Max made sure there was no lipstick on his face. He knew he must've smelled like Joy, but this was all right because a few months ago he had bought Deirdre some of the same perfume, in the smaller one-ounce size, so she wouldn't be suspicious when he came home reeking of it. If the police asked, he could just say he picked up the odor from Deirdre. He was covering all the bases.

In the bathroom, Max put a coat of spray-on hair fibers over his bald spot. The fibers could only be detected on very close inspection or by touch. The only problems were when it rained or when he was nervous—sometimes the fibers melted and dark streaks dripped down his neck.

At 5:25, Max left the office, still feeling very relaxed. Janet, the receptionist who was temping this week, and Diane from Payroll were nearby so Max made sure he said "See you tomorrow" to Angela, loud enough so Janet and Diane could hear how casual and professional he was being.

"Good night, Max," Angela said, not even looking away from her computer monitor. If they'd been alone, she'd have added *God bless* in that crazy way the Irish did. Psychos blew up half the UK and added, *God bless*?

Max hailed a cab on Sixth Avenue and instructed the driver to take him to Fifty-fourth and Madison, the building where Jack Haywood worked. Out of habit, Max memorized the driver's name—Mohammed Siddique— and medallion number—679445. As he got out, he said, "Thanks, Mohammed. God bless."

Max told Mohammed to wait double-parked while he went into the building to call Jack from the concierge's desk. Back on the sidewalk, waiting for Jack to show up, Max couldn't help thinking about the break-in.

He'd told Deirdre that he wanted to take her out to dinner tonight and to be sure to be home at six. Deirdre was usually good about keeping her appointments, but now Max was worried that something might go wrong. Deirdre had said she would be going shopping this afternoon, but Max wondered what would happen if she came home early or had decided not to go at all.

A car horn honked. The sudden noise jolted Max, made his heart skip a beat. He took deep breaths, trying to relax. If he looked nervous tonight and Jack Haywood or someone else noticed, it could also lead to some big problems later. He had to just trust Popeye. After all, the guy was a pro and a pro would know how to handle any complications that might come up.

A few minutes later, Jack strolled out of the building, wearing the jeans and sports jacket he had changed into for his night on the town. As Director of Operations for Segal, Russell & Ross, a big law firm with over two hundred employees, Jack was one of Max's biggest clients. He was only a few years younger than Max, but he kept in shape so he looked thirty-five. He was married with two kids and he had a house on Long Island, but he liked getting away from his wife and drinking and seeing naked women. Since he had become a NetWorld client, Max bought him as many table and lap dances and trips to the private fantasy rooms as he wanted. Once in a while, Jack asked Max to fix him up with a call girl. Jack would tell his wife he was out of town on business for the night and Max would book a room for him at one of the big New York hotels. Jack liked Russian women and Max knew two Russian call girls—sisters with monster-size breasts—who charged two thousand bucks for a *menage a trois*. It was above the going rate, but the money was well worth it to keep Jack as a client. He had a two-hundred-and-fifty-user network with four file servers and Max had placed three consultants there on a full-time basis. Including hardware and software sales, Jack was a million-dollar-a-year client. Besides, you had to love a guy who knew how to relax. What was the point of working your ass off and having no fun?

As soon as Jack got into the cab, Max turned on his "business personality." Usually, he hated small talk and phony conversation, but when there was money involved, man, Max could turn on the bullshit as well as anyone. During the ride across town to Legz Diamond's, Max managed to hold a conversation on golf, wine, real estate and the upcoming mayoral election, and half the time he didn't know what the hell he was talking about. But, shit, he knew that he was selling it well.

Legz Diamond's was on Forty-seventh Street near Eleventh Avenue. It was an upscale strip club—dark and glitzy, like a cheesy, suburban wedding hall. Although it was still early, the place was at least half filled with businessmen trying to keep their male clients happy. That's how the big city worked. You had a problem with it, get the fuck back to Boise, pal.

The host, a Mafia-looking guy with slicked-back hair, was on stage introducing the girls one by one, holding their hands and kissing them on the lips or cheek after he said their names. Max sometimes wondered whether all the girls screwed around with the host, but he was positive that the ones who kissed him on the lips had. Max was a known regular at the club so he and Jack got the VIP seats, right in front of the stage. Immediately, Max bought Jack a rum and Coke and a table dance with the girl of his choice. Jack picked a Puerto Rican with a big smile and a nice set of 38 or 40 triple-Ds. Perfectomundo. That was the way to get 'em in the mood.

Max was watching Jack enjoy himself when he heard someone call out his name. It was Felicia, a black stripper with 46 triple-Ds whom Max had bought dances from many times before. She was on the stage, leaning forward so that her implants hung down off her bone-thin dancer's body.

"How are you?" Max said.

"Wait up, baby," Felicia said. "Let me come down there and talk to you personally."

She climbed down off the stage and sat on Max's lap. Max knew that she was just being nice to him because he had tipped her a lot of money in the past, but he couldn't help but let the special treatment go to his head. He felt like Hugh Hefner, sitting there with a gorgeous girl on his lap. He wondered if Hef listened to Mozart. Guy spent his life in silk pajamas, smoked a pipe, he must listen to real music.

"That's better," Felicia said, wiggling her ass as she settled in on his lap. "So how you been?"

"All right," Max said.

"Yeah? I ain't seen you around here too much lately."

"I've been busy. You know how it is."

Max remembered once telling Felicia about his business and how this had impressed her.

"That's right," Felicia said, "you got some kind of company—computers or something, right?"

"That's right," Max said.

"That's cool, baby. Hey, anybody ever tell you how cute you are?" That lifted him in every sense. Who needed Viagra?

"Nobody who looked like you," Max said.

Felicia kissed him on the forehead and Max felt her hard implants pressing against his chest.

"I got an idea," Felicia said. "Take down my number. You can give me a call some time when I'm not working.

We'll go out and have a good time. Or I can just come over to your place and we'll party there."

Max scribbled Felicia's number on the back of one of his business cards, then leaned back as she gave a nice, slow table dance. First she crouched backwards with her butt high in the air. Then she turned and danced with her breasts in Max's face. The bags were so big they were stretching the skin around them, and her nipples were sticking out like pencil erasers. In the middle of the dance, Max looked at his watch and saw it was 6:08. If all had gone according to plan, Deirdre had been murdered eight minutes ago. Felicia saw him looking at his watch and said, "You got a date tonight, baby?"

"No, I'm just checking the time. It's a little after six," he added so she would remember if anyone asked.

"A little after sex?"

"*Six*," Max said.

"Oh. I musta heard you wrong, baby."

"Right side," Max said to Asir Aswad as the cab turned onto East Eightieth Street. In the middle of the block, Max said, "Right here," and the cab came to a stop.

The meter read $9.70. Max gave Asir a twenty and took back the entire ten dollars and thirty cents change. He never tipped cab drivers and wasn't going to start now. He didn't want the police to think he had been acting in any way unusual minutes before discovering his wife's body.

It was 10:27. Max had dropped Jack off at Penn Station twenty minutes ago. Jack had seen Max writing down Felicia's phone number and it had impressed him a great deal.

"You gonna call her?" Jack asked.

"When I get around to it," Max said.

"If I were you I wouldn't wait on that," Jack said. "I'm

getting a little tired of that Russian coffee cake. I might be in the mood for some chocolate pudding one of these nights. If you don't use that number, why don't you hold onto it for me?"

Jack was drunk, but not so drunk that he wouldn't remember that Max was with him all night while Deirdre was being murdered.

Of course Max had no intention of calling Felicia. Seeing those big gazongas in his face had definitely got him thinking, but before he had sex with a cheap stripper he'd need to see some blood work. He was just egging Jack on, trying to maintain his swinger image since Jack seemed to like it. It was part of the sales technique that he had perfected—*never show the client that you are in any way above him.* In other words, if the client sleeps with cheap hookers, then you have to come off as a guy who sleeps with cheap hookers. Besides, Max had Angela and he'd probably be spending the rest of his life with her. Although, he had to admit, it would be nice if Angela had knockers as big as Felicia's.

Max headed up the stoop to his townhouse. Through the lace curtains in the front windows he could see that there were no lights on inside. As he put his key in the first lock, he remembered what Popeye had said to him when they'd met in the pizza place, about how he might kill Max, too, if Max came home while he was still in the house. Max looked at his watch—10:29. Popeye must have left more than four hours ago. There was no way in hell he could be inside there now.

Seven

After Angela's mother died, her father suddenly started
telling Angela she had to find her Greek roots so last
summer, partly just to shut her father up, she figured,
Why not? and found a package on the Internet and went
for a visit.

Bad idea. Real bad.

She thought she'd chill on the beach, work on her tan,
but it turned into the trip from hell. All everyone kept
asking her was when she was going to get married. She
was twenty-eight, for god's sake, she didn't even have a
serious boyfriend. One of her aunts made her promise
that when she got back to New York, she would call
Spiros, the cousin of someone on the island who was supposed to be a very nice guy. Just to get her aunt and
everyone else off her back, she took Spiros's number and
promised to call him. Jeez, a Greek got on your case, you
were going to agree to anything.

A few months later, when she was back in New York
and had just broken up with the latest dick she'd met out
clubbing, she found the piece of paper with the phone
number in the bottom of her suitcase and figured, What
the hell?

Spiros was weird on the phone. He asked all kinds of

questions—who was she, why was she calling, why did she wait so long to call. Angela was about to hang up when he suggested that they go to dinner Friday night. It wasn't like her social diary was overflowing so Angela went to meet him after work, figuring she'd go for the free meal.

Spiros was short with bad skin, a crooked nose, and a bushy black mustache. He looked sort of like Saddam Hussein. Angela wanted to ditch him right then, but they were at a very expensive Greek restaurant in midtown so she figured he must be loaded. During dinner, he was very polite and kept telling her how pretty her smile was and how her eyes were the color of the Aegean Sea, but Angela was more interested when he started talking about his money. He said he was in "the restaurant business," but he wouldn't tell her the name of the restaurant or where it was located.

He tipped big and, like all New Yorkers, Angela watched for that—it was a good sign.

They went out a few more times and he kept spending a lot of money on her and buying her presents. Whenever she brought up his restaurant he'd say, "Don't worry, I'll take you there some time," but he never did. Then, one afternoon, walking along Sixth Avenue, she spotted Spiros working at a souvlaki cart on the corner of Fifty-third Street. When she confronted him, he confessed that his plan was to marry her and put her to work selling souvlaki while he moved back to Xios. Angela's Irish temper came out in full force as she roared at him, "You fooking bollix!" He'd muttered that was a nice way for a lady to speak and she'd exploded, "I'm not a lady, I'm Irish yah cunt!"

Angela decided that she'd had it with Greek men. A couple of weeks later, she and her friend Laura went to Hogs & Heifers, a biker bar in the meatpacking district. They were having a blast, getting ripped on beer and shots of Schnapps, playing old Aerosmith on the jukebox. She'd had a thing for Steven Tyler years ago and still would've humped him in a heartbeat. Hell, the mood she was in, she would've humped any guy with money and decent breath. A few college girls, egged on by the surly bikers, stood on the bar during "Walk This Way" and started dancing topless. It was an informal ritual at the bar for girls to dance topless and the bikers started chanting for Laura and Angela to get up and join them. So Laura and Angela stood on the bar and did slow stripteases as the guys cheered them on. Laura stopped at her stockings, but Angela went all the way, pulling off her stockings and tossing them into the crowd of cheering men.

After dancing for about a half an hour, Angela got down from bar, suddenly exhausted and dizzy. A sweaty Puerto Rican guy came over, holding Angela's stockings, and said, "Yo, I'm Tony. I think you dropped somethin'."

Angela was drunk and everything else that happened that night was a blur. As she put on her stockings and bra and the rest of her clothes, Tony bought her a shot of tequila. Then he said, "I like the way you was dancin' up there—you got all the moves. I like that accent too. You sound like that bitch from *Braveheart*."

They started making out, touching each other all over, then Tony brought her back to his place in Spanish Harlem. She wound up spending the weekend.

It turned out Tony made good money, as a union plumber, and Angela thought, Sex, money, a big apartment—she had it made. Then, one night, they were hanging out, watching a DVD of *24* when Tony pressed pause and said, "Yo, I got a wife in San Juan." Just like that, like it suddenly occurred to him.

Angela looked at him, said, "So you can divorce her, can't you?"

"Naw, naw, it ain't like that," Tony said. "I got three kids too and they all comin' over to live with me next week. Sorry 'bout that, yo."

Angela couldn't believe it. She'd spent all this time with this prick and let him do all that shit—tying her up, giving her a golden shower—then he says he has a fucking wife and kids! She literally became her mother, going at him like the very best of Irish women—clawing at his eyes, kneeing him in the balls, tearing out clumps of his hair. After she tore a bracelet off his hairy wrist, she took off and left him crying in front of the paused scene of Keifer Sutherland screaming at somebody. A couple of days later, Angela had the bracelet appraised. She expected it to be a fake and was stunned to discover it was white gold from Tiffany's, worth a couple thousand bucks. It cost five dollars to have the clasp fixed and she wondered if maybe her luck was changing.

As it turned out, her luck was changing all right, but not necessarily for the better.

The first change was that Dillon arrived from Ireland and bought her a silver Claddagh ring and a bottle of Black Bushmills, "the cream of the barley," he said. Dillon had that sly smile and those gross yet irresistible lips and said, "Mo croi, I'm stony."

He had to translate, that she was "his very heart" and what girl could resist that shit? A few weeks later, after they decided to move in together, he said, "Trust me, allanna, and we'll be in the clover."

Then the second change came—she caught herpes. Dillon swore he didn't have it, so she figured Spiros or Tony must've given it to her.

Then the third change: A job came to her out of nowhere. She'd applied for the position weeks ago and sick of would-be employers focusing on her shitty typing skills (she could only do twenty-four words a minutes *with* mistakes) and lack of experience (she'd never had an office job above receptionist), she decided, To hell with it, she'd get the job like she got men—with her body. She dressed for the interview in sheer black pantyhose, patent heels, and a killer short skirt.

Dillon, reading his Zen book, looked up at her, smiled, said, "That position for typing or fucking?"

She'd answered, "Either way, I'm good to go."

Her appointment with Max Fisher, CEO of NetWorld, was for two o'clock and Angela arrived at the office half an hour early. The receptionist kept her waiting on the couch in the lobby for over an hour, and Angela got so pissed off she was about to leave. Then Max came into the lobby. Angela watched his gaze shift from her face down to her legs, then slowly back up again. When his eyes fixated on her bust, she thought, *Gotcha*.

She had.

During the interview, Max continued to eye her with his jaw hanging partly open. Angela thought Max was probably the most disgusting and pathetic guy she'd ever met. He was like some overgrown thirteen year old, with that picture of the blonde on the Porsche on the wall and the way he kept staring at her tits, with the tip of his tongue showing between his teeth. Angela said to herself, There's no way in hell I'm working for this loser. Then Max offered her a salary of sixty-four thousand a year plus full health benefits and three weeks vacation.

On her first day, Angela could tell that Max was seriously into her. It was more than just staring at her all the time and flirting. A couple of times when they were alone in his office he put his hand on her leg and one time he said he had knots in his shoulders and asked her to give him a massage. She figured, What the hell? The man had money, money she wouldn't get by blowing him off. Also, she liked the attention. Dillon hadn't been around very much lately. He was always staying out late, saying, *I need to hook up with the boyos.* The boyos meant the guys from the *Ra,* Dillon's name for the IRA.

But after only a few weeks, Max started to disgust her again. She couldn't stand his old, flabby body, and she hated the way he never stopped complaining. If he wasn't talking about his wife, saying things like how he was "ready to trade her in for a newer model," then he was whining about his heart or some other medical problem. And what was with all that crap music? One day he'd told her he'd teach her to appreciate "the nuances of the composers." She'd had to look up nuances in the dictionary, then realized how full of shit he was.

Max was like somebody's grandfather. She didn't know why she'd ever gotten involved with him. After taxes, sixty-four thousand dollars wasn't as much as she'd thought it would be. Max had bucks, she knew that, but he was a real tightwad. Yeah, he had the townhouse and the Porsche, but he never took trips or bought nice clothes. And when it came to tips he had deep pockets, but short arms. If she was going to see any serious amount of money out of the relationship, it wasn't going to be by just sleeping with him.

Meanwhile, Dillon still hadn't gotten her an engagement ring or talked about setting a wedding date. One night, Angela brought it up while they were lying in bed in the dark and Dillon said, "Mo croi, I gave you a Claddagh ring, that's as married as it gets. We get some green together, I'll bring you down to Vegas, do a Britney special, okay?"

Angela didn't want a fancy wedding. She just wanted to go to City Hall, maybe invite her father, her friend Laura and a couple of cousins and that's it. But Dillon wouldn't hear of it till they were, as he always said, "loaded."

He said it *low-dead* and she wondered for the hundredth time, was he fucking with her mind? She was Irish, and she knew how that worked. They did it just because they could, it was the national pastime. It explained the national sport, hurling, that cross between hockey and murder, played with no helmets unless you were, like, "a fag" or something. Talk about head-fucking.

To get revenge, Angela went with Max for a weekend to Barbados, telling Dillon she was going to Greece for an aunt's funeral. She came back more confused than ever. She didn't like Max any better, but she was still pissed off at Dillon. She wanted things to work out with him, but she knew they never would, because of money. He was always talking about how he wanted to have expensive cars and to live on the beach and not have to worry about working.

One day, Max's wife Deirdre came into the office and had one of her fights with Max. Deirdre was a nasty spoiled rich hag who'd probably never worked a day in her life. She wore designer clothes and expensive jewelry and always seemed to be coming and going from a manicure or an appointment with her hairdresser. Angela didn't know what they were fighting about today, but it didn't matter because it was always about something stupid. Angela heard Deirdre cursing at Max, then Max called her a "fucking bitch" and then, finally, they were both quiet. Max had told Angela that Deirdre was manic-depressive and was on medication, but Angela thought Max was just as pathetic for fighting with her all the time. She was sick—what was his excuse?

On her way out of the office, Deirdre stopped by Angela's desk and ordered, "Call Orlando at Orlo and confirm my three o'clock appointment."

Deirdre was wearing the same perfume that Max had bought her, but she used so much of it that she stunk up the whole office. She was overweight, but confident, swinging her big butt, walking on her three-inch pumps, a push-up bra making her chest look like a freak cartoon. Her short hair was dyed a blond that seemed almost orange and she was wearing her usual full face of makeup, like someone had just hurled it at her, letting it stick wherever.

"Why don't you call him yourself?" Angela said, wanting to add "yah dumb cunt."

Deirdre stopped and looked back at Angela with her mouth open, like she was shocked. "What did you just say?"

"Call him yourself," Angela said. "I'm not your fookin' slave."

"I would suggest you not speak to me that way," Deirdre said, "if having a job is important to you. You girls, you come over here, think you have cousins in the NYPD, think that dumb accent is the ticket to the good life. Well let me tell you, Maureen O'Hara is no Halle Berry, if you get my drift."

Deirdre laughed snootily then marched out of the office.

"Fuck you," Angela whispered then, the mick blood boiling, added, "yah fecking hoor's ghost!"

Angela knew that Deirdre couldn't get her fired—Max would just laugh if Deirdre complained to him—but she still didn't like being put down by some uppity bitch. It just didn't seem fair that Deirdre and Max had all that money and lived in that great townhouse. Angela knew if the shoe were on the other foot, and she was the rich lady, she'd be gracious, treat her inferiors with respect, helping out the poor, giving her old Donna Karan or whatever to Goodwill. She'd do a lot of stuff straight from her heart like that.

It was so frustrating—if only Angela had Max's money, she knew her life with Dillon could be perfect. Then the thought came to her for the first time: why *couldn't* they have Max's money? All he had to do was divorce Deirdre—whom he hated anyway—and then he and Angela could get married. Max would eventually have a heart attack and die and Angela and Dillon would be set. But when Angela brought up the divorce idea to Max the next day he said he'd never even consider it. He was so cheap he'd rather stay with a wife he hated than give half his money away in a divorce settlement.

What could you expect from a bollix who didn't tip?

That was when Angela came up with the murder idea. The way she saw it, it was the only way things could ever work out with Dillon. The key was, she had to explain it to Dillon the right way. She couldn't say, "I've been screwing my boss for three months, you want to help me kill his wife?" She'd have to bring it up another way, tell him, "I know a way to get all of my boss's money, you want to help me?" Naturally, he'd say yes, once he found out exactly how much money he stood to make. He'd drop that Zen book in a hurry, replace it with a gun in jig time, that was for sure. Then she'd say that it would mean she'd have to fool around with Max a little. She'd say "fool around with him a little" on purpose, make it sound like it wasn't something serious.

When Angela told Dillon, he said he thought it was a great idea. He didn't even have a problem when she got to the part about "fooling around a little." He said, "But you can't say I'm gonna do it. You gotta tell him it's a friend of yours or some shite like that."

"I'll say you're a friend of my cousin's, but I need a name."

"Tell him I'm Popeye."

"Why Popeye?"

" 'Cause he ate spinach and we should keep the deal green."

Angela laughed.

"What's so funny?"

"I'm just imagining my boss's face," Angela said, still laughing, "when he finds out a guy named Popeye is gonna kill his wife."

"It was dumb to ask for ten," Angela said to Dillon. "You should've just stayed at eight."

Angela and Dillon were sitting in the dining area of her apartment eating Apple Jacks and milk. The place was maybe four hundred square feet and there was no separate kitchen or living area. There was just a small area against one wall for the kitchen appliances and a countertop and a larger area with barely enough room for a full-size bed, a dresser, a small table and folding chairs from Bed Bath & Beyond, and a fourteen-inch color TV.

"He said yes, didn't he?" Dillon said. "You should be thankin' me. I got us two thousand extra dollars. You know how many Protestants I'd have to kill for that? A lot."

"You could've blown everything," Angela said.

"Blowing stuff is what I do, it's me birthright. That stupid fooker is going to bring us all that money. You should have seen his face—how scared he was."

Dillon's mutilated lips looked even uglier when he said this, as if he relished putting the fear of be-jaysus into someone.

"He was scared?"

"Fook yeah." Dillon started laughing. "You know what I told him? I told him he better not be home when I was there 'cause if he was home I might pop him too." Dillon was laughing harder. "I don't know how I didn't start laughing my arse off right then. But I kept looking at him like this…" Dillon made a serious face, his ruined lips making his features even more horrific. "It was like I was feckin' Michael Collins when he was arranging to kill the

Brit agents, you should see that fillum, it's mighty. It was like I could see him thinking, Uh-oh, this fellah wouldn't be codding. It's amazing how somebody so rich could be so feckin' stupid."

"He's stupid all right," Angela said, "but he's not as stupid as you think. I mean a guy doesn't make so much money, own a company like that, being stupid."

"That's not true," Dillon said. "Look around sometime. There're a lot of stupid people in this city, and a lot of feckin' rich people too."

Dillon took his last bite of Apple Jacks, slurped down the flesh-colored milk, then reached for the bottle of Jameson. He poured a shot, called it his eye opener, and drained it. He waited for the liquid to hit his stomach, then gave what he called his *delicious shudder*.

Angela had a minor scare when Max said, "The only thing I'm worried about is this Popeye character." Everything had been going well, but now she was afraid that he would find out about everything.

Later that day, Angela had another scare when Diane in accounting came up to her at the coffee machine and said in a hushed voice, "Can I ask you a personal question?"

Angela knew that when a woman asked another woman that, it was a given that some kind of bitchiness was on its way.

"Sure," Angela said.

Diane was always trying to lose weight—lately she was on The Cabbage Soup Diet. Maybe she was going to ask for some diet advice, get some crack in that Angela should try the diet too, not that she needed to lose weight or anything because she looked *so good*. Yeah, right.

But instead Diane said, "Is there something going on between you and Max?"

"Max?" Angela said.

"You know…" Diane said, "I mean you're always going into his office, locking the door…"

"Who told you that?"

"No one. I just noticed it myself and I was just wondering, that's all."

"There's *nothing* going between me and Max," Angela said as though the idea repulsed her. But, just for effect, she held her stomach like she was going to throw up and said, "That's really disgusting. I mean, how gross is that? Could you imagine going down on that flabby belly?"

"I knew it couldn't be true," Diane said. "I mean, it's bad enough working for him. Who would want to sleep with him?"

Angela hoped Diane would forget all about it, but she'd have to watch her closely just in case. Then, walking away, she thought, *And hon, the diet, it's like, not working*.

That night Angela said to Dillon, "You know what that asshole said to me today? That I should add a cup size to my breasts."

They were in bed, passing a joint back and forth. Dillon took his hit and passed the joint to Angela then said, "So?"

"So?" Angela said. "What do you mean, So?"

"I mean, So? Like so what so."

Jesus, he sure knew how to annoy the shite out of a person.

"What? You don't like my breasts either?"

"I didn't say that," Dillon said. "I happen to like your tits, but I like your arse better."

"Thanks a lot," Angela said.

"You're welcome."

Angela sat up, looking down at her breasts. "I don't care what anybody says—I like them just the way they are."

Dillon sat up and started rolling another joint under the lamp on the night table. Angela, leaning over, started kissing his back and stomach. He had the smell of peat, the smell of the bogs, but she liked it. She said, "You know what else he told me. He said he wants to marry me."

"So?" Dillon said. "You gotta marry him so we get his money, right? That's the plan, right?"

"Yeah," Angela said.

She'd been hoping Dillon was going to propose himself one of these days. Dream on.

Dillon licked the edge of the rolling paper and sealed the joint. He lit up and took a long hit, then passed it on to Angela. Dillon said, "Dunno why I smoke this shite, it hasn't had an effect on me since the eighties. Now you give me a double of Bushmills, I can whistle the whole of the Star Spangled Banner."

She'd always gotten a big kick out of this—Dillon claiming that pot had no effect him. Meanwhile, he'd smoke a joint, then pick up a shot of Bushmills and try to put it in his ear.

His voice already getting really slow, he asked, "See…what…I…mean?"

The day of the murder Angela kissed Dillon goodbye before she went to work, knowing it would be the last time she'd see him before Deirdre Fisher was dead. Dillon was in the dining area, sitting on a chair reading his book.

He held up a finger, said, "Listen to this." Then in his richest, most gorgeous voice intoned, "This is from Shunryu Suzuki…What do you want enlightenment for?…You may not like it."

She didn't get it, said, "I don't get it."

He laughed, said, "'Tis few do."

Dillon said he loved New York, called it his *twisted*

city, and she wanted to add, "Yeah, matches your lips," but never did because she was afraid of his temper. Although Dillon had never hit her, she thought he was the type who could. Violence simmered in him. It was never turned off—just went dormant sometimes.

"I'm going to take this town by the balls," he said, and she said, "Good luck."

He stood, produced a green emerald brooch, and said, "Back home, on Paddy's day, we have the wearing of the green." He pinned it on her breast, hurting her a little, but she didn't even flinch. She figured, like all his countrymen, he was truly fucked up and wouldn't give a shit anyway.

He put on a pair of very snazzy shades and said, "One time I was in Lizzie Bordello's in Dublin. U2 were holding court and I nicked Bono's glasses, you think I look like him?"

He looked like a horse's ass but being a woman, she said, "You kidding? You make Bono look like Shrek."

Dillon smiled, said, "Hold that thought, allanna."

Eight

I had to give the guy credit. He didn't back down easy.
I'd have to watch him closely. His type could sneak right up
and bite you in the ass.
REED FARREL COLEMAN, *The James Deans*

Sixteen years ago, when he got back from Desert Storm, Bobby took an acting class at some place downtown on Broadway. He didn't want to be an actor— no, that pussy *Hamlet*, *Streetcar*, Death of a Whatever shit wasn't for him. He just wanted to learn how to play a role, make people know right away he was the type of guy who didn't take shit from nobody.

He knew he needed some acting lessons big time when he pulled his first bank job, out at a Chase in Astoria. He went up to the teller, slid the note under the window, and stood there, trying to look like a guy who didn't fuck around, like Ray Liotta in *Something Wild*. But the girl looked at him, just for a second, like, Are you for real? Bobby thought he even saw her start to smile for a second there, like she didn't believe a guy looked like him could pull a bank job. His crew got away with the cash, no problem, but the girl's reaction still annoyed the hell out of Bobby. He wanted instant respect.

Before the next job, Bobby watched *Scarface* like a dozen times, trying to get the whole Pacino badass shit down cold. He thought he had it, but when he went up to the window at the bank the same thing happened. He thought it must be nerves or something. When he pulled smaller jobs, at grocery stores and supermarkets, it was even worse. He'd whip out his piece, say, "This is a stick up," and his mouth would be dry and the words would come out sounding all wimpy.

So he figured enough was enough and he signed up for the acting class. He felt out of place around all of the artsy-fartsy types, like he was crashing a party or something. He would've bailed but the teacher was this hot-looking little thing named Isabella. She'd been in something on Broadway and was in some soap opera for a couple of years. She knew her shit about acting and she gave great head too. Bobby stopped going to the class and got private lessons from Isabella. When she wasn't going down on him, she was teaching him how to emote, use stuff from his past, shit like that. Sometimes they'd read lines from plays to each other. It took him a while, but he finally got good at it. Isabella said he should start auditioning and that's when he knew it was time to dump her. From then on, whenever he pulled a job all he had to do was look at the fuckers and they knew what was going down. He probably could've robbed anyplace he wanted without ever showing a weapon.

Since Bobby got paralyzed he hadn't tried to act at all. But he knew that for what he had planned with Victor at the hotel, he was gonna have to have his acting skills sharp as a fucking tack or the plan would have zero chance of working.

Bobby opened his old *Riverside Shakespeare* book to a random scene in *Macbeth*. He took a couple of minutes to memorize the line, then he looked in the mirror, trying to look tough, like DeNiro in *Taxi Driver,* and said, "Come to my woman's breast and take my milk for gall you murthering ministers, wherever in your sightless substance you seek peace…"

He tossed the book away, realizing this was a waste of his fucking time. He still had the magic.

°

The townhouse was a lot bigger than Dillon had expected. He knew it would be big, but he didn't know it would be like *big* big, like a feckin' palace. There were three floors and the whole place was filled with all kinds of rich, ugly shite—couches, tables, chairs, mirrors, God-ugly paintings on the wall. Dillon couldn't wait till he was livin' in this gaff—then he'd make some *serious* changes. First he was going throw out all this ugly shite. Then he was going to put in a Shebeen bar downstairs with one of them giant screen TVs—like the kind they had in the sports bars—and then he was going to have his own feckin' club—call it A Touch of the Green. Every night he'd be blasting the Pogues with his own private DJ, and he'd invite all his boyos to come down, and they'd rock the place with jigs and reels. He might even teach some bollix how to play the spoons. He already knew how to play the odds.

Dillon still couldn't believe that all this was going be his just for killing some rich old lady. Jesus, he'd offed fookers for the price of a pint.

It was funny—before all this started he was getting tired of Angela and was thinking about dumping her when she came to him with this great idea. At first he thought it must be some kind of joke—it all seemed too easy. She said all she'd have to do was "fool around" with the guy and get him to want to marry her. The funny thing was, he didn't care if she took him on and ten of his friends, just as long as he got the dosh.

Dillon didn't know why Angela thought that they were going to get married someday. Yeah, he had considered asking her to marry him, but what the hell did that mean? He'd asked lots of colleens to marry him—it was just something fellahs said to women to make them shut up. He'd a supply of silver Claddagh rings. Angela also wanted to have kids, buy a house in the country or some shite. Dillon had three kids already, that he knew about, and he had four separate wallets with snaps of them. And if he really wanted to have a wife and kids, he would've stayed with Siobhan, the girl he got pregnant in Ballymun. There was woman, fiery and able to sink the jar like a good un and cook, she made black pudding to die for.

The only reason he was with Angela at all was because of the way she was in that pub that night. Usually, he liked dumb women, but Angela looked good there, giving mouth to the ugly bartender. He'd been planning to take off after a couple of weeks, but he couldn't afford rent yet, so he figured he'd live with her till he found a decent score.

He told Angela a lot of lies, afraid if she knew the truth she'd throw him out. He told her he was a scout for the RA, thinking sussing out schemes for the boyos was a patriotic ideal she'd understand. The truth was he was what is known in Ireland as a Prov-een. When the Irish want to diminish something, somebody, they add *een*, making it diminutive. You call a man a man-een, you're calling him a schmuck, a wanna-be. The Ra had many guys who hung on the fringes, did off jobs for The Boyos but were never seriously considered part of The Movement. They were mainly cannon fodder, used and discarded and if they managed a big score, no problem. Dillon had actually made some hits for the Boyos, but it didn't get him inside, not in the inner circles where it mattered. He knew where they hung out in New York but he didn't know what the level of operations was. They kept him on a strictly need-to-know basis and a loose demented cannon like Dillon, he needed to know precious little.

There were two other other things he lied to Angela about—one was big, the other small. The small thing was herpes. He said he'd caught it off her, but the truth was he'd caught that shite a long time ago, back in the eighties. The big lie was that he'd only killed a few people before. Actually, he'd killed at least seventeen people—some memorable, some not. Like all his race, Dillon was deeply superstitious. All that rain, it warped the mind, added a mountain of church guilt. What you got was seriously fucked up head cases or as they called them in Dublin, "head-a-balls," which doesn't translate in any language yet discovered.

The one that gave Dillon pause was a tinker he'd killed, not that the guy didn't need killing; he did, but you didn't want to mess with a clan who knew a thing or two about curses. It was in Galway, a city of serious rain, it poured down with intent and it was personal. That town had swans and tinkers, and culling both seemed like a civic duty. There'd been a case in the place, swans and tinkers being killed, and the citizens were outraged about, yep, *the swans*. Dillon had been drenched, lashed with wet, the week of the Galway Races. Fookit, he'd lost a packet on a sure-fire favorite and then in Garavans the tinker had snuck up on him, doing the con, going, "How are ye, are ye winning, isn't it fierce weather?" Like that. The whole blarneyed nine and then lifted Dillon's wallet, headed out of the pub. Dillon caught him at the canal, rummaging through the wallet, so intent on his fecking larceny, he never heard Dillon coming. A quick look around, no one about, then Dillon gave him the bar treatment, a Galway specialty. You zing the guy's head off the metal bars lining the canal for as long as it takes to say a decade of the rosary, keeping the deal religious. Thing is, you murder a tinker, you're cursed—they have a way of finding out who did the deed and then damn you and all that belongs to you. Still gave Dillon a tremor when he thought about it.

Todd, that was the tinker's name. Dillon would like to have lots of things in his past changed, and knowing the tinker's name topped the list. Knowing the name made it, like, personal and shite. You didn't ever want murder to be personal, you might start to take it serious, think it meant something. He felt the karma would come down the pike and hit him when he least expected it. He never shared this hibby jibby with anyone, but Todd was engraved in whatever passed for his heart forever. Wasn't that curse enough?

Oh, yeah, and he'd committed one murder in New York. He cracked some guy's head open against a brick wall because the guy had that plummy Brit accent.

Dillon had only gotten busted for one of his murders— a guy he'd cut for looking at his woman—and did five hard years in Portlaoise, where they kept the Republican prisoners. His first day, he'd found the Zen book on his bunk, left by the previous inmate. He'd picked it up from boredom and got gradually hooked. Hooked up quickly too with the Provo guys and got his arse covered though again, he wasn't privy to any of their councils. They'd look out for him but didn't feel any great need to stretch it.

He continued to ransack the downstairs of the townhouse. It was fun turning things over, destroying shite. A rush like when he was in his teens and the Brits came at them with rubber bullets, those suckers bounced off you, you hurt like a pagan for a week. The first time they got an armored car on fire and got the soldiers to crawl out, crying for their mammies, with a sniper picking the fookers off, one by British one. Fook, it got him hard just remembering. Those Brit accents, sounding polite even as they roared. Dillon was convinced then that he was one of the real Boyos. In fact, there was hardly a kid in the city who hadn't been bounced by a rubber bullet—it came with the territory.

When everything on the ground floor looked good and wrecked, he went upstairs. He found the bedroom Max had told him about, which was filled with more ugly old shite that looked like rubbish his grandmother would buy. Everything was made of wood and they had some fierce gold-colored bed. Dillon imagined what the room was going to look like when he put mirrors on the ceiling, put down some reed mats, like home, get one of them waterbeds, and put a jacuzzi in the bathroom. He broke all the glass stuff from on top of the dresser and night table and dumped all the clothes out of the drawers. Then he found the old lady's jewelry box and stuck all the diamond- and gold-looking stuff into a plastic bag he found.

On the wall, there were some pictures of a fat old lady—he guessed this was Mrs. Fisher. There was also a picture of Max Fisher standing on a beach somewhere. He looked the same as he did at the pizzeria and in Modell's, except he had a bit more hair. Dillon couldn't wait till he got to do Max too. He knew the plan was to wait for him to die but, fook, Dillon wanted to get on with his life. He hated that old bollix, the way he was sitting there in his posh suit. He reminded Dillon of Fr. Malachy, his principal in school. Dillon never understood what the priest was saying but nothing about school made much sense to Dillon. The only reason he went was to keep the Social Services away. But Fr. Malachy was always calling him down to his office for whatever, or suspending him. Malachy thought he was God almighty because he was the principal and could do whatever he wanted. Now Max Fisher was trying to pull that same deal, trying to call all the shots, but this time Dillon named the jig—now he was the man in charge and Max Fisher was the little Irish schoolkid sitting on the other side of the desk. When Dillon had heard that Malachy died in real agony from cancer Dillon had muttered, *hope he died roaring.*

Dillon heard voices and a noise—a key turning in a lock. He took out the .38 he'd gotten from the Boyos' place down off the Bowery. When he'd showed up there, they'd rolled their eyes, like, here's this mad annoying fook again. But he had money to pay for the piece and, what the hell, he'd brought some decent bottle of Jameson. They treated him like a younger brother who's always hanging on but is never, like ever, going to be in the gang.

Heading downstairs, he remembered what the Yanks said and used it now like a prayer, albeit a dark one, *Lock n load.*

Nine

Straight to Hell
THE CLASH

As Max was feeling for the light switch, he slipped and fell. The way he landed and the way the pain was shooting down his side, he thought he'd broken his hip. When he started to get up he realized he was okay, but wondered what the cold wet stuff on his hands was.

For some reason, this whole time he'd been planning the murder, Max hadn't thought about what the body would look like. He thought Deirdre would die like people in old westerns died. In those movies you never saw any blood—the cowboys and Indians just fell off their horses and lay there nice and still. In modern movies, they always showed the blood squirting out of people's heads, gushing from their mouths. Max always thought it was just Hollywood exaggerating things, but now he realized that those movies didn't show half of the real horror.

If it weren't for her short, blond hair, Max might not have recognized Deirdre at all. Blood had leaked from her head into a two- or three-foot-wide puddle around her body. Although she lay on her back, Max could barely make out the features of her face. He thought, This can't be fuckin' happening. It was part of a dream—soon the alarm clock would ring and he'd wake up. When a ringing actually started, Max thought he really *had* been sleeping. But then he realized that the noise wasn't an alarm clock, it was the burglar alarm. Shit, it nearly gave him a coronary and his heart was in bad enough shape.

After he shut off the alarm, he glanced back at the scene, shocked again by all the blood. When he realized that the wormy stuff on the wall was part of Deirdre's brain he started to throw up. No one told him it was going to be so…gross.

He went into the downstairs bathroom where he took off his blood-covered clothes and washed the blood off his hands. He still couldn't believe this was happening. What the hell had he been thinking, planning this murder like some kind of lunatic you read about in the tabloids? The *Daily News* today had two twins on the front page, the ones who'd murdered their parents, with the screaming headline, TWIN KILLING. Wait till they got hold of this.

He wondered if he was insane. He didn't think he was insane, but what the hell did that mean? Insane people never think they're insane so how did he know if he was insane or not? He certainly felt fevered and needed a drink—a whole bar of them.

He had to get a grip. He could worry if he was insane or not later—right now he had to do what he was supposed to do or he was going to spend the rest of his life in jail, possibly on death row.

Trying not to look at Deirdre's body, he walked back out toward the front of the house. He went upstairs to make sure it was ransacked like the downstairs was. He saw that most of Deirdre's jewelry was gone, then noticed that Popeye had broken the jar that held his kidney stones. Now he'd have to get on his knees later and look for the fucking things. In the center of the room was a turd. Max squinted at it, truly horrified. Somehow it even seemed worse than the murder, that the animal went to the toilet on his carpet. How fucked up was that? Murder was one thing but this, this was a goddamn liberty.

He went back downstairs, just to make sure everything was right before he called the police. He was about to dial 911 when he saw something that made him freeze. Sticking out from the hallway into the living room was another pair of feet—a woman's feet in high heels. He thought, Jeez, it's just like *The Wizard of Oz*. Then nausea returned fast as he inched toward the hallway, shaking, covering his mouth. When he saw the second blood puddle he gagged, coughing up stomach acid. He couldn't recognize this woman's face either, but something about her body looked familiar. She was heavyset, wearing jeans and a light blue sweater. Her long curly brown hair looked familiar, too, like...

Fuck, it was Stacy Goldenberg—his niece, on Deirdre's side. She was living in New York, going to school at Columbia. Sometimes she and Deirdre went shopping together and, for some reason, she must have come home with her tonight.

Max fainted. When he regained consciousness both hips were killing him. He remembered the dead bodies and how he needed to call the police. He thought about confessing—getting a shrink to say he was nuts. They'd medicate him, lock him up for a while, and he'd eventually get out. Or he could pin the murders on Angela—say it was all her idea. It *was* all her idea, wasn't it?

He shouted, "Get me the fuck out of this!"

Max couldn't remember anything. Suddenly, his whole life was a fog. Then he heard Popeye saying how he would get to him if he ever went to the cops. This Popeye was a total psycho—there was no doubt about that—and Max had a feeling he meant everything he said.

Max went into the kitchen, chugged some vodka, the booze burning like a son of a bitch. Then he did some deep breathing, pulling himself back together, and dialed 911.

◦

Max was staring through the lace curtains at the red strobe lights outside the townhouse and he didn't hear the last question Detective Simmons had asked him.

"Sorry," Max said, "What was that?"

"The alarm," Simmons said. "Could you please tell me what happened with that again?"

Detective Simmons was a stocky black man, about forty years old. He was wearing a wrinkled white shirt, obviously discount, sweat stains on the armpits, with a tie wound on loosely. Max was wearing the navy sweat suit he'd changed into before the police came. He knew it was stylish and made him look slim and athletic.

Other officers, forensic workers and a crime-scene photographer were gathered in the hallway, creating a din of voices and confusion.

"Like I told that other officer," Max said. "I tripped it off by accident. I mean I forgot to disarm it."

"So the alarm definitely wasn't ringing when you got home?"

"No," Max said.

Now Simmons was looking in a small notepad, saying, "And what about the other victim—Stacy Goldenberg. Did you know that your wife was going shopping with her today?"

"No," Max said. He was starting to feel nauseous again, thinking about how he was going to have to face his brother-in-law and sister-in-law—Stacy's parents. The vodka in his stomach was shouting, *Yo, buddy, how 'bout some more down here?*

"When was the last time you spoke to your wife?"

"Like I told the first officer—this morning."

"You didn't talk to her at all during the course of the day?"

Max shook his head, trying for that devastated look.

"The past few days, had your wife told you about anything strange that happened around the house while you were gone? For example, did she say any strangers came to the door or rang the bell or anything like that?"

Max, still shaking his head, said, "No. Nothing like that," acting weighed down with grief.

"So far we haven't found any sign of forced entry," Simmons said. "What about keys? Do you keep a spare set with any friends or neighbors?"

"No," Max said, letting his voice choke a little.

"What about the code to your alarm? Do you share that with anybody?"

"No one knew the code except me, Deirdre, and the alarm company." Damn, if he could just squeeze a few tears out. How did they do that shit?

"You see what I'm getting at, don't you, Mr. Fisher? There are only two likely possibilities for how the killer got inside the house. He either broke in before the women arrived, or he forced his way in with them. If he broke in, he would have tripped off the alarm, and if he forced his way in with the women, the alarm would still have gone off unless he forced your wife to disarm it. But even if he did that, it wouldn't explain how the alarm got set again when he left, and you're telling me that when you came home the alarm was set. So the only logical conclusion is that the killer—or killers—somehow knew the code to your alarm."

Simmons gave him a look that seemed to scream, *I know you did it and I'm gonna hang you for it, you schmuck.*

Trying to ignore the look, pretending he was imagining it, Max said, "You know, I'm really not feeling too well. Is it possible we could do this tomorrow?"

He wiped his dry eyes, as if he were on the verge of some hysterical weeping.

"I understand," Simmons said, "but it's true what they say, you know—the first twenty-four hours after a crime is committed is when most criminals are apprehended. If we could just clarify a couple of other things, I think it could help us a great deal."

An officer came over and started talking to Detective Simmons. Max wasn't paying attention, staring blindly again toward the activity outside the house.

"This is just routine," Simmons continued, "but can we go over your whereabouts tonight one more time just to make sure we got everything down right?"

He had a little edge in his voice, making it clear that this wasn't really a request.

"I was at Legz Diamond's entertaining a client."

"And what time did you get there?"

"I don't know. Somewhere around six o'clock."

"And you were with a gentleman named Jack Haywood?"

"That's right."

"And where does Mr. Haywood work?"

Max told him. Simmons wrote the information down then asked, "And how long were you at Legz Diamond's?"

He stressed the *Legz*, leaning on it, letting it show what he thought of those kinds of places.

"Like I said, I got home around ten, ten-thirty, so I was probably there, I don't know, till about nine forty-five, ten o'clock."

"And you say you took a cab home?"

"First I dropped Jack off at Penn Station." Suddenly, Max felt lightheaded again, a little dizzy. "I really don't think I can handle any more of these questions right now. I'm sorry." He couldn't wait to get back to that vodka bottle.

"You want to see a doctor?"

"No. That's all right. I think I just need to be alone."
Alone with vodka.

"You might want to think about staying at a friend's house or at a hotel tonight. We'll have to be here for a while longer, working on the crime scene."

"That's all right," Max said. "I'd rather stay here."

Simmons gave him a look, like, *Why would you want to stay at the scene of a goddamn bloodbath?* Max wondered if he'd fucked up.

Trying to temper it, Max said, "I mean, of course it'll be difficult, but I'm gonna have to deal with it eventually, right?"

Shit, that didn't help. Work, brain, work.

"You sure about that?" Simmons said. "Those reporters are like goddamn vultures out there. This is going to be a big news story, you know."

"I know," Max said.

"Your number listed?"

Max shook his head.

"Well, that's one good thing anyway. If you want, I could have someone call Mr. and Mrs. Goldenberg, spare you that at least."

"It's okay," Max said. "I'll call them."

That was good, letting the cop know he was a standup guy. Yeah, it was going to be a difficult call but hey, that's what Max Fisher did, the difficult stuff.

Yeah, right.

Simmons stood, putting his pad away in his shirt pocket, and said, "I'll be in touch with you again, let you know how the investigation is going. You're not planning to leave town or anything, right?"

Max thought this over carefully then, as if his whole life had ended, said, "Where would I go?"

Calling Claire and Harold Goldenberg was a whole other nightmare. For Claire, Deirdre's sister, the murders were a double tragedy. After Max told her, she screamed, "No!

No! No!" then broke down, crying hysterically. Jesus, Max should have had that drink first. What the hell was wrong with him? Did he think she'd take it well?

When Harold got on the line Max had to go through the whole rigmarole again. He felt worse for the Goldenbergs than he did for himself. He'd always liked Harold, who had his own practice as a chiropractor in Boston, and he had nothing against Claire either. He didn't want to hump her or anything, but she was inoffensive. They were both nice enough people, and they definitely didn't deserve to lose their only kid in a tragedy like this.

Stacy wasn't so bad either. He never saw her very much when she was growing up, but when she started at Columbia she got closer with Deirdre, her "rich aunt in the city." It was horrible that she had to die, especially like this. She hadn't ruined anybody's life, caused misery for anybody. She was just an innocent college girl who probably didn't have an enemy in the world. Christ, she was only twenty.

Max felt his entire body getting hot and starting to shake—he wanted to call Angela, remind himself why he went through with all this crap in the first place. But as he picked up the phone and started to dial he stopped himself. That was exactly what Detective Simmons was waiting for. Max knew that Simmons suspected him more than he'd made out—why else would he have asked him if he was planning to leave town? The police had probably tapped his phone lines, put a cop on surveillance to watch his every move. They probably already knew about Angela, and her cousin, and Popeye, and now they were just waiting for Max to give himself away.

That alarm business had done them in, Max decided. That cocky Irish prick obviously wasn't as much of a pro as he claimed to be. Max kicked himself for not doing some kind of background check on Popeye before agreeing to all of this. He'd been thinking with his dick and that was never a smart move.

Max finished the bottle of vodka, the alcohol doing wonders to relieve his panic. He decided he was just acting paranoid, which was probably normal after you've paid to have your wife killed. He decided he couldn't have handled the situation any better than he had and the only thing he could do now was get some rest.

Surprisingly, Max slept like a baby, dreaming about Felicia the lap dancer.

In the morning, feeling clear-headed and alert, he resolved to keep his mind focused. He showered, shaved, and got dressed. The bedroom was still a mess so he did a little straightening up—he was able to retrieve all of his kidney stones—and decided he would have his maid come in later, or sometime soon, to finish cleaning. He was hungry and went downstairs to make a pot of coffee and some oatmeal. With a glass of water he swallowed a Mevacor and one of his little blue Viagra pills. The police had gotten someone to clean up the blood late last night, although there was still a faint stain on the wall where Deirdre's brains had splattered. Max decided he would have to have the maid deal with that too. He'd also have to get someone to repair the two bullet holes in the walls. Or maybe he could just hang pictures over them.

As Max ate his breakfast, the doorbell rang several times. Looking through the peephole, he saw the reporters outside his door. Finally, when he finished his food, Max opened the door and made a brief statement to the TV cameras.

He said, "This is a tragedy that no one who hasn't experienced the violent death of a loved one, or loved ones, could possibly comprehend. I just hope the police find the bastard who did this and that he's punished to the fullest extent of the law."

He knew he'd achieved the right blend of outrage and deep sorrow and that his face would look great on the news. Hell, he'd probably get letters from women asking to marry him.

The reporters shouted questions, but Max apologized politely and shut the door. He was proud of himself for handling the situation so well. He sounded exactly the way he was supposed to sound and he'd even managed to force out some tears. He'd put drops in his eyes beforehand and those suckers always stung him.

Keeping with Jewish tradition, Deirdre's funeral would have to be as soon as possible. Max calmly took care of all the arrangements, scheduling the service for Monday morning at the Riverside Memorial Chapel on Amsterdam Avenue, where he had gone for his aunt's funeral last year. The whole deal cost him a pretty penny but, hey, he wasn't no cheap date. He spent the rest of the day on the phone with friends and relatives, accepting condolences and sharing sympathies.

No one from the police department called all day, but Max didn't know whether this was good or bad. Late in the afternoon, he wondered if he should call Simmons to find out what was going on. It seemed like the natural thing to do, right? On the other hand, would that be something an actual grieving husband would do? Finally, he decided not to call and just wait and see what happened. This was more like the old Max, making informed decisions.

At six o'clock, he watched the local newscasts. All the stations had the murders as their top story—after all, it wasn't every day that two affluent white women were murdered in New York City. He watched himself on TV, again proud of his performance. According to the reports, there still weren't any suspects in the case, but police were conducting "a thorough investigation."

The next day Max woke up early to prepare for his guests. His brother Paul and Paul's wife Karen from Albany were coming down and so were Harold and Claire Goldenberg. The Goldenbergs were only going to stay for one night, and they were going to stay in a hotel. Tomorrow they would attend Deirdre's funeral in the morning and then fly back with Stacy's body to Boston for her funeral on Tuesday. Max was looking forward to seeing his brother and sister-in-law, but he was dreading having to face the Goldenbergs. He hated to admit it, with them grieving and all, but they were dull as hell.

The Goldenbergs arrived first, but fortunately they didn't want to stay long. Claire said she wanted to see the spot where her daughter had died, but when Max showed it to her she lost it and Harold had to take her back to the hotel. An hour or so later, Paul and Karen arrived. Max and Paul had never been very close, but Max always felt good about himself when he was around Paul. He had six years on his brother and, although their age difference didn't mean as much now that they were both in their fifties, Max felt that same superiority over his brother that he'd felt when he was sixteen and his brother was ten. Now Paul was an English professor at some college in Albany. He taught Shakespeare and Chaucer, or something like that, and he and Max had zero in common. Max loved watching Paul drool over the fine house, the expensive furnishings. Try pulling that down as a goddamn teacher.

The phone was ringing constantly through the day. Relatives and friends he hadn't heard from in years came to the house to pay their respects and to find out about the funeral arrangements. A couple of reporters rang the bell, too, but Max had Paul explain that the family needed to be alone. Karen went food shopping and came back and cooked a huge roast-beef-and-potatoes dinner. Max felt guilty about eating the meat, but he decided to hell with being health conscious—this was a special occasion. And, fuck it, he was hungry. All that sympathy gave you an appetite. He even had a slice of cherry cheesecake for dessert. It was delicious, too, worth every goddamn milligram of cholesterol.

Finally, Max was starting to feel some of the relief that he'd thought he'd feel after Deirdre was gone. With all these people around, Max imagined how aggravated he would have felt if Deirdre had been there, going on and on about herself and her problems or confronting people like some kind of maniac. Now, for the first time in years, Max felt like he could relax in his own house. The way he was handling his grief, his whole attitude, was having an impact too. Was it his imagination or was he standing a little more erect? Posture had always been a problem but, hey, murder your old lady, you didn't need a chiropractor. Radical therapy, maybe, but it worked.

Max was also starting to feel less guilty about Stacy's murder. Yeah, it was horrible that she had to die, and yeah, he was upset about it. But it wasn't as if *he* had killed anybody. Popeye was the crazy one—he'd pulled the trigger. Stacy's death was just an accident, no different than if she had been walking across a street and been run over by a bus. The fact that she was murdered in Max's house, by a hit man whom Max had employed, was an unfortunate coincidence that Max had had no way of preventing.

And, besides, she died with her dreams intact, no major disappointments yet. He'd kind of done her a favor, when you thought about it.

On the news that night, there were reports about a woman in Brooklyn who had strangled her two children and set them on fire and a janitor in a Bronx elementary school who was discovered having sex with a nine-year-old girl.

It was a good thing New York was full of sickos, Max decided—it meant that the stories of Deirdre and Stacy's murders would be quickly overshadowed.

The next day, Monday, was the funeral. Max wore a Hugo Boss suit, one he knew made him look good. Harold and Claire were at the chapel, along with the rest of Deirdre's relatives and friends. Many of Max's relatives were there too. Some people from the office came, including NetWorld's CFO and Vice President. Although Max was hoping Angela would show up, he realized it was probably better that she hadn't. Probably no one would have noticed, but it might have seemed slightly unusual for someone who had been with the company less than a year to take such a strong interest in her boss's personal affairs. Besides, they wouldn't have had a chance to talk in private anyway.

Max was barely listening to the rabbi's eulogy, but when he realized that everyone was breaking down in tears, he knew he had to show *some* reaction. He couldn't force out any tears, so he just put on his sunglasses and just stared down at his lap. He tried to emit some loud sighs but feared it sounded like he was breaking wind. He decided to let it slide, let the shades do the talking, like rock stars did.

After the rabbi, Claire stood at the podium and made a long sad speech about how she had lost two of the most important people in her life. This actually made Max cry and he took off his sunglasses for everyone to see. He was going for that swollen eyelid look that women seemed to pull off naturally.

Deirdre was buried in her family plot on Long Island. Max was glad they hadn't bought plots together and that he would never have to be anywhere near Deirdre again. After Deirdre was lowered into the ground, each family member covered the coffin with a shovelful of dirt. Max felt another wave of relief when the dirt he dropped clattered on top of her coffin.

Then came his moment, the grand slam, the slam-dunk. He approached the grave, letting a slight tremor rack his body, then produced one white rose. He'd planned to let it flutter into the hole as he gave a perfect moan but, fuck, he missed and the flower landed on the side. He had to bend down, dirtying his new suit, then muttered, *Fucksake*, and threw the goddamned thing in.

The *shiva* sitting was at Max's house. During the next few days, people dropped by the townhouse, bringing food, and sharing stories about Deirdre. As much as Max had enjoyed the mourning bit at first, it was getting old. Besides, it made his jaw hurt, having to wear that hangdog expression day after fucking day.

Paul and Karen stayed until Tuesday night and then drove back to Albany. On Wednesday, a condolence card arrived from the office, along with a bouquet of flowers. Although the card was signed by almost everyone, Max didn't read anyone's note except Angela's. It read:

> *With My Deepest Sympathy, Angela*
> *Gra go mor*

What the fuck was with that, Greek or something?

Seeing her handwriting made Max suddenly desperate to see her in person. Again, he wanted to call her—just to hear her voice, that accent he loved, and hang up—but he knew that would be stupidest thing he could do. But he was becoming restless. He couldn't wait to go back to work, to get back into the swing of things.

On Thursday, Berna, Max's West Indian maid, came and scrubbed the wall and the floor in the downstairs hallway. A repairman came to fill in the bullet holes and now it was impossible to tell that anything had happened. Kamal had come back from India and on Thursday he came by to prepare Max's macrobiotic meals for the next several days. He hadn't heard anything about the murders. When Max told him he broke down crying.

Max hadn't realized how close Kamal and Deirdre had become. Max had hired Kamal a couple of months ago, after he had been referred by the massage therapist at his health club. Kamal had often come to the house while Max was at work.

When Kamal was composed enough to speak he invited Max to come with him sometime to an ashram on the West Side to meditate. Max said he'd think about it, although he couldn't imagine himself sitting in a lotus position and chanting like some hippie.

"Remember, people don't die, because they aren't born," Kamal said. "Birth and death are merely illusions. All people and objects exist now and forever in the universal unconscious."

Max stared at him, thinking, *What a crock*.

Max liked Kamal's cooking and he thought he was a nice guy, but he decided that if kept forcing this religious crap on him the guy would be history.

On Friday, Max couldn't stand being cooped up any longer. He took a cab to his gym in the Claridge House on Eighty-seventh and Third. He swam his usual forty laps, then sat in the steam room, reading *The Wall Street Journal*. After he showered, he weighed himself and was thrilled to see that he'd lost four pounds.

He had a relaxing weekend at home—eating Kamal's food, taking short walks around the neighborhood. On Saturday—a gorgeous seventy-degree day—he walked to Central Park and sat for most of the afternoon on a bench in the shade, reading networking magazines, trying to keep up on new developments in the industry. There'd been nothing about the murder or the police investigation in the newspapers or on TV. Max remembered how

Detective Simmons had promised to "be in touch soon" and now more than a week had gone by since the murder. While Max was glad that the story seemed to be fading, he didn't like the way Detective Simmons was staying away from him. As he walked home from the park, Max had a funny feeling he was being watched.

Ten

Bobby was watching the girl with the blond hair and the big rack check into her room at the reception desk of the Hotel Pennsylvania. The way she kept looking around, twirling her hair with her index finger, Bobby could tell she was uptight about something. She was wearing low-slung jeans and a tight tube top and high heels. Bobby tried to imagine what she looked like naked and, man, he liked the picture that popped into his head. He wished he could whip his camera out right there. She had a slutty look to her, but there was something innocent about her, too, like she was afraid of something. She didn't look like a hooker, but she definitely looked like a girl who was someplace she wasn't supposed to be.

As she walked past the table with the big arrangement of red flowers, Bobby wheeled across the lobby to the Bell Captain's desk and said to Victor, "The girl near the elevator. Find out if she's expecting anybody."

Victor looked beyond the flow of people and said, "You mean the skinny chick with the knockers and the big hair? I never seen her before in my life."

"I didn't ask you if you've seen her before. I said find out if she's expecting anybody."

Victor went to the reception desk. A minute or two later he came back to Bobby and said, "She's meeting her husband up there, they're staying the night."

"I'm going up," Bobby said.

"You hear what I said? The girl's married."

"Married my gimp ass. She wasn't wearing a rock—she had some other weird fucking ring on her finger."

"That doesn't mean she's not married."

"I'm telling you, there's something going on with her."

"Look, let's just wait for a real escort to come along."

Bobby, looking at Victor in that dorky bellhop uniform, wondering if something had really happened to the guy's balls, if they fell off in the chemo or something, said, "Just get me the key to that girl's room."

"Come on," Victor said. "I really don't think this is a good idea."

"Look, if this is gonna work you're gonna have to trust me. You know I wouldn't do anything stupid, right?"

"Hey, I'm not calling anybody stupid, but you said we were gonna go after pros."

"I'm telling you, I have a hunch about this girl. She looked scared, the way she kept playing with her hair. If she's not a pro, I bet she's cheating on her old man or the guy's cheating on his old lady. We could make a mint with one good picture. I know when something's off and this smells to hog heaven, they're cheating, on someone."

"Whatever," Victor said. "But I'm telling you—I think you're making a big mistake."

When Victor came back with a maid's plastic keycard Bobby said, "So what name did they register under?"

"Brown," Victor said.

"See? Now tell me that isn't a bullshit name. I'm telling you, stick with me and you're gonna go places."

Bobby got off the elevator on the eighteenth floor. He wheeled himself one direction, took a few towels from a maid's cart, then went back the other way to room 1812. He could hear Mr. Brown's moaning from two doors away. Fuck, you could of heard him in Queens. After making sure the coast was clear, he slipped the keycard Victor had given him into the lock and slowly pushed the door open.

Room 1812 was long and narrow, with the bed against the wall at the far end. The light on the night table was on so Bobby had a clear view of the action, which was good because the light from the hallway didn't make it too far into the room. Bobby went about halfway over the threshold and gently let the door rest against his chair. Then he raised his camera with a towel over it, the lens peeking out underneath.

Mr. and Mrs. Brown were going at it, but all the noise was coming from Mr. Brown—Mrs. Brown wasn't making a peep. As Bobby snapped a few quick shots, he had a feeling that he knew Mr. Brown from somewhere. Then he remembered seeing him pass by in the lobby earlier in the night. But downstairs the guy had had curly blond hair and now he was nearly bald. He almost muttered, *The fuck happened to you?*

Mr. Brown must've heard the snapping camera or seen Bobby out of the corner of his eye because he looked up and after staring at Bobby for a couple of seconds said, "Hey, what the hell?"

Bobby let the corner of the towel drop over the camera's lens.

"Jeez, I'm sorry, mister," he said. "I'm really, really sorry. I just came to bring you your towels—"

"Get the fuck out of here!" Mr. Brown shouted.

Wheeling toward the bathroom, Bobby said, "It'll only take a minute, mister. I gotta put fresh towels in every room two times a day or they get really mad at me—"

"Just get the hell outta here!"

"You don't want your towels?"

"Get out, you fucking moron!"

"What about your soap?"

"Leave!"

"Please, Mister," Bobby said, wheeling back toward the door. "Don't get me fired. I need this job. I need it real bad." He took a last look at the blonde, who'd pulled the sheet up around her tits and turned her back to him. "I'm real sorry about bustin' in on you, I didn't see nothing…" He scooted out the door and let it shut behind him.

Riding the elevator down, camera tucked in his bag, Bobby was smiling, proud of his performance. He was better than fuckin' Dustin Hoffman in *Rain Man*. Maybe he should've listened to Isabella, gone on some auditions. Maybe it wasn't too late. There had to be roles for guys in wheelchairs, right?

Nah, he decided, acting was too fucking boring. He needed the buzz, the action. Crime was where it was at.

As he wheeled out into the lobby, he started thinking about Mrs. Brown.

She was a good-looking girl all right. She had to be a pro—why else would a girl like that spread her legs for some middle-aged bald guy looked like that?

In the lobby, Bobby met Victor near the Thirty-second Street exit, said, "So far, so good."

"Yeah, sure" Victor said, all panicked, like he didn't believe it for a second. "What the fuck happened?"

"Stop shitting your pants, will ya?" Bobby said. "I got some good pics. Now we just gotta get the payola."

Bobby took the Eighth Avenue bus uptown. When he got back to his apartment, he developed the film as fast as he could. Two of the shots had come out blurry and one had the towel in the way, but two were clear as fucking day. In the one he was going to use, you could see Mr. Brown with his mouth open, staring at the camera, while Mrs. Brown was just starting to cover those big knockers of hers. Bobby thought for a moment, trying to come up with a good name, then on the back of the picture he wrote a note telling Mr. Brown to leave ten thousand dollars at the hotel's front desk for "Tommy Lee." He stuck the photo inside a manila envelope and sealed it.

When he arrived back at the hotel, Victor said, "I got some bad news for you. The guy and the girl—they both took off."

"Fuck, when?"

"Half hour after you left. Why don't you keep your fuckin' phone on? Goddamn phones—everybody's got 'em, but nobody's got 'em turned on."

"I thought you said they were staying the night?"

"That's what they told the girl at the desk, but that doesn't mean they're gonna do it. It's not like they're *obligated* to."

"Shit."

"And that's not all—the cops were here."

"The cops?"

"There an echo in here?"

Wanting to smack Victor, Bobby said, "What the hell'd the cops want?"

"Got me. When I first found out I thought, That's it— I'm fired. F 'n' F. Fired and fucked."

Now Bobby remembered seeing a big black guy in a gray suit in the lobby earlier in the night, thinking the guy had a cop look to him. Bobby had always had great cop-dar.

"Was he asking about us?" Bobby asked.

"No, that's just it," Victor said. "It was the couple. He was asking all kinds of questions about them. Who are they, have they been here before, what's the girl's name— shit like that."

"The girl? Not the guy?"

"That's all I know," Victor said. "Then when the girl

left the cop followed her. Look, Bobby. I mean I like working with you again and everything, but we can't do this shit no more. Now with the cops coming down here, this is getting crazy. I can't lose this job, Bobby. It has nothing to do with you—I just can't lose this fucking job, I've too much riding on my paycheck."

Bobby, starting to wheel away, said, "The whole thing was a dumb idea anyway. Forget about it."

"Hey, come on," Victor said. "Don't be like that. Wait up a second."

During the bus ride home, Bobby was thinking about the cop, wondering why he was asking questions about the girl. He also wondered why Mr. Brown arrived at the hotel wearing that blond wig. Then he thought, What the fuck difference did it make? Even if the guy had paid the money it wouldn't've changed anything. Right now Bobby had enough money. He owned his apartment outright and had some savings safe with loan sharks. What would an extra ten grand do for him? It wouldn't get him outta the goddamn chair, wouldn't let him get up and walk to the deli or whatever. He wasn't doing this for the money. The money was, like, a *bonus*. Just to show he wasn't completely fucking useless.

A few months after he was paralyzed a vocational counselor at Mount Sinai Hospital asked Bobby if he was planning to return to work and Bobby said, "Hell yeah."

The woman went on about the different services available to him, how he could learn how to use a computer and maybe get some bullshit office job, and Bobby said, "I don't wanna do *that* kind of work—I wanna do *my* work. Can you guys help me do that?"

"And what kind of work do you do, Mr. Rosa?" she'd asked.

Bobby had mumbled something like, *Never mind*, and hightailed it the fuck out of there.

Bobby was lost in thought and suddenly realized that the bus was passing the Eighty-ninth Street stop. He started screaming at the driver, "Hey, what the hell's wrong with you, asshole! Didn't you hear me ring the goddamn bell? Jesus Christ, what the fuck does a guy gotta do to get off a fucking bus these days?" If he'd been packing, he might have shot the fuck.

Bobby continued to curse as the driver lowered him on the wheelchair lift. He heard the driver shout after him, "You're welcome."

Yeah, Bobby would have shot him.

When he got home, Bobby tried to relax on a tub chair in the shower. Then he flipped around on the TV awhile, but nothing was on. He ate a couple packages of Cup-a-Soup and then hit the sack.

The next day Bobby took a bus uptown to visit his mother at the Jewish Home for the Aged, a nursing home on 106th Street. He'd moved his mother up there last year, from a nursing home in Brooklyn, because it was only seventeen blocks from his apartment and he wanted to visit her more often.

For a while, he went every day, bringing her ice cream and Chinese food and getting one of the orderlies to wheel her out to the garden so she could get some fresh air. But then his mother had another stroke, a bad one, and now she just slept most of the time. Bobby still visited her three or four times a week; he would've gone more often, but it was too depressing to see her so out of it. He was afraid that when her time came and she died that was how he'd remember her—with her eyes closed and her toothless mouth sagging open.

As usual, his mother was in bed asleep. Her body had shriveled, especially on her left side. She'd always been short, but under the blanket she looked like she was four feet tall. There were tubes connected to her arms, meaning she probably had another infection. Bobby was gonna raise hell, find out why nobody called to tell him, but he knew this wouldn't do any good. It would just get him all worked up and his mother would still be lying in bed like a vegetable. Sometimes Bobby thought his mother would be better off dead and he even thought about taking her home and shooting her.

More and more, he just wanted to shoot somebody, go postal, let them know how goddamn angry he was.

He might've done it too, offed his Mom, except she was Catholic and he knew she wouldn't want that. She was probably already pissed off at him for putting her in a Jewish nursing home. But, hey, she was past complaining.

Bobby shook his mother's arm until her eyes opened. She couldn't smile anymore, but Bobby could always tell she was happy to see him. The dribble from the corner of her mouth could be a sign of happiness, he figured. Like she was trying to smile.

After sitting next to her for a while, Bobby took the elevator down to the cafeteria and bought a little container of ice cream. Then he went back up to his mother's room and shook her awake. She turned toward him, but this time only one of her eyes opened.

"Look, Ma, I got your favorite—vanilla."

His mother turned away, like she was angry, but Bobby kept the little wooden stick with the glob of ice cream on it in front of her face until she turned back and started eating it. Some ice cream dripped down her chin and Bobby wiped it off with the sleeve of his shirt. He took a lick himself and that shit wasn't half bad.

When she finished eating, Bobby stayed with her a while longer, watching her sleep. Then he realized that it was past one o'clock and her soap operas were on. He turned on the TV in front of her bed to channel 7 and cranked the volume. He leaned over the bed, kissed her, and then left the room quietly.

When Bobby got back to his apartment he realized he had nothing to do. He would've gone to Central Park with his camera and scouted for some new prospects, but it was getting cloudy outside and the air felt like rain. Maybe he'd just go out to the video store, check out the new releases, pick up some food at the supermarket, and then come back home and call it a day.

Bobby came back from the supermarket and cooked himself dinner—baked beans, powdered potatoes, and two cans of Beefaroni. Even Def Leppard couldn't get him out of his funk. When the Def couldn't crank you, it was way past time to shoot someone.

While he ate he stared at the pictures of Mr. and Mrs. Brown, thinking that the guy was starting to look familiar again. He didn't know if he was imagining it—maybe it was just that he was staring at the pictures for so long, of course the guy was starting to look familiar. But, no, there was more to it than that. Bobby had seen that face before. Then, suddenly, it clicked. He wheeled out to the hallway, to the incinerator room, and when he didn't find what he was looking for there, he rode the elevator down to his building's basement. In one corner, the porters stacked the old newspapers they picked up from the recycling bins on every floor. Once a month they'd tie them up and cart them off, but recycling day must have been a couple of weeks off because the pile was pretty big. Bobby fished through the papers until he found the week-old *Daily News* he was thinking of. But he didn't really get excited until he turned to page three and saw the big picture of Mr. Brown, and the story of the two women who were murdered on the Upper

East Side in this very expensive-looking townhouse. Max Fisher, the article said, was the founder and CEO of NetWorld…

Bobby took the paper with him back to his apartment. Suddenly, Leppard sounded okay again. Thanks to a millionaire named Max Fisher, Bobby was back in business.

Eleven

Sutter looked at him. "I prefer tough, rich and
a pussy magnet."
"As a cop, you might get two of those three."
Sutter smiled and said, "You never know."
JAMES O. BORN, *Walking Money*

On May 12, 1989, Alexis Morgan, a thirty-six year-old
former model, was walking her two pet chihuahuas
through a secluded path near Belvedere Castle in
Central Park when she was brutally stabbed to death by a
mysterious assailant. The single wound to her throat had
nearly decapitated her, and police believed she was
grabbed from behind and cut with a large knife or
machete. There were no witnesses to the attack but several people reported seeing "a suspicious white man" in
the area minutes before the killing and hearing her chihuahuas barking moments afterwards.

Although he didn't fit the description of the "suspicious
white man," Ms. Morgan's husband Henry, a wealthy real
estate mogul, was a prime suspect. The Morgans had had
a stormy two-year marriage, marred by loud public fights
and Mr. Morgan's accusations that his wife was having an
affair. While Mrs. Morgan's pocketbook was stolen in the
attack, police believed this may have been "a decoy," to
make it appear as if robbery had been the motive.

Mr. Morgan had a rock solid alibi—he was playing
tennis with a friend at the Wall Street Racket Club at the
time of the murder, and the friend and workers of the
club vouched for him. However, the police still didn't

rule out Morgan completely. They believed he may have hired someone to kill his wife. They created a composite sketch of the suspect and began a citywide manhunt for the killer. A few weeks later, police tailed Morgan to a meeting at a diner in Chelsea with Vinny "The Blade" Silvera, a killer known to have connections to the mob. Later that night, Silvera was brought in for questioning, but wouldn't confess to anything. Morgan was arrested separately. Under heavy interrogation, Morgan—who had his own business links to organized crime—was told that Silvera had confessed and then Morgan, falling for the ploy, promptly gave a taped confession, implicating Silvera. Both Morgan and Silvera were tried and sentenced. A few months later, Morgan was found beaten to death in a bathroom on Riker's Island.

Of course there were many obvious differences between Alexis Morgan's murder and the recent murders of the two women in the East Seventy-fourth Street townhouse, but there were many similarities as well. In both cases, robbery was the apparent motive. In both cases, the victims had been killed brutally, as if murder was the sole intention. And in both cases the husbands had convenient airtight alibis.

Kenneth Simmons, Detective Investigator at the 19th Precinct, had had nothing to do with the Alexis Morgan case. He was only in his second year on the force in 1989 and he was still spending most of his time doing clerical work. But, like everyone else who lived in the city at that time, he had followed the details of the case closely in the news. Several years later, at a promotion ceremony at One Police Plaza, he met Lieutenant Anthony Santana, who had broken the case, and Santana filled him in on many of the details. In particular, Kenneth recalled how Santana had told him that he would have broken the case much sooner if it weren't for all the media hype. "It was like a zoo," Santana said. "The suspects always knew they were being watched twenty-four hours a day." He believed that if Morgan didn't know he was being watched, he would have led them to Silvera much sooner. Santana said, "You can't shoot a deer when he hears your footsteps, you gotta sneak up on the fuck, know what I'm saying?"

Kenneth knew.

While he wasn't going to rule out any possibility, Kenneth was ninety percent certain that the townhouse murders were Alexis Morgan all over again. Max Fisher had hired somebody to kill his wife and Stacy Goldenberg was just in the wrong place at the wrong time. When he interviewed Max at the house he had a feeling Max was holding out on him and Kenneth's detective instincts were rarely wrong. But he also knew that the important thing was not to press him. Like Santana said—you can't let them hear your footsteps.

Kenneth was hoping that the townhouse case would be his big case, the one that comes along once in a detective's life. Solving the murders of two white women would also be great P.R. and could lead to a promotion to Sergeant or Lieutenant in a couple of years. Kenneth had been married for eight years and five years ago had had a baby son with Down Syndrome. The baby's condition had near destroyed his wife. And people's comments like

> *Mongoloid*
> *Retard*
> *Damaged goods*
> *Handicapped*

had ignited a rage in Kenneth that simmered close to the surface every waking moment. He was searching for an outlet to vent and Max Fisher was going to be it. He hated the prick anyway, with his freaking designer suits, fake hair, smarmy attitude, and that collection of classical music. Kenneth was a closet opera buff—not a fact you advertised as a New York City cop—but when he saw Fisher's classical collection he knew right away that the man was full of shit. He had all the big names out, like he was trying to impress, but it was obvious he had no true respect for the music.

And what was up with that navy tracksuit he'd been wearing during the first interview, acting like he thought it made him look all that? Kenneth wanted to put the man in another kind of suit—an orange one.

Fisher was going to be Kenneth's ticket to a promotion all right. His goal when he came on the force was to make Lieutenant before he was forty and to start collecting his pension by the time he was forty-five. He was thirty-nine now, so time was running out. He already had a time-share at a condo on the Jersey shore, but he couldn't wait until he was retired, and could spend all his days on the golf course.

Two days after the murders, Kenneth and his partner, Detective Louis Ortiz, were in Kenneth's office. Louis said, "Gluckman from Ballistics just called. They ran the bullets and shells through Bulletproof and Brasscatcher and came up dry."

Kenneth finished a long sip of coffee, said, "But they still say it was a .38, right?"

"Yeah, but get this—they think it was a Cold Lady .38. Our killer wouldn't be too smart if he bought a broad's gun on the street."

"Unless the killer *is* a broad."

"You really think so?"

"I doubt it sincerely. But I think the guy might've fucked up on purpose—sets the alarm and buys the pussy gun because he wants to give us a lot to think about."

"You really think that's what happened?"

"You know what I think. The job was sloppy—the guy who did it wasn't a pro. He was a friend or someone Fisher had met. We got any priors with this gun?"

"*Nada* so far."

"Any word on the street?"

"They've been debriefing everybody they bring in, all Manhattan precincts, but so far nothing. Nothing from Forensics either. They said the women died somewhere between five-thirty and seven-thirty—probably closer to five-thirty, and both right around the same time. Nothing to go on with the blood either—it all came from the victims. The coroner also said the perp liked what he did. Some of the wounds were unnecessary, the victims were already dead. He called it overkill."

"And Fisher's alibi?"

"Rock-fucking-solid. A stripper remembered him—said she was giving him a lap dance around that time. Gave me her business card, too, by the way. She said she likes giving freebies to cops. You should've seen his friend, the client he was 'entertaining.' The guy was shitting bricks, man. He was like, 'You gotta promise me—this won't go back to my wife, right? This won't go back to her, will it?' Man, and I thought *I* was p-whipped." Then, smiling, he added, "But maybe we'll get lucky and get some DNA off the turd the shooter left."

Kenneth got up from his desk and stretched. He'd helped his wife move some furniture last night and he'd thrown his damn back out. He said, "Let's give it a couple of days—see what happens. At least the media isn't jumping all over this case the way I thought they would. Gives us a little more room."

"Yeah," Louis said. "It's lucky that crazy bitch set her kids on fire in Brooklyn."

"Hey, I'll take a break anyplace I can get it." Then Kenneth, rocking his hips to keep his back loose, added,

"We still got one big problem—motive. Why did Max Fisher want his wife dead?"

"Wild guess—she was fucking some other guy."

"That's the obvious answer, so where's the other guy? And how come none of her friends or relatives ever heard her talking about a lover? I'm telling you, there's something about this case that just doesn't fit. The answer's out there—we just gotta find it."

As he always did when he was distracted, or when he was angry or frustrated about something, Kenneth touched the gold pin in his lapel. It showed two hands reaching out to each other, never quite touching and looking like they never would. It was the symbol for Down Syndrome, and one night on CNN he was thrilled to see Bill Clinton on there wearing the pin. Kenneth had done a little Google search, and discovered the pin had been given to Clinton by some obscure mystery writer. When he told his wife all she could say was, "I don't read mysteries."

Kenneth looked up, saw Louis watching him playing with the pin.

"You really wanna nail this motherfucker, don't you?" Louis said.

"Yeah, I really do," Kenneth said.

The next few days brought a couple of new developments. It was discovered that Max Fisher had made several withdrawals from his bank accounts the few days before the murders, but it only added up to several thousand dollars—something worth thinking about, but it wasn't enough money to prove that he had hired a hit man. Ballistics' Brasscatcher database determined that the Lady Colt .38 may have been the same gun used in the unsolved homicide of the owner of a shoe store in Queens a year and a half ago. At first, Kenneth thought this could be the big break, then he found out that Brasscatcher couldn't be one hundred percent about the match. And, even if the same gun was used in both crimes, it didn't mean that the gun hadn't changed hands on the street one or more times since the Queens murder. It was suggested that the Boyos, who had a front in the Bowery, were selling these guns on the street but it was almost impossible to pin anything on them. Worse, people liked them, because everyone had seen *In The Name Of The Father* and thought that's the way it really was. Trying to arrest an IRA guy was like trying to arrest a Mafia guy, you were messing with the public's romantic notions.

Louis questioned people at Max's office and friends and family members of Deirdre Fisher and Stacy Goldenberg and came up with no new leads. Jeez, it was going cold already.

Kenneth and Louis were having lunch, sitting at one of the back tables in Pick-a-Bagel on Second Avenue, when Louis said, "We gotta start looking at other possibilities, man."

Kenneth swallowed a bite of bagel with tofu scallion cream cheese, then said, "Like what?"

"Like maybe it was just what it looked like at the beginning—a guy was robbing a townhouse, the women came home, he panicked and shot them."

"The alarm was reset," Kenneth said. He hadn't been able to sleep for the past two nights, his frustration with the case getting to him. "Fisher set the alarm off when he went into the house. Unless Fisher was lying—and I see no reason why he would lie about that because it just makes him look more guilty—then Fisher must've given the alarm code to whoever killed those two women."

He'd gone over this a hundred times till his wife had roared, "You're obsessed."

She was right.

"Hey, that makes sense to me," Louis said. "So why don't we just bring Max Fisher in?"

"If I thought that would help—believe me, I wouldn't be sitting here on my fat ass eating bagels. But we gotta make Fisher think he's safe, let him get complacent. Every day that goes by that he doesn't hear from me he gets a little more nervous. Right now he's probably thinking, 'Why isn't Detective Simmons calling? He said he'd call.' But pretty soon he's gonna think we forgot all about him and that's when his big shot side is gonna come out. He's gonna think he's above the law, king of the world, and that's when he's gonna slip up. And that's when I come in and go for my knockout punch. That's when he gets the new tracksuit."

"Tracksuit?" Louis asked.

"Trust me on this one," Kenneth said. "We keep up with the silent treatment a few more days and start tailing him. Who knows? Maybe it'll be like Alexis Morgan all over again. Maybe he'll dig his own grave."

Kenneth put a twenty-four hour surveillance on Max Fisher, but this didn't turn up any new leads. Fisher went to the park, the supermarket, his health club, and other normal places. Then, just when it seemed like the case was going nowhere, there was a breakthrough. Some of the jewelry that was stolen at Max Fisher's apartment turned up at a pawnshop in Chinatown. The owner of the shop, Mr. Chen Liang, didn't speak a word of English, but through a translator swore to Kenneth that he didn't know who the man was who'd sold him the jewelry, he'd never seen him before. The man had allegedly come into the shop on Saturday afternoon, the day after the murder. He dumped the jewelry on the counter and said "How much?" Liang said he offered the man five thousand dollars, even though the jewelry was worth ten or twenty times that much. The man must've not known jack about jewelry because he didn't complain, didn't even try to negotiate. He happily took the cash and left the store.

Liang gave a complete description of the man. He was about five-eight, one-thirty, dirty grey hair, funny-looking mouth, and was wearing a leather jacket with what looked like a bullet hole in it. He spoke English with some kind of accent. Liang was very cooperative and polite until he found out he'd have to give back the jewelry. Then he started screaming like a maniac in goddamn Chinese, carrying on so much Kenneth almost had to cuff him.

Kenneth put out a citywide alert for the man. He knew that this guy might not be the killer—he may have just been a fence the real killer or someone else had sold the jewelry to—but finding him would definitely be a good start. Also, Kenneth now knew for sure that this wasn't a professional job. A pro wouldn't be dumb enough to unload jewelry he'd stolen from the scene of a double murder. And a pro wouldn't be dumb enough to sell off jewelry for a fraction of its worth. The alarm business meant that it couldn't have been random either, so the only logical conclusion was that Fisher had hired a non-pro to bump off his wife—either an acquaintance or a small-time hood. Fisher had gone cheap and that would cost him.

Later in the day, Kenneth got word from his cop on surveillance that Fisher had gone into work. Kenneth drove down to Fortieth Street in his tan Coup-de-Ville and took over the stakeout himself, hoping that this might be the day Fisher slipped.

Finally, after seven o'clock, Fisher left his office. He looked nervous—like a man who's guilty as hell, Kenneth thought—looking in both directions as he headed toward Fifth Avenue. Kenneth drove around the corner, making a right on a red, and made it to the corner of Fifth and

Fortieth in time to see Fisher getting into a cab. The cab continued downtown on Fifth, so at least it didn't look like Fisher was going directly home. At Thirty-third, the cab turned right. It continued, inching along two traffic-congested blocks, pulling over in front of the side entrance to the Hotel Pennsylvania.

Kenneth stopped and double-parked about four or five car-lengths behind the cab. It was getting dark and he couldn't see clearly into the back of the cab, so he was surprised when Fisher got out wearing a curly blond wig. He looked so ridiculous that Kenneth almost started to laugh, asked aloud, "The fuck's with that?"

He got out of his car and followed Fisher into the hotel.

Fisher was at the reception desk, checking into a room. There was a lot of activity in the lobby, but Kenneth stayed a safe distance away anyway. After Fisher headed toward the elevators, Kenneth waited to see what would happen next. He wondered if Fisher was planning to meet his hit man to make his final payoff, just like Henry Morgan. He was already imagining himself in front of the mikes and cameras, explaining to the reporters how he had cracked the case. Then he saw himself, *Lieutenant Kenneth Simmons*, on the podium at One Police Plaza, shaking the Mayor's hand. His gold pin matching the new gold shield.

After about fifteen minutes had passed, Kenneth decided to go to the desk, start asking questions. The short woman with thick glasses behind the desk seemed uncomfortable, like she might be hiding something. He asked her if the man with the curly blond hair was meeting anyone in his hotel room and the woman pointed toward a good-looking white woman with big, blow-dried hair who was about to get on the elevator. For some reason, she looked familiar to Kenneth and a couple of seconds later it clicked. Earlier in the evening he had seen her leaving Fisher's office building. So Max Fisher was the one having the affair, not the wife. This was definitely getting interesting.

Kenneth asked the woman at the reception desk whether the couple came to the hotel frequently. The woman shrugged, then said, "I don't think so. At least not during my shift."

The woman told Kenneth that the couple had registered at the hotel under the name Brown and that they were planning to stay overnight.

Kenneth thought, *Brown? Are they kidding?*

About forty-five minutes later, the white woman with the big hair came out of an elevator and headed toward the Seventh Avenue exit. Kenneth considered stopping her and speaking to her, but decided it might be more valuable to follow her, see where she was going. Who knows? Maybe Fisher had met her in the hotel room to give her the money, and now she was on her way to make a final payoff to the hit man. Or maybe *she* was the hit man, or hit woman.

On Seventh, the woman hailed a cab going downtown. Kenneth didn't have time to get his car so he hailed another cab, presented his badge, and ordered the driver to follow the other car. It went across town to First Avenue and stopped on the corner of East Twenty-fifth Street. The woman got out and walked quickly up the block, toward Second. Kenneth followed her on the opposite side of the street, jogging to keep up with her.

About midway down the block, the woman went up the stoop into the vestibule of a tenement. Out of breath, Kenneth hurried up the stoop and followed her into the building. The woman turned around, startled. Kenneth was used to this reaction from white women in vestibules and elevators.

She was reaching into her purse—maybe for pepper

spray—when Kenneth said, "It's all right, I'm a Detective—NYPD." He showed his badge. He always got a rush out of that.

"Jesus Christ," the woman said. She was breathing heavily now too. "You just scared the bejaysus out of me."

Kenneth registered the brogue and had a fleeting thought about the murder weapon's possible connection to the Boyos.

Kenneth said, "You mind if I ask you a few questions?"

"Questions about what?"

"Do you live in this building?"

"Yeah. Why?"

"Can I have your name please?"

"What's this all about?"

"Can you tell me your name, please?"

The woman, still breathing heavily, said, "Angela. Angela Petrakos."

"I saw you at Hotel Pennsylvania before. You went into a room with Max Fisher, didn't you?"

"No."

"There's no use lying about it—I saw both of you. Is he your boss?"

Angela didn't answer so Kenneth asked the question again.

"Yeah, he's my boss."

"How long have you two been seeing each other?"

"We're not seeing each other."

"You realize his wife and niece were murdered last week. Now I'm not saying you had anything to do with that, but you're gonna have to answer these questions sooner or later. We could either do this here or down at the precinct. Take your pick. I could be wrong but a nice lady like you, I don't think you'd like the Precinct, it's a bit…rough."

Angela waited a few seconds, looking scared as hell,

and Kenneth almost fell sorry for her. She was good looking, with that blond hair and that great rack, and Kenneth wondered how she got mixed up with Fisher, what she saw in that sleazebag.

"Can we go inside and talk?" she said. "I have to go to the bathroom."

"Actually, I wouldn't mind using your bathroom myself," Kenneth said. "If you don't mind."

Following her upstairs he was thinking, Love that brogue, but what's with the Greek name? Then, watching her swing her hips back and forth, he thought, And she has a fine ass, that's for damn sure. Kenneth was faithful to his wife, had never cheated on her in eight years of marriage, but that didn't stop him from looking. And he'd heard cops talk about Irish girls in the locker room at the precinct. Word was they were like banshees in the sack.

The building was a typical tenement—the paint on the walls was peeling, there was a faint ammonia odor. Two floors up she stopped in front of apartment 5. She opened the door, said, "I still don't understand what you think I have to do with those people getting killed, this is really crazy," and then went ahead into the kitchen area. The lights in the apartment were on. Kenneth stepped inside and took a look around. It was a small place—a studio.

Angela said, "Can I get you something to drink?" and Kenneth said, "No, that's all right."

Then Kenneth noticed the shut door at the end of the apartment and the crack of light underneath. He was about to ask Angela if she lived alone when the door sprung open and a thin, pasty guy with long gray hair came out firing a handgun. Kenneth recognized the man as fitting the description of the suspect who'd hocked Deirdre Fisher's jewelry in Chinatown. Falling backward, he tried to reach into his holster for his own piece, but it was too late. He was already down.

Twelve

Of course it all went to shit. I should have known better.
VICTOR GISCHLER, *Gun Monkeys*

Dillon was watching *The Flintstones* on the Cartoon Network. It was one of his favorite episodes, with the Great Gazoo, and he was laughing like he'd been on the weed for a week. He'd had a wee dram of Jameson too, nothing lethal, when he heard voices in the hallway. It sounded like Angela talking to some guy, but he didn't think she was stupid enough to bring someone back to the apartment with her.

Dillon turned off the TV, hearing Angela say, "I still don't understand what you think I have to do with those people getting killed, this is really crazy."

Shite, Dillon thought, she brought home a Guard.

Cursing to himself, he took his gun out of his dresser drawer and went into the bathroom. The apartment door opened and Angela said, "Can I get you something to drink?" The guy said, "That's all right," and Dillon swung open the door and shot the feckin' cop two times in the chest, watching the fat bollix fall back, hit his head on the refrigerator, and land on the kitchen floor. If he wasn't so angry at Angela for bringing the cop home—what was the feckin' cunt thinking?—Dillon might've thought it was funny.

Angela was covering her mouth, trying not to scream. Dillon told her not to make a fecking sound. He didn't want the neighbors coming over, banging on the door. But then a minute went by, and another, and no neighbors showed up. Maybe they thought the shots came from TV or something. Angela was sitting on the bed, crying. The cop was in the puddle of blood on the kitchen floor. Dillon noticed a shiny gold pin on the wanker's lapel. He reached down, removed it, and pinned it on his own self.

Dillon knew he had to do *something*—get rid of this bollix fast. He couldn't carry the body down himself without breaking his back. Besides, where would he take it? Then he had a great idea. He heard this shite on TV once, or read it or some fuck. A guy was fighting with his wife or something and he hit her so hard she died. He didn't want the police to find out so he put her in the bathtub and poured battery acid all over her—covered her with it. When she dissolved, he just washed her down the drain.

Dillon had never tried that shite himself, but he thought that putting battery acid on the cop would be a great way to get rid of him—keep the gig nice and clean anyway. The only feckin' problem was he didn't know where he was going to get battery acid. He thought about it for a little while longer, then wondered, If battery acid could dissolve people, could Drano do the trick too? He didn't see why not. But he'd probably need a lot of Drano to get the job done and he couldn't go to the store now. Somebody might've heard those shots and by the time he came back cops could be raiding the feckin' place.

Angela was still crying like a Brit. Dillon went in the bathroom to take a leak and think, admired the way the pin caught the light when he tousled his hair in the mirror. He asked his own self, "Do I look like I just killed a cop?" The tinker's curse crossed his mind, but he shook himself free of it and said, "You look a poet me man."

When he came out, Angela was staring down at the cop, her eyes getting wider. Dillon looked over and said, "Jaysus, fuck me."

The cop's eyes were open and blood was dripping out of his mouth. He was trying to talk.

Dillon went into the drawer in the kitchen cabinet and took out a big butcher knife. He came back and jabbed the knife into the cop's chest. The cop's shirt turned redder, and the blood puddle grew, but his eyes closed for good. Dillon nearly admired the way the fooker had clung on to life, had tried to hang in there. But a butcher's knife, it doesn't do argument.

Angela was still crying, making noise now. Dillon slapped her in the face and said, "Shut up, yah hoor's ghost," and then went into the bathroom and washed his hands.

Dillon didn't know how things had gotten so fucked. After he sold the jewelry he'd taken to that Chinaman, he was planning to leave Angela and New York City. He'd always heard Miami was nice. He saw himself chilling out down there, smoking dope, lying on the beach and writing poems all feckin' day. To hell with moving into that rich fellah's house uptown. It was a stupid plan anyway—never would have worked. He was just going to hang out with Angela a little longer, till things cooled down, then it was *slan, alanna*. But, now, the stupid woman had fucked everything up—bringing home a cop right into her kitchen. Now, all of a sudden, Miami was in jeopardy.

He came out of the bathroom, went to the closet and took out two bed sheets. He tucked one of the sheets under the cop's fat body and then rolled the body onto the rest of it. Then he put the second sheet around the same way and went to the phone and called Sean, one of the other Prov-eens that hung around the boyos. Luckily, Sean was home. Sean was second generation Irish—thus more Irish than the real thing, used to be in the FDNY—and now he drove a livery cab. He said he'd definitely come to the city from Queens to help Dillon out, saying with his stutter, "N-n-nothing to pray about."

"Is the trunk of yah cab empty, Sean?" Dillon asked.

"W-w-why?"

"You'll find out me man."

After Dillon hung up he got two blankets out of the closet and he took the blanket and the sheet off the bed. Blood was soaking through the sheets that were currently wrapping the cop. Grabbing the cop by the feet, he dragged the body into the bedroom area, out of the blood puddle. He wrapped the body up the best he could. It didn't look very neat, but at least the blood wasn't leaking through anymore. Next, he got the mop and started mopping, wringing out the red water into the kitchen sink. He could mop like the best of them, prison taught you that. He got rid of most of it, but there was still a big red stain on the floor.

Dillon had nothing to do except wait for Sean, so he watched more *Flintstones* and some *Bugs Bunny*— American cartoons were feckin' mighty—then had another wee dram of Jameson. Well, you would, wouldn't you, after killing a Guard? After *Bugs Bunny* he watched some of the Knicks. He was gradually teaching himself about American sport, mainly to fill in the hours. He had learned that when you lose a game *you choke.* Jaysus, he loved that, *you choke.* And even better, if you lost a game, they said, Y*ou got your arse handed to you.*

He glanced at the trussed body and said, "You got yer arse handed to yah, fellah."

Finally Angela stopped crying. She went into the bathroom and came out, wiping her face with a towel. She sat down next to Dillon, held his hand, and said, "I'm sorry— I really, really am. I didn't mean to do any of this. He followed me home—I had no choice. It'll be all right, won't it? I mean nobody's come to the door so maybe nobody heard the bloody shots. If they did, maybe they didn't know what it was. Maybe they just thought it was a car backfiring or firecrackers or some shite. I mean the plan's still gonna work, right? We'll still get married, won't we? And we'll still get all of my boss's money too. You'll see. It's just gonna take a few months, right?"

He vaguely wondered why, all of a sudden she was speaking like an Irish version of Tony Soprano's wife.

"Whatever," Dillon said. He knew none of this was going to happen, but he never saw the point in telling a woman what he was thinking.

During the Knicks post-game show, the buzzer rang. First Dillon made sure it was Sean, then he buzzed to let him up.

Sean was like a caricature mick, red hair, skinny as a rail and with that death-white skin and freckles. He spoke with a stammer, especially when he was drunk, which was most of the time. He drank Guinness like water and spiced it up with Jameson. In the bag, he'd pick the hottest woman in any pub, sidle up to her, and go, "I-I-I d-d-d-dr-drive a c-c-cab. W-w-will you g g-go ou-ou-out wif me?" Then the left side of his face would begin to twitch, ensuring that any dim hope went right down the toilet. But he had a streak of ruthlessness that rivaled Dillon's own. It was rumored he'd killed a priest, the worst sin of them all, and said, "I'm going to hell, going to have me own self a time first. The priest will be waiting for me, keep the fire nice and toasty."

At the door Dillon said, "You leave your cab double-parked like I told you to?"

"Y-y-y-yes," Sean said. Then he noticed the body on the floor. He said, "Ih-ih-ih-is it a nun?"

"No, tis nothing," Dillon said. "Just a rent collector."

You want an Irish guy on yer side, kill a snitch or a rent collector, and you have their undying loyalty.

"G-g-good on yah," Sean said.

Angela was scrubbing the stains off the kitchen floor with a sponge and Mr. Clean. She said hello to Sean. Dillon said, "Sean, say hello to Angela."

Sean said, "I d-d-drive a c-c-cab. Will you g-g-g-go ou-ou-out wif me?"

Dillon shook his head, said to Angela, "We're just going to drive uptown, dump it somewhere, and that's it." And to Sean, "You'll be back home in like a half hour."

Then Dillon and Sean picked the body up—Dillon lifting from the head, Sean from the feet. The body wasn't as stiff or as heavy as Dillon expected.

"W-w-w-w-what if s-somebody sees us?" Sean asked.

"We have to be quiet, that's all," Dillon said. And then, remembering Lauren Bacall, he said, "You can be quiet, can't yah, you just put your lips together and shit the fook up."

Jesus, he loved that broad, Bacall, she was a real dame, a ball-buster and with serious edge. Dillon wondered if she had any Irish in her. If not, he'd have been glad to supply some.

Dillon opened the door and listened closely to make sure nobody was in the hallway or coming up or down the stairs. Then he said, "Let's go."

They went down the two flights of stairs like they were carrying a piece of furniture. At the bottom of the stairs Sean walked too fast and the cop's head banged into the wall.

"Jaysus, yah bollix," Dillon said. "Take it easy, will yeh?"

They opened the first door into the vestibule then Sean stopped suddenly—his eyes staring ahead. Dillon turned around and saw a man coming up the steps into the building. There was no time to go back upstairs. They just had to move to the side of the vestibule and let the man pass.

Dillon had seen the guy in the building before. He was a typical nancy white guy—wore a suit every morning, going to work. He'd never said a word to Dillon before, but this time he smiled and said, "Moving out?"

He looked drunk and he smelled like alcohol. He was wearing one of his suits, but the tie was on loose.

"No," Dillon said. "Just tossin' away me old rug."

"Cool," the man said.

He passed by Sean and disappeared up the stairs.

Sean said, "L-l-l-l-l-let's just g-g-g-g-g—"

"Just shut yer stammerin' mouth and start movin'," Dillon said.

They carried the body out to the street. There was no one passing by and no cars were coming. Moving fast, they stuffed the body into the trunk and got inside the car, a dark blue Chevy Caprice. As they were driving up First Avenue, Sean went, "W-w-w-what if that guy c-c-calls the c-c-c-c-cops?"

"No, he was fucked up and he's a pillow biter, they don't do cops, if you follow me drift?" Dillon said. "He saw fooking nuthin."

"Nobody's s-s-s-s-stupid enough to think that w-w-w-was a rug."

"Just move it along, yah arsehole," Dillon snapped.

Cursing to himself and shaking his head, Sean continued to drive uptown. Dillon couldn't stand the quiet anymore and turned the radio on to a good local Irish station and cranked the volume. When they got to Eighty-sixth Street, Sean said, "Where are we headed?"

"Harlem," Dillon said. "St. Nicholas Avenue."

Dillon had used his idle time to walk around Manhattan and he already knew the city as well as a native. At 125th, they cut over to St. Nicholas and continued uptown.

At 144th, he said, "All right, this looks about right. Slow down."

They turned on 144th and stopped in front of an empty lot of rubble. The streetlights were burnt out on the entire side of the street.

"Come on," Dillon said. "Let's do this fast as we can."

Sean opened the trunk and they lifted the body out. It was so quiet they couldn't even hear the traffic noise from St. Nicholas Avenue. There were only the sounds of a dog barking and some kids screaming, maybe a block or two away.

Stepping over the garbage and rubble, they continued walking into the darkness. A few times Dillon, going *Fookin thing*, slipped and almost fell. Sean was beginning to whine, asked, "How m-m-much farther?"

"Shut yer trap," Dillon said. Then, when he thought they were far enough away from the street, he said, "All right, right here. Drop it."

They let the body fall, then they started covering it with whatever garbage was lying around. It was impossible to see anything, but Dillon picked up what felt like wood, paint cans, dirt, whatever. When it seemed like the body was covered he said, "That's all right. They'll never look for a dead Guard here anyway."

"A dead *w-w-w-what?*" Sean gasped. He was almost out of breath. "Are you d-d-d-d-demented?"

"What?" Dillon said.

"You s-s-s-said it was a r-r-r-rent collector."

Thinking, *Vive la difference*, Dillon said, "Yeah? So?"

"J-J-J-Jaysus," Sean said like he was going to go for Dillon. "I don't believe it, I c-c-c-could murder yah. The Boyos told us s-s-s-s-stay clear of the G-G-G-Guards."

"It doesn't matter now, does it?"

"B-b-but G-G-G-Guards. That's like b-b-b-blasphemy."

Dillon stepped back and felt a sudden piercing pain in his foot. He almost screamed, but stopped himself in time. He realized he must have stepped on a nail or something, but didn't want to look at it until he was back in the car. Then he said, "Let's just get the bejaysus out of here." He was thinking, *Just me fooking luck to get that tetanus thing.*

Back in the car, the pain in his foot was even worse. He turned on the car's overhead light and saw the head of a thick nail coming out of the bottom of his sneaker. He had no idea how deep it was wedged into his foot, but it felt like it was hitting bone.

Driving down St. Nicholas Avenue, Sean said, "There b-b-b-b-better not be b-b-b-blood in the b-b-b-boot of the v-v-v-vehicle."

Dillon yanked off his tennis sneaker—a three-inch-long rusty nail came off with it. He said, "Fook, and I just bought these shites at Modell's."

Thirteen

*He had made someone else's world a hell, and someone
had made his world a hell. Supply-chain management
for human suffering.*
JOSEPH FINDER, *Company Man*

In the back seat of the cab, Max Fisher put on his curly
blond wig. He knew he looked ridiculous—like a goddamn clown—but he figured it was better than nothing.
He was still paranoid about why Detective Simmons
never came back to talk to him and the last thing he
needed was to be seen checking into a hotel room with
his executive assistant.

When he went to work this morning he had no idea
he'd wind up where he was now. His plan was to have a
normal day at the office, get back to work, keep his mind
occupied. But he had no idea how fucking tempting it
would be to see Angela sitting at her desk, wearing one of
her skirts that barely covered her butt-cheeks. Usually,
he'd find some way to get her into his office and they'd
have a quickie, but he knew that anything like that would
be impossible today, and probably for a long time. Everyone was talking about how a detective was here last week,
asking everyone questions about him and Deirdre, and if
anybody had any "theories" about what might have
happened. This proved to Max that he wasn't being
paranoid—Simmons was definitely on to him.

Trying to bang Angela now would be nuts, but Max
couldn't help himself. Knowing she was so close by,
wanting her so badly, was driving him wild. Before

lunchtime, he called her into his office, but left the door open. As she went over Max's schedule for the rest of the day, Max winked at her. Angela saw him, immediately smiled as Max wrote, "I have to be with you" on a pad and slid it across the desk to her. She wrote back, "How?"

Like two students passing notes back and forth in a classroom, Max and Angela plotted out their strategy for meeting later on at the Hotel Pennsylvania. He figured it would be better to meet at a big hotel, where there was a lot of activity, than at a small hotel where they were more likely to be noticed. He often set his clients up with call girls at the Hotel Pennsylvania and they never had any problems. Besides, they were planning to take precautions. They'd arrive separately, check in under phony names, and he'd wear a wig. The wig was his idea. Angela wrote that she could go buy him a nice one during her lunch break. He tried it on in his office, knowing right away that it made him look like Harpo Marx, but deciding that it was worth it to be alone with Angela.

When he entered the hotel lobby, he looked around, made sure he wasn't being followed. Surprisingly, people passing by didn't give him funny looks—maybe the wig didn't look as ridiculous as he thought. He'd already called the hotel from work and found out there were plenty of vacancies tonight and there wouldn't be a problem booking a room at the last minute. He checked in under the name "Brown" and told the woman who was working at reception that his wife would be meeting him, when she arrived to please send her right up. Then he paid for the room in advance, with cash.

In room 1812, Max made himself comfortable—showering, and then lying in bed, relaxing, watching TV, his right hand slowly sliding under his boxers down to his crotch, touching what felt like a spot where the skin was irritated. He quickly took off his underwear to examine the area more closely. He discovered it wasn't really irritation—shit, it was more like a blister, and there were several smaller ones there as well. They itched and hurt like hell. How could he not have noticed them before?

He rushed into the bathroom, sat on the toilet bowl, and leaned over his lap, examining himself more carefully. The longer he looked at the blisters, the larger they seemed to grow. He tried to squeeze them, but this only made the itching and pain worse. Soon the discomfort was unbearable. As usual, he thought the worst first and imagined he had ebola, smallpox, that flesh-eating virus. It had to be something horrendous.

After a few more minutes of total panic he realized he wasn't dying, but the word "herpes" crept into the back of his mind.

When Angela came into the room, Max was still in the bathroom. He had started crying. Although he'd washed his face with cold water, when he came out of the bathroom Angela immediately knew something was wrong.

Max's lips quivered—he couldn't get the word out. Then he dropped his boxers and held out his penis for Angela to examine. He was trying to see if she seemed surprised, but she didn't show any particular reaction, saying, "What's wrong?" Then she said. "Oh, I get it. It's some kind of joke, right?"

"Look closer," Max said.

Angela got on her knees, said, "Is that all you're worried about?"

"It looks like…" Max still couldn't say the word.

"What?" Angela said.

IIis face turning red, starting to cry again, Max blurted out, "Herpes!"

"Herpes?" Angela said, like it was the most ridiculous idea possible. "That's just a little rash, that's all. Knowing

you, you probably made it worse from all your feckin'
scratching."

"They look like blisters to me."

Angela laughed, said, "Jaysus, listen to you. You
should go back to worrying about your heart, a wee rash
and you're blubbering like a big baby."

Continuing to examine himself, Max said, "It hurts."

"What do you expect, scratching yourself like a feckin'
monkey?"

"What about you?" Max said. "I mean you haven't
been having any symptoms, have you?"

Angela was sitting on the edge of the bed, taking off
her shoes. She froze for a moment then said, "What do
you mean?"

"I mean this," Max said. "I mean you've never had any
pain or seen any blisters or—"

"Are you asking me if I have feckin' herpes?"

When Angela turned around Max was staring at her
with a deadpan expression. She said, "You better stop
this, yah bollix, before I really start getting upset."

Now her eyes had all the fire and rage of an angry
Greek woman in them. Max didn't realize until now how
lethal this Irish-Greek-combo thing could be. It was one
dangerous mix.

Figuring he'd better soothe her, he sat down next to
her on the bed and put an arm loosely around her back.
He started kissing the back of her neck, under her hair,
until she started to giggle.

"I'm sorry, sweetie," he said. "I really am glad you're
here. You don't know how horrible it's been—being in
that house all alone all week. A couple of times I almost
gave in and called you. When I saw your name on that
card the office sent me I couldn't stop staring at your
handwriting. It just made me miss you even more."

Max turned Angela's head toward him, started kissing

her lips. Then he moved his right hand down her back, over that great ass and said, "God, you don't know how much I missed this."

Angela freed herself. "I have to go pee."

"Yeah, can I watch?" Max asked.

"You're so funny," Angela said without smiling as she went into the bathroom. He wondered, *That was a joke?*

Still sitting on the bed, Max said, "Have you heard anything from Popeye?"

"Why would I hear anything?"

"I mean through your cousin."

"No. And I think it's better if we don't know anything, don't you?"

"I guess you're right," Max said. "But I was ready to send a hit man after him a few days ago."

"Really?" Angela sounded shocked or confused—Max couldn't tell which. "Why?"

"The lunatic killed my niece. I mean she was just a young kid. When I found her lying there I was almost going to call the police and confess everything."

"Well, thank God you didn't do *that*."

"You're telling me," Max said. "After the funeral, the whole picture started to come into focus for me. I mean it was a terrible thing that she had to die and everything, but it wasn't as if Popeye didn't warn me. What was the word he used? *Pop*. He said he was going to pop me if I got to the house early, so I guess he had to pop Stacy, God rest her soul. I mean if he didn't pop her then we all would've been arrested by now, right?"

"Right," Angela said.

"But the thing that still ticks me off is that whole alarm business. It was supposed to look like he was waiting for them outside, right? Like he forced them to disarm the alarm. But then what does that jerk-off do? He arms the alarm before he leaves. What was the guy thinking?"

"Maybe he was trying to make it look like nobody was there."

"With two dead bodies in the foyer? This way, the cops know somebody gave him the code. I don't even know why he bothered to steal that jewelry. Like the police were gonna believe it was a robbery?"

"Maybe they'll think he made your wife tell him the code, or he memorized the code when your wife disarmed the alarm."

Max thought about that, then said, "Eh, maybe, but it was still a boneheaded thing to do. And why, why did he have to take a crap in the house, on my Oriental rug? You know how much it cost to clean that thing?"

"Oh, stop with your worrying," Angela said. "You'll see. A few months from now, when we're married, you'll look back on all this and think how crazy you were acting. Oh, and about the shitting, I heard once that it's not because burglars are, like, being disrespectful—it's from adrenalin."

Max thought Angela was full of shit, said, "You're full of shit."

"No, I'm serious. I read it in a book once."

Max, who had never seen Angela read anything except magazines and the *New York Post*, said, "I thought you said you heard it?"

"No, I read it, in a book about burglars. It was the history of burglary in America and there was a whole chapter about shitting on the floor. Great book—you should borrow it sometime."

Now Max was positive that Angela was just being all Irish again, spinning one of her stories that got more and more exaggerated with each telling. He didn't think Greek women did that. He didn't know a whole lot about Greek women and he was beginning to think he didn't know a whole lot about women, period. Why couldn't they just do lap dances and shut the fuck up?

Angela came out of the bathroom naked. She climbed into bed and pushed Max back, pinning down his arms.

"This is your night," she said. "You can have anything you want." The word *want* had that whole Irish accent thing going on, and it was so fucking sexy.

"I *want* you," Max said, trying to mimic it.

"How?" Angela asked.

Max flipped her over and pinned her down hard. He said, "You know we won't be able to do this again for a long time. It was way too risky to come here."

"In that case," Angela said, "you'd better make it good."

Max started on top, then ordered her to turn over. His blisters—or whatever the hell they were—were hurting, but he decided to ignore the pain. Doggy-style was his favorite position. He liked grabbing onto Angela's hair or squeezing her butt cheeks and imagining she was anyone he wanted her to be. For a while, he imagined she was Felicia, the stripper from Legz Diamond's. That worked great, especially when he had his eyes closed. Then he heard something off to his right. He looked over and saw in the shadow near the door some guy in a wheelchair with what looked like an armful of towels.

"What the hell?" Max said.

"Jeez, I'm sorry, Mister," the guy said. "I'm really, really sorry…"

Jesus Christ, the guy wasn't just crippled, he sounded retarded, too.

Max told him to get the fuck out of the room and the guy started babbling about how he had to replace the towels and the soap and some other bullshit.

Max yelled, "Get out, you fucking moron!" and that got rid of him.

Max wanted to call downstairs and get that jerk fired but Angela said, "Oh, give him a break. He's handicapped."

"So?" Max said. "He should still know better."

"He's gone now. I'm sure he's not going to say anything. He's probably scared out of his wits."

"Eh, I guess you're right," Max said and let himself fall back onto the bed. "Where were we?"

Angela turned around. Max grabbed onto her shoulders and squeezed hard, picturing Felicia.

Fourteen

"It's herpes all right," Dr. Alan Flemming said to Max the next morning. "Simplex Two."

Dr. Flemming was Max's General Practitioner and they were in Flemming's Park Avenue office. Although Dr. Flemming was probably only a few years older than Max, Max hoped he didn't look *that* bad. Flemming had white hair, a hunched-over posture and a thin, wrinkled face. As Max had heard Angela once say about her Irish grandfather, *his wrinkles had wrinkles*.

This morning, Max had made an emergency appointment with Flemming when he woke up and discovered that the blisters on his penis seemed to have grown larger.

"You're sure it's herpes?" Max said. "I mean don't you have to wait for the lab results before you can tell?"

"Of course I'll need to confirm it with a Pap smear," Flemming said, "but I'm ninety-nine percent certain of the diagnosis. But there's no reason to panic—herpes isn't exactly a life-threatening virus. All you have to do is keep the lesions dry and apply some alcohol or witch hazel. You also might want to wear loose clothes. If you wear jockeys, you might want to consider a switch over to boxers. It also might be a good idea to blow dry your genitals from now on rather than toweling dry. But whatever you do, don't feel like you're a bad person or something's wrong with you because you contracted this. You can rest assured—millions of people in the world are going through the same thing that you are and it's really not as bad as many people think. I've had patients who've gone for months, hell, years even, without experiencing any symptoms whatsoever. The outbreaks will usually only occur when you're under a high level of stress or anxiety. With the tragedy involving your wife and niece, I'm not at all surprised to see you having an outbreak now. By the way, have you…been with anyone recently?"

"What do you mean?"

He knew exactly what he meant but he knew he couldn't let on.

"The only reason I'm asking," Flemming said, smiling assuredly, "is that herpes, in almost all cases, is a sexually transmitted virus. In all likelihood, you contracted it from someone and if you did it might be a good idea to warn that person."

"Maybe my wife had it," Max said. "I mean maybe she had it, but didn't tell me."

"Well, the only way she could've gotten it would be if she had—well, I don't think that's really important now anyway. After I have Christine do a Pap smear—and we'll also do some blood work—I'm going to put you on a medication to help suppress the virus and a painkiller for your itching and discomfort. Within a few days you'll be as good as new."

Max doubted that, doubted it a whole lot.

Flemming picked up his clipboard and started to leave the examination room. At the door, he turned back, smiled and said, "By the way, just as a precautionary measure, if you've been having unprotected sex you might want to think about an HIV test."

"HIV?" Max could barely move his lips to say it, frightened to fucking hell. "Why? You think I have—"

"No, no, I'm not suggesting that at all. I'm just saying

it's best to err on the side of caution. Many people who have herpes also tend to be HIV-positive. That isn't to say that you're likely to be HIV-positive. But, given that you have already contracted one sexually transmitted disease, it might be a good idea to check for others."

"Yeah well, I think I'd like to hold off on an AIDS test," Max said.

"Are you sure?" Dr. Flemming said. "The sooner you know—"

"I'm not taking the goddamn test."

Later, riding in a cab to his office, Max could barely breathe. There was no way in hell he was ever going to take an AIDS test. It scared him enough to have to call for his blood work from his cardiologist—he couldn't imagine making a phone call to find out if he'd been sentenced to death.

Max had heard somewhere that the first sign of AIDS is sometimes lumps on the lymph nodes. Max wasn't sure where the lymph nodes were, but he thought they were somewhere on his throat. Feeling around, he was convinced that he had lumps.

He screamed silently, *Fucking lumps!*

When he arrived at his office he hadn't calmed down much. He marched past the receptionist's desk toward Angela and said loud enough for everyone nearby to hear, "Excuse me, could you come into my office with me, please? I need to dictate a letter."

When Angela came into the office Max asked her to close the door behind her. Then, after she sat down with her pad, he said in a low, but serious voice, "Thanks for giving me herpes, you stupid bitch."

Angela seemed surprised, but Max was pretty sure she was acting.

She said, "Herpes? What the hell?"

"You don't have to deny it anymore—I just came back

from my doctor. Irritation my ass. You knew you had herpes and you didn't even tell me."

"You went to a *doctor*? When?"

"This morning. Come on, I don't have time for this bullshit. Just admit it."

"Are you sure he isn't making a mistake? I mean how can he tell without a blood test?"

"They don't take a blood test, they take a Pap smear, but it's herpes all right. He's treated tons of cases before."

"Well, I didn't…" Angela lowered her voice and continued, "I didn't give it to you."

"Then where did I get it, a fucking toilet seat?" Max noticed that the left side of her face looked slightly purple, said, "What the hell happened to you?"

"Oh, it was nothing," Angela said. "My roommate opened the bathroom door last night and it hit me. I'll live."

But Max, not paying attention, said, "Well, if I didn't catch it from you, you got it now, so you better go see a doctor and pretty damn soon."

"Maybe your feckin' whore of a wife gave it to you," Angela said.

Her temper was coming out and the fire in her eyes was ferocious.

"My wife?"

"Yeah. How do you know she wasn't doing it with some bollix behind your back?"

Max considered this for a moment. Deirdre having an affair? It seemed crazy. Then he imagined Kamal naked, on top of her, and a sick feeling started to build in his stomach. Kamal was the only other man he knew about who'd had any sort of contact with Deirdre and he remembered how unusually upset he'd been to hear about her death. But that was crazy. He'd never heard Kamal even *talk* about a woman before and, besides, he was almost positive the guy putted from the rough.

"That's crazy," Max said. "No guy would've been interested in Deirdre and besides—you have to have sex to get herpes and Deirdre and I didn't exactly have an active sex life."

"I'm telling you the truth," Angela said. "If you don't believe me it's your feckin' problem, not mine."

There was quiet knock on the door. Max said, "What is it?"

The receptionist who was temping this week poked her head into the office. She said to Max, "There's a man here to see you."

"A man?" Max said, looking at Angela. "I don't have any appointments this morning, do I?"

Angela shook her head. Max said to the girl, "Did he say what his name was?"

"No. But he said it's very important that he speak to you."

"It's probably a fucking salesman. Tell him to leave his business card and we'll get back to him if we're interested."

"He said he's not a salesman."

"That's what they all say."

"I think he's telling the truth. He's in a wheelchair. He said he won't leave till he sees you."

"A wheelchair? Jesus H., he's probably working for some handicapped charity. He's—" *A wheelchair. Jesus fuck.* Max looked at Angela, then quickly looked away and said, "I'll go see him."

Max went toward the front of the office, rubbing the back of his neck to help ease his suddenly pounding headache. He managed not to scratch his groin but, Jesus Christ, he wanted to.

The man in the wheelchair was waiting near the reception desk. He had a thick black beard and dark, serious eyes. He was a big guy, stocky, looked Italian or maybe Spanish. Was it the same guy? Max wasn't sure. The retard at the hotel had been in shadow. But two guys in wheelchairs showing up in one week? What were the odds?

Max said, "Can I help you with something?"

The man extended his hand, said, "You certainly can. Name's Bobby Rosa."

"What the hell do you want?"

"I want to talk to you and I got a hunch you're gonna want to listen."

It was the same guy, all right. Wanting to break the bastard's teeth, Max said, "Look, I don't know why you're here, but you're lucky I don't get you fired for what you did. I would've but we felt sorry for you because you're retarded."

Bobby smiled proudly. "You really thought I was retarded, huh?"

Shit, Max thought. If the guy wasn't a retard maybe he wasn't a housekeeper either.

Looking around, Bobby said, "Nice place you got here. You must have, what, ten thousand square feet? What kind of rent you pay?"

Max looked over at the temp who seemed to be busy typing. Lowering his voice and stepping away from the reception desk, Max said, "Look, if you don't get the hell out of here right now, I'm going to get someone to take you out. Got that?"

Bobby said, "You got a good set of balls on you for a little guy. It's no wonder you're such a successful businessman."

Max said, "You want me to call the cops, I'll call the cops."

"You're not gonna call anybody." They were both talking in low mutters now, but the fucking temp was probably listening to every word. Still, it'd look worse if Max asked her to leave them alone, wouldn't it?

"Yeah?" Max said, leaning close to Bobby's ear. "And why won't I?"

"Because," Bobby said, "I have some pictures here that I doubt you're gonna want the cops to see."

Max noticed now, for the first time, the manila envelope on Bobby's lap.

"Why don't you come into my office?" he said.

Max went right to the bar and started making a stiff vodka tonic, his groin itching like hell. Bobby wheeled in behind him, stayed by the door.

Without looking at Bobby, Max said, "Now what the fuck are you talking about, pictures? Is this some bullshit joke 'cause if it is, I'm not laughing."

"Sit down," Bobby said.

Max, holding his drink at the bar, turned around slowly.

"What did you say?"

"I told you to sit down."

"Look, if you think I'm gonna let you get away with any more of this bullshit just because you're paralyzed, you're out of your mind."

Bobby took out a five-by-seven glossy and slid it across the desk. Max looked back and forth between Bobby and the photo several times, then walked slowly toward his swivel chair. Although he was scared out of his mind, he tried to keep his cool. But when he sat down his hands were already shaking. He looked up at Bobby, whose face was expressionless. Who was this guy, some detective? The only explanation Max could think of was that Harold and Claire Goldenberg had hired him to investigate the murders.

"So who the fuck are you?" Max asked.

"Under the circumstances I think I should be the one asking the questions, don't you?"

"Are you a detective?"

"No, I'm not a detective."

"Then who are you?"

"I'm the guy's got a picture of you fucking your secretary while your wife's not even cold in her fucking grave. Might get some people thinking, you know what I'm saying?"

"What do you want?"

"What do you think I want?"

Max stared at Bobby for a few seconds, wondering if the guy was crazy—he sure as hell looked crazy—then he got up and went back to the bar to make another drink. He said, "You like vodka?" thinking that maybe he could warm the guy up.

But Bobby said, "I don't drink."

"You have liver problems?"

"Excuse me?"

"You don't drink. Is it because you have a bum liver?"

"No, no, nothing like that. I just don't like what alcohol does to my brain." He touched his index finger to his head, said, "I like to stay sharp upstairs."

"I know what you mean," Max said, turning on the charm, starting to schmooze with the guy. "The only reason I drink is to keep my HDL up and my LDL down—doctor's orders." Max drank half the drink in one gulp. "What's your LDL?"

"My what?"

"Your bad cholesterol level."

"I don't pay attention to that shit. But yours…I figure yours is right off the goddamn chart. Am I right or am I right?"

Max, walking back to his desk with the drink, said, "I hope you're kidding, Bobby. I mean, you must be in your forties, right? I probably have about ten years on you, but you should still start thinking about HDL and LDL. Believe me, problems can sneak up on you, especially if you have a high-fat, low-fiber diet. And you especially need to watch yourself, I mean being crippled and all. You probably don't get your heart rate up a lot."

Bobby, glaring, said, "Thanks for the medical advice."

"No problem," Max said, resting the drink on the desk. "Now, Bobby, look. You can see I'm a nice guy, can't you? I mean I'm concerned about your health and everything. And you seem like a pretty nice guy to me. We're both older guys, been around the block a few times—we probably have a lot in common we don't even know about. So what I want to know is why can't you just be straight with me and tell me exactly who you are and why you took that picture."

"Why I took that picture? Because if I didn't have that picture you wouldn't pay me the quarter of a million dollars you're going to." He seemed like he was getting a big rush from this, fucking with a big shot businessman. Yeah, this was probably the highlight of this loser's life.

Max's hand was shaking, but he said, "Why the hell would I pay you one cent? So you have a picture of me screwing my executive assistant. Big shit. I could've hired someone to take that picture myself if I really wanted it."

Max forced a laugh, but Bobby stayed deadpan.

"You're going to pay me a quarter of a million dollars cash on Monday morning at nine o'clock," Bobby said. "If not, a copy of that picture's going to the NYPD."

Max stared at Bobby. Finally, he smiled, said, "That was a joke, right?"

"I'll be here at nine o'clock sharp," Bobby said. "I want the money in one suitcase, two at most. How you get it in there is your problem."

He started to back away from the desk.

Max said, "Whoa, whoa, hold up a second. This is all bullshit. I mean you're kidding, right?"

Bobby started wheeling away. Suddenly, Max was feeling light-headed and he wasn't sure whether it was drunkenness or panic. He said, "Hey, get back here."

Bobby stopped, turned around slowly.

In a hushed voice, Max said, "Look, usually I'd tell you to take a hike, but I really don't need this bullshit in my life right now, so here's what I'll do—the picture for a thousand bucks."

"My price is non-negotiable," Bobby said.

"Come on, a quarter of a million dollars? You have to be out of your fucking mind."

"I know a lot more about you than you think," Bobby said. "I read the papers, but I also use my head, I put two and two together. 'Grieving husband' my gimp ass."

Max said, "Look, even if I wanted to give you that kind of money, I don't have it."

"Monday—nine A.M. sharp. Oh, and you can keep that copy of the picture." Bobby looked up at the poster of the blonde on the Porsche. "Maybe you wanna hang it on the wall."

After Bobby left, Max poured himself another vodka tonic. His head was spinning and he had lost sensation in his face. Feeling dizzy, he opened his door and called for Angela to come into his office. When she came inside, Max was lying on the couch, holding his head.

"What's wrong?"

Max told her to lock the door, then motioned with his hand weakly toward the desk and the picture. Angela picked up the photo, stared at it for a few seconds, said, "That bollix." Then she started smiling, said, "I look pretty good, don't I?"

Max snatched the photo and said, "I can't believe this day is happening. First herpes, now this!"

"What did he ask for?"

"The bastard wants two-fifty K or he's going to the police."

"So?"

"So, did you hear what I just said? Are you an idiot or something? Once the cops find out about me and you they'll be on our backs for good."

"That wasn't nice."

"What?"

"Calling me an idiot. You do that in Ireland, you better be holding more than a fookin drink."

"Jesus, I feel like I'm gonna throw up," Max said. "What the hell are we supposed to do now?"

"I'll get you some coffee."

"Fuck coffee! There's only one way out of this," Max said, and he covered his face with his hands. How the hell did it come to this? "Can you get in touch with your cousin today?"

"My cousin?"

"I think we have another job for his friend Popeye."

Fifteen

"What about your coffee?"
"Fuck the coffee."
"I would, but I don't fancy the blisters."
ALLAN GUTHRIE, *Two Way Split*

The coffee burned Dillon's tongue. He was in the Starbucks beside Penn Station, and he spat out the scalding liquid, going, "Fookin thing."

A guy, yuppie-looking, gave him a long stare. Dillon was up for it, was he ever, glared at the guy, snarled, "The fook you looking at?" He was delighted how his New York accent was coming along, and the brogue still riding point. The guy quickly looked away. But Dillon was antsy, needed to wallop someone, some bastard needed a hiding and soon. When the compulsion hit him, as it did more and more, he had to have an explosive interlude, blow the cobwebs out.

He got out of there, an employee asking, "Everything okay, sir?"

Dillon paused, then said, "Hunky fucky dory yah wanker."

Translate that.

It was evening, the darkness bringing out the predators, skells in abundance. Even though Forty-second Street was now more a tourist attraction than a sleaze zone, it still had pockets of peril and Dillon had quickly found them. He stood in a doorway near Ninth Avenue, saw a lost Japanese tourist, camera hanging from his neck, a T-shirt with "Giuliani Rules" on it.

Dillon moved fast, hit the guy from behind, his knife out and the nip's throat sliced before he could mutter, "Banzai."

Dillon said, "Call it quits on Pearl Harbor a cara."

But, for fook's sake, all the guy had was plastic. Where were the bucks? He also had a packet of Menthol Lights and a Zippo, with the inscription *Small change.* No truer words. Dillon kicked him in the head for good measure and, as he headed up the block, he lit a menthol, enjoying the crank of the lighter, thinking, Johnny Cash and Zippos, it was a mighty country.

He began, like a mantra, the sports lingo he'd been learning, measuring out the phases like a new language. You grew up in Ireland and hurling was the sport of necessity, this American deal was a whole new territory. But he loved the sound of it, like praying but without the guilt or the bartering you had to do with god. He started, "Them Knicks need to take it to the next level, what to plug in and take out, they need a point guard, Isaiah Thomas better get his head outa his arse, the old days, Patrick Ewing, John Starks, they had a core, then the Bulls, ah they had it, the fookin Lakers, what was going on there, and the Sox, way to go boyos." Like that. No idea what he was saying but getting off on the melody.

No one paid him any heed, just one more crazy fuck, with a menthol cig and a bug up his ass.

New York, you gotta love it.

Walking down Fifth Avenue, all Angela could think about was the way Bobby Rosa had looked at her. On his way out of the office, he'd winked at her and smiled and said, "Goodbye, sweetheart." He wasn't really her type. She didn't mind the wheelchair, but guys with beards had always kind of disgusted her because they reminded her of her uncle Costas from Astoria who used to try to feel her up when she was thirteen. But Bobby didn't seem like a bad guy. She felt bad that they were gonna have to kill him.

Angela didn't know how everything had gotten so screwed up. It was bad enough that that innocent girl had to die, but then Dillon had to go and kill a cop. Getting Max's money was turning out to be a lot harder than she'd thought it would be. Besides, after hearing on the news about how brutal Dillon had been with the two women and then seeing him stick that knife into the cop's chest like he was getting off on it, she wasn't sure she wanted to marry him anymore anyway. You marry a whackjob like that, were you expecting white roses? Yeah, right. She didn't know where all that rage came from. One minute, he was talking about all that Buddhist peace shit or quoting the poetry of that Yeats guy, and the next thing he'd smack her across the face.

She'd go, "The fook did I do?"

Nothing, was the answer, but he'd laugh, go, "Just in case you were thinking of fooking me over, and there's more where that came from—call that a taster."

Then he'd take out a knife and start cleaning his nails with it, staring at her with that deadeye look.

But she couldn't break up with him now. She had to wait until this mess was over with and then decide what to do.

It started to rain as Angela continued along Fifth Avenue. She didn't feel like taking a bus or paying for a cab so she just kept walking, hardly realizing that she was getting soaked.

When she got home Dillon was sitting in his underwear on the bed watching music videos saying, "You brung me fookin dinner, I hope."

"I figured we'd just order in or something," Angela said.

"You said you were gonna pick it up, yah bleedin bitch."

"So I forgot. What's your problem?"

"I've been trapped here all day and guess what, I'm

starving—that's what my problem is, so get in the kitchen, get me some stew—you're Irish, stew is yer birthright. Put lots of cabbage and bacon in there, and don't forget the spuds, you got that, bitch?"

"I'm not your bitch," Angela said.

Now, his voice getting all gentle again, he asked, "What's that, mo croi?"

"Shut up."

He laughed. "That's funny," he said. "I really like that, mo croi."

Angela sat at the kitchen table and started taking off her wet shoes.

"Food, now!" he roared.

"You could've ordered in something yourself," she said.

"And have a delivery boy come up here and ID me? It's all on the news and shite. They're talking about how that cop *you* brought up here is missing and they got a cartoon of me in the paper, tis the spit of me too. That Chinese hoor informed on me arse, the one I dumped that jewelry on in Chinatown. What if the cop I did told other cops he was following you last night? I've been sitting here all day, waiting for the cops to show up—Jaysus, it's worse than the Falls Road, waiting for the Brit patrols."

"I told you you shouldn't sell that jewelry."

"Well, I did and get this right in yer dumb head, you don't *tell* me dick. You have two jobs, and both begin with f. One is food."

"Fuck you."

"Yeah, and that's the other one."

"If we wind up in jail now it's because you sold that jewelry."

He got up suddenly, a bad sign, and said, "I don't do jail, get that?"

There was something in his voice. "That's it," Angela said. "I've had it."

She marched past Dillon and went into the bathroom, slamming the door behind her. He banged on the door, demanding that she come out, going, "Where the hell's me dinner?" Angela covered her ears with her hands and sat down on the toilet seat, squeezing her eyes shut.

He was pounding on the door, now saying, "I'm too hungry for this shite. I'm going to ring for some takeout but you have to go to the door to pay for it. I'm not kiddin' yah."

Angela turned on the shower to drown him out, but it didn't work till she got in. As long as she kept her head under the water, his ranting was just part of the white noise.

When she came out, wrapped in a towel, Dillon was still in his underwear, now watching a basketball game.

Noticing the layers of Band-Aids over the bottom of Dillon's right foot, Angela said, "Did you put peroxide on that like I told you to?"

"You addressing me?" Dillon asked.

"Yeah, I'm talking to you," Angela said. "Why wouldn't I talk to you?"

Dillon went back to watching TV. He muttered along with the play-by-play, "Move yer ass mothfookers," trying to sound like a New Yorker.

"So?" Angela said, putting on a bra. "Did you or didn't you put peroxide on that?"

"Couldn't be bothered," he said.

Angela leaned forward, taking a closer look at the foot.

"You probably need a shot for that, you know, or you'll catch tetanus."

"I'll catch anorexia if I don't get me grub," he said.

Angela finished getting dressed—putting on jeans and a black T-shirt with "My Boyfriend's Out of Town" in red across the front. She sat down on the bed next to Dillon and rested a hand on his lap. For a while there was silence except for the sports commentator babbling, then

Dillon said, "I was watching *South Park* before and Kenny is dead again, you see that one?"

"I think so," Angela said.

The food arrived and Angela and Dillon sat on the bed together eating the shrimp lo mein and barbecued spare ribs directly from the cartons. Finally, Angela decided it was a good time to break the bad news.

"Something happened today," she said, "but before I tell you you have to promise not to get mad at me."

"What?"

"You have to promise."

"What is it?"

"You're gonna get angry," Angela said. "I can tell it already."

"Just tell me what the fook it is, you're spoiling me dinner." Christ, she thought, she never saw a man eat so much and still stay skinny as a wet rodent.

Dillon's nostrils flared. He looked the same way he did before he stabbed that cop.

"All right," Angela said. "Remember how I told you I was with my boss last night at that hotel?"

"Yeah," he said.

"Well something happened that we didn't know about. Something that could be bad."

"Stop whining and tell me what it is."

"Well, there was this guy," Angela said, "and he took some pictures of us."

"You mean like a Guard?"

"No, not a cop—definitely not a cop. He was in a wheelchair and—anyway, he came to the office today and he showed the pictures to Max."

"What were the pictures of?" Dillon asked.

"Just of us, you know...in bed together."

"So? What's he going to do with them, beside play with his own self?"

"If the police see them it'll show that me and Max were together, that we could've planned the murder."

"But the police haven't got the pictures, the gimp in the wheelchair does."

"That's where the bad part comes in. He wants money for them. A lot of money."

"You mean he's trying to blackmail you?"

"He's trying to blackmail Max."

"And you're sure this fooker isn't a Guard?"

"I don't know what he is," Angela said, remembering again how Bobby Rosa had looked at her. "But Max thinks it's a big problem. He wanted me to get you to get rid of him."

Dillon sat calmly for a few seconds and Angela thought, Hey, that wasn't too bad. Then he suddenly threw his carton of food against the wall on the other side of the room. Angela covered her ears as Dillon stood up and kicked the top of the TV set with his right foot, then roared as the pain hit his already inflamed sole. He said, "You're going to get the hiding of yer life, you hoor's ghost!"

Dillon began hitting her in the face, slapping her with his open hands. Angela didn't know how she got out of the apartment. She ran down the stairs, nearly tripping several times. She walked toward Second Avenue, not realizing for several minutes that she was barefoot.

She went into the Rodeo Bar, on Second Avenue and Twenty-eighth Street. She sat at the dingy half-empty bar and then realized she had no money. She told the bartender she was "waiting for a friend" and stared at the hockey game on TV.

She became aware of a guy sitting on the stool next to her. He was young, around twenty-three, in a business suit and she saw a couple of other guys—his friends— giggling to each other. The guy said, "Hey, is this Woodstock or something?"

Angela was confused for a second then realized he was making fun of her for being barefoot.

"Just leave me the feck alone, yeh arsehole!"

The guy, looking terrified, went back to his friends.

Angela left the bar and headed toward home. She approached her apartment building, hoping Dillon had calmed down a little. Food and weed usually took his edge off, but she knew it was only a matter of time before he really lost it. Then she thought about Bobby Rosa again. The guy was really into her—that much was obvious. And, yeah, he was in a wheelchair, but there was something about him that made her think he could take care of himself. But could he take care of Dillon?

Angela didn't have the key to her apartment. She kept ringing the buzzer, but Dillon wouldn't answer it. Finally, after nearly an hour, someone leaving the building let her in and she went upstairs. The door to her apartment was open.

Dillon was sitting on the bed, watching videos and reading his damn Zen book. He said, "I wouldn't go in that bathroom if I were you. That fookin Chinese food, it was off."

Angela went to the fridge and poured herself a glass of soda.

Dillon said, "While I was in there on the bowl, shittin' out me organs, I was thinking this guy in the wheelchair is our problem too. I don't trust that bollix, Max. If he cracks, he's taking us down with him. You know that, right?"

Angela didn't answer.

Dillon said, "So my question is how much should I charge?"

"Charge?"

Dillon glared at her like she was stupid.

"For blasting a guy in a wheelchair."

Sixteen

Muggers are plain creepy.
DUANE SWIERCZYNSKI

Max said to Kamal, "Have you ever had herpes?"

They were in Max's kitchen where Kamal was busy cooking Max's macrobiotic meals for the rest of the week. Three pots were going on the stove and Kamal was chopping up beets and potatoes.

"Herpes?" Kamal said pausing with the cutting knife in his right hand. "Why do you ask that?"

"No reason," Max said. "I mean it's not like I think you're gonna infect the food or anything like that. It was just something that was on my mind."

"No," Kamal said, still looking confused. "I do not have any venereal diseases."

"Ah-ha," Max said. "So you haven't been tested for herpes."

"No, I do not believe so. Unless it was part of my regular physical examination."

"Very interesting," Max said. "Very very interesting."

Now Max was almost one hundred percent sure that the little Indian guy had been banging Deirdre, probably had been banging her for some time. The last time Max had had sex with her must have been three or four months ago and he must have caught the virus then.

"You can just admit it," Max said.

"Admit what?" Kamal asked.

"That you and Deirdre were, you know...a couple. Don't worry, I won't fire you or anything like that."

"I have no idea what you are talking about," Kamal said.

"Come on," Max said, "you think I'm blind? I saw how much time you and Deirdre spent together. It's obvious you two were very close."

"I admired your wife a great deal," Kamal said, "but I could never imagine having relations with her."

"Not even one time," Max said, "just for the hell of it?"

"I'm offended that you would even ask me such a thing. I am a Sikh from Punjab—we are very spiritual people. We don't sleep with other men's wives, not even if we wanted to, and I did not want to sleep with your wife. No offense but, western women, they have a peculiar odor—it's from eating meat perhaps. I like the smell of curry and spices, if you can understand."

Max stared at him deadpan, thinking, Is this guy for real?

Then Max demanded, "You swear to God?"

"Why should I—"

"If you didn't do anything you shouldn't have a problem swearing to God about it."

Kamal slid the potatoes and beets into the steamer then said, "I do not believe in God the same way you do."

"Yeah, yeah, whatever," Max said. "Then do you swear to the Buddha about it?"

"The Buddha does not ask anything to swear to it. The Buddha is not a singular being or concept. The Buddha is all things."

Max picked up a plate and held it up. He said, "Fine, so let's say this plate is the Buddha. Do you swear to this plate that you never banged my wife?"

Kamal looked at Max like he was crazy, then said, "I did not do anything with your wife. I'm giving you my word which should be enough, now please, do not say any more disrespectful things about the Buddha. It is very, very hurtful to me."

The little rice eater looked like he was about to cry.

Max stared at him for a few seconds and decided that he was probably telling the truth after all. But if Kamal didn't give the herpes to Deirdre that meant that Max must have gotten it from Angela.

"Eh, just forget about it," Max said. "What difference does it make anyway?"

Max went to the fridge and poured himself a glass of skim milk.

"You know, you should really consider joining me at the ashram sometime," Kamal said, stirring the big pot of brown rice. "I think it would very healing for you."

"I'm Jewish," Max said.

"Our guru welcomes people of all faiths," Kamal said. "And meditating and chanting can be very cleansing. It can help you to become at peace with your inner self."

"I'm not gonna sit on the floor and chant like some hippie," Max said. Then he wondered if he could meet some classy Indian woman at the ashram. Hell, he could do rice and, for a decent lay, he'd chant till the crows came home or till the whatever fucking birds they had in India came home. Besides, what the hell was he doing with Angela anyway? He used to think he was in love with her, but lately he wasn't so sure. She had a nice body and that great accent, but there wasn't much more going on there. What had he been thinking?

"Lemme ask you something," Max said. "Do women come to these ashrams?"

"Yes, of course," Kamal said. "The spiritual journey is not just for men."

Kamal was trying not to smile. Was something funny?

"Yeah, lemme ask you something else," Max said. "Are they well-endowed?"

"Excuse me?"

"Tits. Do they have big tits?"

Kamal waited a few seconds, checking the vegetables, then said, "Some of them do, yes."

"In that case, maybe I'll give the hippie shit a shot," Max said. "I mean after I get through with my mourning of course."

Then he looked away and glanced at the copy of the *Daily News* on the table. Some Jap tourist got his throat cut on Forty-second Street and the police had no suspects. Max chuckled, thought, *I guess Times Square ain't no Disneyland after all.*

Seventeen

*I lose it, flapping about in the rain and kicking the hell out of
the dog. I don't deserve this. I don't fucking deserve all this
fucking bad luck and this stupid fucking life.*
RAY BANKS, *The Big Blind*

The next day another Manhattan murder was the lead
story on the six o'clock news. The rat-gnawed body of
forty-one-year-old Homicide Detective Kenneth Simmons
of the 19th Precinct had been discovered by some children
in an empty lot in Harlem. The body had two gunshot
wounds and a stab wound to the chest. The police had
released a police sketch of a suspect in the case—a white
male, approximately five-five or five-six, maybe 130
pounds, with gray hair, last seen wearing an old leather
jacket and dirty blue jeans and new sneakers. On Monday
morning, the suspect had been spotted in a pawnshop on
Bayard Street in Chinatown selling jewelry that was
stolen during the recent murders of two Upper East Side
women. Police believed that he might be a suspect in
those murders as well since Detective Simmons had been
working on that case when he was killed. People with
any information regarding the case were urged to call a
special police hotline number or 577-TIPS.

Watching the news report on the TV in his living
room, Max had no doubt that the guy in the police sketch
was Popeye. His face was too fat and his eyes and nose
looked different, but everything else, down to the leather
jacket, was definitely him. Max didn't know what that guy
was going to fuck up next. Was the stupid prick deter-

mined to wipe out the population of Manhattan? He'd
read once that the Irish were truly demented. Well, no
argument there.

Sitting at a table in the back of Famiglia Pizza on Fiftieth
and Broadway, Max saw Popeye limping up the aisle. After
Popeye sat down, diagonally across from Max, with a big
cupful of ice, Max said, "What happened to your foot?"

"Fook me foot, yah suited prick," Popeye said. Then
looking around nervously he said, "Nobody followed yeh
here, right?"

Dillon was fingering a gold pin in his leather jacket,
like it was a talisman or something. The Irish and their
goddamn superstitions.

"Not that I know of," Max said.

"Yeah, well you better be sure," Popeye said. "I
shouldn't even be here now. I should be in Florida,
writing me poetry."

The idea of this bloodthirsty animal writing poetry was
too much for Max. What was that old joke? If you threw a
stone in Ireland, you'll probably hit a poet, usually a bad
one.

Smiling, Max asked, "How do your poems start? Roses
are red?"

Popeye had the cup up to his mouth, sucking out an
ice cube. When his eyes peered over the cup, Max said,
"Don't look at me."

Sucking on a cube, Popeye said, "What?"

"You heard me, you little cocksucker." Max laughed.
"Just sit there and keep looking straight ahead and don't
look at me. If you look at me one time I'm getting up and
leaving here and you'll never see me again."

"I like that, the little bollix showing some spunk,"
Popeye said. "But are you on medication? *You're* the one
who can't look at *me*."

"Not anymore," Max said. "Now *I'm* calling the shots."

"You'll be calling the fookin mortuary, I haven't time for this shite."

"Then find time, because you'll be here as long as I want you to be here."

"Yeah, and if I get up, walk out, what will you do, use more obscene language?"

"Go ahead. You're the wanted criminal, not me."

"If I'm fooked, you're coming to hell with me."

"You can't prove anything," Max said. "What are you going to do, say I hired you to kill my wife? I really doubt that the police'll take your word over mine. I'm a re-spected businessman. Who the fuck are you?"

"Did you say fook to me?"

"I told you not to look at me."

"Bollix, I'm legging it."

"I don't think that would be a wise idea."

Popeye paused, half-standing, then sat down again and said, "Why not?"

"Think about it. You need this guy out of the way as much as I do. You don't know what evidence the police have on you. Maybe you left something in my house that night—something you forgot. Or maybe they found some of your blood or hair there or they got something off that piece of shit you left on my rug—thanks very much for that, by the way. What was that, your idea of a fucking housewarming present? It wasn't very bright, with DNA and all that other shit the cops have these days. I don't know what it feels like to die by lethal injection, but I imagine it's not very pleasant."

Popeye stayed still for a few more seconds then settled back down in the seat and stared straight ahead. Finally he said, "So where does the crippled fuck live?"

"First let's talk about the important *shite*," Max said, trying to put on a brogue, wanting to give Popeye a taste of his own. "My money. I want to revise the offer I made to you over the phone this morning."

"You said twenty large."

Max loved the way Popeye's tone was weakening. Jesus Christ, Max felt the power going straight to his head.

"Yeah, well, a lot has changed since then," Max said. "For instance, you've made it on to the NYPD's Most Wanted list, so I've decided you owe me a freebie for this one."

"Like fuck I do."

Max ignored this, said, "You have as much stake now in this as I do. You can't disappear until this Rosa guy is out of the way and you know it."

Popeye's eyes narrowed into slits.

"How will you find his address?"

"I already called Information," Max said. "They told me they didn't have any Bobby Rosas. I said, what about Robert Rosas? They had one in the West Village—the fudgepacking district. The Rosa I met didn't look like a guy who talks into the mike, if you know what I mean. They also had one at one hundred West Eighty-ninth so I said gimme that one."

"But how you know it's the same fellah?"

"I did something you're not used to doing—I used my fucking head. I called the building and said to the doorman, 'Does a Robert Rosa in a wheelchair live at your address?' The guy said 'Yeah,' and I hung up. You have any more stupid questions?"

Popeye started to say something, but Max interrupted and, with his best Oirish accent said, "Good, then you can get the *bejaysus* out of here."

Popeye looked stunned for a couple of seconds, mumbling something about "tinkers." Then he stood up and said, "You shouldn't take the Lord's name in vain, tis bad luck."

❖

About twenty minutes later, when Max got out of the cab in front of his townhouse, a man said, "You Max Fisher?"

Looking at the guy, Max thought, Jesus Christ, what now?

The guy took out his shiny gold badge and said, "Ortiz—Homicide. I think you better come with me."

Eighteen

I wanted to say they busted apart as do dried-up dreams,
or public trust, but, truly, they flew apart exactly like
yesterday's shit.
DANIEL WOODRELL, *Give Us a Kiss*

The doorbell rang and Bobby said, "Come in," sitting in
his wheelchair about ten feet from the door, his Glock 27
compact pistol resting on his lap. In walked Max Fisher's
executive assistant. She was wearing a short red leather
skirt, matching pumps and a tight top. Like the other
night at the hotel, her hair was big and blown dry, but
tonight she had on thick red lipstick, plenty of eye makeup, and silver hoop earrings.

After looking her up and down again and then waiting
a couple of seconds, Bobby wanted to say, *Holy fuckin'*
shit, but went with "Can I help you with something?"

"Sorry to bother you like this," she said. "I mean I
would've called, or tried to call and tell you I was coming
over, but I didn't think I'd have time. It's just I heard my
boss talking on the phone today and I had to come over
to warn you."

Man, that Irish accent was sexy as hell. He was trying
to remember whether he'd ever banged an Irish chick.
He had—a few of them—but they were Irish-American.
They didn't sound like this girl, that's for sure.

"Warn me about what?" he asked, hiding the gun
between his leg and the side of his chair.

"I think you're in big trouble," she said. "My boss said
he's sending somebody over here to hurt you, or maybe

worse. I don't know what's going on, but I heard him
mention your name and address."

Bobby stared at her for a few seconds. She was biting
her lower lip, in a naughty schoolgirl way, and he wished
he could give her something else to bite on. He wondered if she'd dressed up just for him. The other night, at
the hotel, she'd been wearing jeans and a tube top.

"So who's this guy that's gonna come after me?" he
asked.

"He calls himself Popeye."

"Popeye? I gotta look out for Olive Oyl too?"

Angela smiled, said, "I just heard Max talking about
Popeye."

"And how does Max know a guy like this 'Popeye'?"

Angela shrugged.

"Is he the guy with the gray hair and the screwed-up
mouth I saw a sketch of on the news?"

"I really don't know anything else," Angela said. "I
mean I guess it could be the same guy."

Bobby looked her up and down again, said, "Wanna sit
down?" and Angela said, "Sure."

As Angela passed by Bobby caught a whiff of her perfume and said, "You're wearing Joy."

"Yeah," Angela said, smiling. "How'd you know?"

"I bought some of it for an old girlfriend one time. I
love that smell."

Bobby watched her sit down on the couch. He liked
the noise her leather skirt made when she crossed her
right leg over her left. She was exactly the type of girl
Bobby would have gone crazy for before he got shot.
He would have taken her to one of those classy Italian
restaurants downtown in the West Village, then to some
club on Seventh Avenue, and then back to his place for
an all-night screw fest.

"This is a really big place you got here," Angela said

looking around. "You live here all by your own self?"

"Yeah," Bobby said. Then he lifted himself up in his wheelchair to do a pressure-relief and said, "But I'll probably sell it one of these days and move into something smaller." Noticing an empty pizza box on the coffee table and glasses half-filled with soda on the end pieces he said, "Sorry it's such a dump."

"Oh, don't be ridiculous," Angela said. "If you want to know a secret, my apartment's a real mess too."

Bobby was staring at Angela's mouth, loving how when she stopped talking her lips stayed slightly apart. He said, "So you know why Max wants this Popeye guy to kill me, don't you?"

"No," Angela said.

"You don't know anything about the pictures?"

Angela shook her head.

"Well," Bobby said, "I sort of took these pictures the other night of you and your boss…in that hotel room."

Bobby was watching Angela's reaction closely. She seemed genuinely surprised, but he couldn't tell for sure.

"You're saying you were the guy who—"

Bobby nodded.

"And you took pictures of me and Max…"

The funny thing was, it almost seemed the idea was getting her hot. He nodded again.

"I can't believe this," Angela said, but not in an angry way. "What are you, a detective or something? Did somebody pay you to follow us?"

Bobby laughed.

"No, it was just chance. It could have been any two people. It didn't have to be you and your boss."

"I don't get it," Angela said. "Why would Max want somebody to kill you?"

"Well, the meeting we had yesterday…I'm not really sure how to put this. I went to Max with a business proposition. I'm a businessman, like he is—except my business is a little different than your boss's."

"I don't get it."

"Yeah, I didn't think you would. Let me put it this way—I was trying to squeeze some money out of him. It was just a racket I got involved with because I had nothing else going on and it got a lot bigger than I ever thought it would."

"A racket? What kind of racket?"

"Taking pictures of people fucking in hotel rooms and trying to blackmail them."

"That's amazing," Angela said.

"What is?"

"That you could be so honest about something like that. I mean a lot of guys would've made up some bullshit story. You just sat there and told me the truth. I can really respect that about a person."

Bobby liked that. "Thanks."

"I mean, I have to admit I'm a little embarrassed that you have those pictures and that you saw me...you know...but on the other hand I can understand why you did it."

"But you don't have to worry," Bobby said, "once your boss pays me the money I'll throw out all of those pictures and the negatives. They won't wind up on the fuckin' Internet if that's what you're worried about."

"Oh, I'm not worried about stuff like that. I really don't care about Max. As far as I'm concerned he can go rot in hell."

"Really?" Bobby said, loving how she said *hell*. You could almost feel the flames. "I thought...I mean, going by the way you two looked that night..."

"I made a huge mistake," Angela said, looking at her lap. "It's the story of my life—things just seem to get really fucked up. I was on the rebound, you know? Max kept asking me out and asking me out and finally I just said yes. I guess I just thought he was a different person than he turned out to be."

Her accent had become full-blown Irish, and had a trace of little-girl-lost in there too, a sucker punch for most men, and for Bobby, who hadn't felt anything for a woman since Tanya, it was a K.O.

"Did he pay this guy Popeye to kill his wife?"

"I don't know for sure, but after hearing him on the phone today…I'm almost positive he did. He was going crazy for me, getting really obsessed, you know? I kept telling him it was nothing serious and that we should end it. But he wouldn't get the message and then he must've gone ahead and got this guy to kill his wife. Believe me, if I had any idea anybody was gonna get hurt there was no way I would've stayed with him."

Angela uncrossed her legs then crossed them again, her leather skirt making that rubbing sound. Her bottom lip was moist and, he didn't know if it was just him or something about the way she was sitting, but her bust looked bigger than it had when she walked in.

"But you were with him the other night," Bobby said, "after his wife got killed."

Angela looked away for a moment, toward the front door. When she turned back, tears were streaming down her cheeks and her face was all scrunched up and ugly.

"I was afraid," Angela said, her voice cracking. "I wanted to break it off, but I've only had my job for a few months and he told me if I didn't keep going out with him he'd fire me and give me a shitty reference. And I was lonely, I guess. Maybe you can't understand, but women get desperate when they get lonely. They do things they wouldn't ordinarily do. Plus my mother was putting a lot of pressure on me."

"Your mother?"

"My mother died a while ago and she was, you know, real salt-of-the-earth."

Bobby loved how she pronounced it *sall-t*. She could even make a condiment sound sexy.

"She had a hard death," Angela went on, "and before she passed, she held my hand and begged me to find a good man someday, not to end up alone." She took a tissue from her bag, dabbed at her eyes, then said, "Maybe you can't understand it, but my mother always had a lot of control over me."

"Actually, I know exactly what that's like," Bobby said.

"You do?"

"My mother and I were very close."

"I'm sorry," Angela said.

"Oh, she's not dead. She's in a nursing home. I still go visit her all the time, but she's really out of it."

"I think that's the most beautiful thing I've ever heard in my whole life," Angela said, starting to cry again. "A son who visits his mother in a nursing home."

Bobby was feeling something he'd never thought possible—he was feeling *noble*, like a fucking good guy. He had no idea how that had happened, but he kind of liked it. He saw himself like Tom Cruise in that flick, *Born On The Fourth of July*, having fucking dignity in his disability.

"I only go a few times a week," Bobby said.

"A few times a week! I hope when I'm old I have a son like you who'll always love me."

Now the tears were starting to flow freely down Angela's cheeks. Bobby noticed that the tissue she had was drenched so he wheeled into the kitchen and returned with some paper towels. He gave one to Angela and she dabbed her eyes a few times and said, "I have a confession to make. There's something I lied to you about before and I feel really bad about it."

"Shoot," Bobby said.

"See, the truth is, I *could've* called to tell you all of this instead of coming here. But after I saw you leave the office, I just couldn't stop thinking about you. I thought maybe if I came over here…I don't know…I just thought maybe something could happen between us. Believe me, I usually don't do stuff like this—I mean get so forward with guys—but after all the hell I've been through lately I figured things couldn't get much worse than they already are. I just think you're a very attractive man and…I feel like such an idiot. I should probably just go home now."

Bobby's face was hot. He hoped he wasn't blushing.

"Well, that's definitely very flattering," he said.

"It is?"

"Of course," Bobby said. "I mean you're a good-looking girl and—"

"You mean that?"

"Mean what?"

"That I'm good-looking."

"Of course. Believe me, if I wasn't in this wheelchair…"

"Oh, I don't care about that."

"You don't?"

"If you want to know the truth I think a wheelchair's kind of sexy. I mean it's not like I'm some bleedin' pervert or anything like that. I don't go out trying to meet guys in wheelchairs, but it's not like I have anything against it and you're so, like, courageous about it. You don't whine or moan—you just go on with your life. Max can use both of his legs and he never, and I mean never, stops whining."

"I don't think you understand—"

"You know who you're like? You're just like Tom Cruise in that movie about the Vietnam vet in the wheelchair. My mother loved that movie. She'd say, God rest her, 'See that? That's a man of character.' "

Bobby couldn't believe she'd said that. It was like they were *fucking communicating mentally*. How great was that?

Angela was gazing at Bobby with her eyes wide open and her lips parted slightly, like she wanted to be kissed. In the old days, Bobby would have sat next to her on the couch, gone in for some tongue action, and the rest would have been history. But now he felt like it was his first time alone with a girl.

"I have an idea," Angela said, maybe sensing his awkwardness. "I'm a really good cook. I could go out and get some stuff and cook you a really great dinner. Are you Greek by any chance?"

"No, but people sometimes think I look Greek. Why?"

"My father's Greek and you sort of remind me of his side."

Shit, why the fuck didn't he just say he was Greek? He could do Greek. Hell, anyone could do Greek. Just don't shave and grunt, what's so hard about that?

"Hey, I have an idea," Angela said, her face brightening. "I know how to make a great pasticcio and I could make a big Greek salad to go with it. How's that sound?"

Bobby said that sounded dynamite. While Angela was out shopping for food Bobby got dressed as quickly as he could. He put on one of his good silk shirts and a pair of chinos. He wished he had time to take a bath and trim his beard, but by the time he finished getting dressed Angela was already back from the supermarket. Bobby had Thin Lizzy going, figuring he'd impress her with some Irish rock.

Angela heard the opening riff of "Whiskey In The Jar," shrieked, "Oh my God, that's like, my favorite song."

Bobby had a feeling she was full of shit. He liked that, though—showed she was into him.

Coming back with some bullshit of his own, he said, "Yeah, I love Lizzy, man. My opinion, they're better than

AC/DC. I got everything they ever did on cassette."

Angela told Bobby to wait in the living room while she was cooking because she wanted the meal to be a surprise. It took a long fucking time, but she finally told him dinner was ready and he wheeled up to the table. By the way Angela was looking at him he knew that after dinner she was gonna be up for some dessert. He hoped he could give it to her. Phil Lynott was into "The Boys Are Back in Town" and Bobby figured, hey, it had to be an omen.

The pasticcio was only so-so—okay, it tasted like horseshit—but Bobby told Angela that it was the best Greek dinner he'd ever eaten. They sat at the table afterwards, drinking Merlot and talking. He told her all the highlights of his life, including how he had wound up in the wheelchair.

"I was dating this black girl named Tanya," Bobby explained. "It was nothing too serious, you know? We were just going out a lot, having a good time. Then one night we were at her place, up in the South Bronx, listening to some tunes. I remember the fucking song that was playing—Guns N' Roses, 'Sympathy for the Devil'—when her boyfriend comes into the room."

"She had a boyfriend?" Angela said.

"It was news to me too," Bobby said. "He was a big black guy, like six-four, and he was angry as hell."

"So what happened?"

"He starts saying, 'Why are you fucking my woman?'—shit like that. I didn't know what was going on. I just said to him, 'Look, you two better settle this yourselves,' and I got up to leave. That's when I heard the shot. Next thing I know I'm on the floor and I can't feel my legs."

"Did he go to jail?"

"No, he ran away and I didn't press charges."

"Why not?"

"What was the point? It wouldn't get me my legs back."

Bobby didn't want to tell Angela the rest of the story, how when he got out of the hospital he took a bus up to the project in the Bronx where the guy lived and pumped six bullets into his back. But just thinking about how he'd plugged that fucking bastard and then put a couple in Tanya when she came home made his blood bubble.

"You okay?" Angela asked.

"Yeah," Bobby said. "It's just the memories are, you know…painful."

Angela shook her head in sympathy then said, "You know what I think? I think you're lucky."

"Why's that?"

"Look at you—you're strong, healthy, not too old. If he shot you in the head you would've died and you never would've met me."

"Yeah, I guess that's true," Bobby said, thinking only somebody who wasn't paralyzed would say a thing like that. He remembered what it felt like, lying on Tanya's floor, realizing he was a cripple. In twenty-plus years, pulling heists and shit, he never got a scratch. Then some jealous fuck walks in a room and shoots him in the back. There was nothing lucky about it.

They started to talk about other things. Then Angela said she had to go to the bathroom, but instead she stopped behind Bobby and started kissing the back of his neck, running her hands over his chest. He had no idea what to do next. He felt sweat building under his arms and he couldn't remember if he'd put on deodorant. He was positive that he reeked and that he was going in his pants. Angela rotated the wheelchair around, away from the table, and climbed on top of him. As she undid his chinos he said, "There's something you gotta know."

He told her how he couldn't stay hard for more than a

couple of minutes and how he didn't think he'd be able to screw. It was hard for him to say all of it, to find the right words and then get them out, but when he finally did he was surprised how much better he felt. Still, he was ready for her to make up some phony excuse and go home. But instead she put her hands over his cheeks, and moved her face right in front of his, looking into his eyes and said, "Don't worry, everything's gonna be okay. Think of my mother looking down at us." Bobby was going to say, Think of that black fuck looking up at us, but managed to keep it to himself.

After about ten minutes had gone by, Bobby was going to tell her that it was a waste of time, that they should just forget about it. But then Angela looked up at him and by the way she was smiling he knew they were finally getting somewhere. She climbed on top of Bobby in the wheelchair and started thrusting. At first, all Bobby could think about was how he was going to shit and make a big asshole out of himself. But then when he saw Angela starting to come Bobby felt a way he never thought he'd feel again.

"See?" she said. "I told you everything was gonna be okay, didn't I?"

Later, they went into the bedroom.

"Hey, who took all these pictures?"

Bobby was afraid Angela would think he was some kind of loser, but he didn't see any point in denying it.

"I did," Bobby said. "Why? You like them?"

"It looks like something they'd have hanging in a museum," Angela said. "You didn't tell me you were an artist."

"It's just a little hobby of mine," Bobby said.

"I love the way they're all different sizes. It's like you're saying that women are different, but they're the same, like—I don't know what I mean, but I like them."

It crossed his mind that maybe she wasn't playing with a full deck.

Now that they had gotten the first time out of the way, Bobby's old confidence was back. They went at it again and this time Bobby wasn't worried about anything. He couldn't believe how lucky he was to meet a girl like Angela who didn't treat him like he was a freak.

Angela lay next to him in the dark. Cool jazz was playing, the soft music seeming to fit the mood. Angela was running her long fingernails through Bobby's thick, sweaty chest hair.

"You know it could be easier for you the next time we get together," Bobby said. "I can use a vacuum pump or get one of those injection devices. You just shoot some medicine into the side of your dick and you stay hard for hours."

"Maybe you could take Viagra."

"Tried it," Bobby said. "Didn't do shit for me."

"You know what would be great?"

"If you moved in here and I could fuck you stupid every night?"

"That too." Angela caressed his chin and stared into his eyes. "But it would be great if you could get rid of Popeye."

"What do you mean, get rid of him?"

"You have that gun. I mean, I saw it. Maybe you could, like, scare him, or do something to make him leave, go back to Ireland."

"That's where he's from?"

"Or maybe you could…I don't know. I'm just worried about him, that's all. I think if he kills you, Max might send him after me next."

"Kill me? Whoa, I did two tours in Desert Storm. Nobody's gonna kill me, especially some crazy, grey-haired Irish fuck. No offense."

"So you'll protect me?"

Angela was twirling the hair below his bellybutton now and he couldn't believe it—he was getting more liftoff.

"Don't worry, sweetheart, I'll take care of Popeye," Bobby said, grabbing Angela and pulling her back on top of him. "Now how about you take care of me?"

Nineteen

*I pictured his mouth open and the powerful cleaning fluid
filling his mouth, his lungs, stomach—pooling in his ears,
penetrating into his skin, burning through the tiny pipe of his
cock, tearing its way like a knife up his asshole. He would soon
be cleaner than any human ever got. His stench would be
filtered and dumped with the toxic waste.*

VICKI HENDRICKS, *Miami Purity*

Homicide Detective Louis Ortiz pressed the RECORD
button on the digital recorder on the desk and said, "As
you might've heard we have a suspect in the case. There's
also been another victim."

"Why are you taping me?" Max said. "I don't get it—
am I being interviewed or interrogated?"

"Maybe you should answer that question for me."

"Look, I don't know what's going on here. I thought
you were going to fill me in on what happened to my wife
and niece. But if this is some kind of—"

"If you want to call a lawyer you can."

"What do I need a lawyer for? Only guilty people need
lawyers."

"Then shut up and answer my damn questions," Ortiz
said. "As you may have heard, my partner, Kenneth
Simmons' body was discovered this afternoon."

"Yeah, I heard about that on the news."

"What did you hear?"

"That a Detective Simmons was killed."

"And you realized that this was the same man who was
working on your wife's murder case?"

"The name rang a bell."

"Did the news come as a surprise to you?"

"Excuse me for getting off topic here," Max said, "but I don't see why you're talking to me. From what I heard on the news the suspect you're looking for is a skinny guy with gray hair. Does my hair look fucking gray to you?"

Max had some extra edge in his tone, letting this prick know he was a respectable businessman, a pillar of the community, the guy who paid the cops' goddamn wages.

Ortiz breathed deeply then said, "Kenneth Simmons was following you when he was killed."

"Following me?" Max said. "What the hell for?"

"That's not important now," Ortiz said. "What's important is we found his car in front of the Hotel Pennsylvania on Thirty-third Street. Can you tell me what the car was doing there?"

"I haven't the foggiest idea," Max said. He had always been a horrible liar, especially under pressure. *Foggiest*. What the fuck was he, British?

"Maybe it'll come back to you," Ortiz said. "I questioned the clerks at the hotel. They said at around eight o'clock on Monday evening, Detective Simmons inquired at the desk about a couple that had checked in under the name Brown in room 1812. You don't have an idea who that couple is, do you?"

Max was shaking his head.

"I don't have to tell you what I think," Ortiz continued. "Unfortunately, the woman who was working at the desk that night said she couldn't remember what the couple looked like, but I have people taking a look at the security video from that night and I think it's going to show you and a woman checking into that hotel. Now if you're as innocent as you say you are you could just save us some time and tell us who that woman is."

"I don't know what you're talking about," Max said as calmly as he could. "I was never in that hotel."

"All right," Ortiz said. He turned off the recorder then got up and went behind Max. Resting his hands on the back of Max's chair, his mouth almost touching Max's left ear, he said, "You wanna do this the hard way, we'll do it the hard way. But I'll tell you right now—if I find out that was you in that hotel I'm gonna make your life a fucking nightmare. You ever get fucked up the ass? Well, I hope you enjoy it because I'm gonna put you in a cell with a psychotic, white-boy-hating motherfucker who's got a big, fat, fourteen-inch dong. Then we'll see how much you like fucking around with Louis Ortiz."

Ortiz stayed there for a few seconds, letting his words sink in, then he returned to his seat and turned the recorder back on.

Max felt wetness on the back of his neck—either sweat or his spray-on hair was dissolving. He wasn't sure what he was accomplishing by not admitting he was in that hotel; when Ortiz saw that surveillance tape that ridiculous wig would be no disguise. But, at this point, he didn't see what he had to lose by continuing to lie.

"Look, I want to do everything I can to help you," Max said, "but I think you're forgetting that my wife and niece are *dead*. You know what it's like to come home and find the brains of your loved ones splattered on your wall? Believe me, it's not very pleasant. But what's even worse is having to put up with some ignorant fucking detective, making up ridiculous stories, trying to implicate you. Don't you people have any sense of decency?"

Max thought that his speech had affected Ortiz and was proud of himself for performing so well, but then Ortiz said, "You want me to spell it out for you, Fisher? I think you hired somebody to kill your wife. I think your niece was just unlucky, got mixed up in it by accident.

Detective Simmons thought the same thing—fact, he was more sure about it than I was. That's why he was following you that night. Oh, and by the way I do know what it's like to lose somebody close, like a partner you've been working with for the last seven fucking years."

Max said, "That's it. I'm not doing any more of this bullshit without my lawyer."

"I thought you told me only guilty people need lawyers?"

"Guilty people and people who are being harassed."

"All I'm asking is that you tell me the truth."

"I'm telling you the fucking truth, but you don't want to hear it."

"All right," Ortiz said, "then tell me—where did you go Monday night after work?"

"I took a cab home."

"You have anybody who can vouch for that?"

"Not unless you can find the cab driver who drove me."

"Speaking of cab drivers," Ortiz said, "we *did* find a driver who claims he picked up a man fitting Kenneth Simmons' description in front of the Hotel Pennsylvania at approximately eight-forty Monday evening. Simmons ordered him to follow another cab which ended up going to the corner of Twenty-fifth and First. A woman got out of the first cab—the driver couldn't ID her except that she was white and had 'big blond hair'—and Kenneth Simmons got out of the cab and followed her. The driver of the cab that the woman was in hasn't been found. You don't, by any chance, know anybody who lives around that area, do you?"

Shit, Twenty-fifth was Angela's block. But she hadn't mentioned anything about talking to a cop that night.

"No," Max said after taking a few moments to mull it over. "I don't."

"What about a gold pin, two hands almost touching? You ever see one of those suckers?"

Max had no idea what Ortiz was talking about, said, "I have no idea what you're talking about."

"My partner had a pin. It wasn't on his body when his body was discovered."

Then Max remembered the weird pin that Popeye had been wearing at the pizza place. Like the idiot didn't have enough heat on him already, he had to steal the pin off a cop he'd killed.

"Lemme ask you something," Max said. "Let's say I was in that hotel with a woman that night—which I absolutely wasn't—and let's say we checked in under—what did you say the name was?"

"Brown."

"All right—let's say we checked in under the name Brown. How the hell would that help you find out who killed my wife?"

"We think the gun that was used to kill Kenneth Simmons was the same one used to kill your wife and niece. He was either killed on Twenty-fifth Street or else he was taken to Harlem and killed up there. But the only reason he ended up in either place was because he followed your girlfriend—excuse me, Mrs. *Brown*—out of the Hotel Pennsylvania. If we know what went on in that hotel it may tell us why he followed her when she left."

"I guess that makes sense."

"So, then, Mr. Fisher," Ortiz said, "are you ready to tell me anything?"

Max thought for a moment, then shook his head.

"What about the man in the sketch?" Ortiz took out a copy of the sketch from his drawer and slid it across the desk for Max to look at. "You ever seen him before?"

Max stared at the sketch of Popeye for a good ten seconds, trying to make it look like he was really studying it, then said, "No, never."

Ortiz glared at Max. "Where were you before you got home today?"

"I was at work. You gonna try to book me for that too?"

Ortiz pressed the STOP button on the recorder.

"Maybe we should do this again," he said. "This time without all the bullshit."

"I'd rather not."

"How about taking a polygraph?"

"Not without my lawyer."

"It won't matter anyway," Ortiz said, "after I take a look at that surveillance tape."

Twenty

*A rotting old woman in the bedroom in black plastic bags
would be a sure tip-off. He had to find a way to get rid of her.
Feed her to some dogs or something.*
JOE R. LANSDALE, *Freezer Burn*

Dillon's book of Zen wisdom wasn't weaving its magic no
more. He poured a shot of Jameson, the bottle nearly
empty. Everything was running down. The tinker he'd
killed crossed his mind and he gave an involuntary tremor.
He downed the whiskey, then waited for the hit and muttered, "That shite burns."

To erase the tinker, he dredged up another memory, a
dog he'd owned. Mongrel called Heinz, cos of the 57
ingredients it had. That mutt loved him, completely. He'd
deliberately starved it for a week, see how it fared. Not so
good—lotsa whining in there. He'd got back to the shithole he was living in then, put out his hand to the pooch
and the fooker, the fooker bit him. He almost admired the
sheer balls of the little runt. But, of course, no one, no
thing, ever bit Dillon, at least not twice. He got his hurly,
made from the ash, honed by a master craftsman. Dillon
had never used it, except to bust heads. He'd stolen it at a
match in Croke Park, and if he remembered correctly,
Galway had their arse handed to them by fookin Cork.

The dog had backed away and Dillon cooed, "Come
on boy, come get yer medicine."

Took him fifteen minutes to beat the little fook to
death, gore all over the walls, the tiny animal not going
easy.

For devilment, Dillon had told this story to Angela, hoping to get a rise out of the bitch.

She'd been horrified and then he asked, "You ever been hungry, alanna?"

She didn't know what he meant and he said. "There's a little moral here mo croi, and it's don't bite the hand that feeds you."

Then, near to tears, she'd said, "I don't know what you mean."

And he laughed, delighted, said, "And isn't that the bloody beauty of it?"

Bobby popped a wheelie coming out of the D'Agostino supermarket on Columbus. He was in a good mood, still thinking about last night with Angela. He couldn't wait to call her later—maybe she'd want to come over and listen to some Ted Nugent.

Then, looking over his shoulder, he saw the guy walking about ten yards behind him. It was him all right—same thin, gray guy with the lips who was in the police sketch on TV and in all the newspapers. He was wearing faded jeans and his hands were tucked deep into the pockets of a leather jacket.

It was cooler than it had been on recent nights and there were still a lot of people on the street, shopping or coming home from work. Bobby didn't think Popeye would try to shoot him here, with all these witnesses— but he might use a knife.

Instead of crossing Columbus, Bobby turned left on Eighty-ninth and headed toward Central Park. It was a darker, emptier, quieter block, with mainly four-story brownstones. Bobby rode at a slow, steady pace and listened closely to what was happening behind him. He had always had great ears. In Iraq, he used to hear the towel-head snipers even when they were a hundred or so yards away. Now he listened to Popeye's footsteps, hearing them get gradually closer. There was something unusual about the way he was walking. He was taking one solid step, followed by a softer dragging step, like he had a limp. But the footsteps were definitely getting closer. Just before he reached the darkest part of the block, which was shaded by dense, overhanging trees, Bobby braked and wheeled around. The bag of groceries fell off his lap and crashed onto the sidewalk, gushing dark purple liquid. He raised his arm in one fluid motion, taking his Glock from his jacket pocket and aiming it between Popeye's eyes.

Obviously surprised, Popeye stopped about ten feet from Bobby, his left arm by his side and his right hand in the lower pocket of his leather jacket.

"Look what you did, asshole," Bobby said. "You broke my fuckin' grape juice."

Popeye started to move his right hand. Bobby went, "Move one more fuckin' inch I'll put a hole in your head."

"Jaysus, take it easy fellah." Popeye said. "No harm, no damage done. Just take it fookin' easy, me man."

Wondering if the guy knew how stupid he sounded, Bobby said, "Take your hand out of your pocket slowly. It comes out with anything—I don't care if it's your fucking house keys—I'm gonna start shooting."

For a moment, Popeye remained still, then he showed his empty hand.

"Now your jacket. Drop it on the sidewalk, and take five steps backwards."

Cursing in Irish under his breath, Popeye slowly took off his jacket and let it fall.

"Now back up."

Popeye backed away a few steps, then Bobby slowly wheeled himself forward one-handed. Keeping the gun aimed, he leaned down, picked up the coat and removed a switchblade from one pocket and a .38 from the other. He put the gun and the knife in the pocket of his windbreaker.

"Okay, dickhead. We're going for a walk."

Bobby said to his doorman, "I want you to meet my cousin Popeye—he's visiting from out of town."

"It's a pleasure to meet you, Popeye," the doorman, an old guy, said.

Inside his apartment, Bobby ordered Popeye to sit on the couch and Popeye said, "Okay, so who told you about me? Fisher?"

"What do you mean?"

"You knew my name. Jaysus, I knew I should never've trusted that prick. When did he put you on to me?"

"I think, under the circumstances, I should be the one asking the questions," Bobby said, aiming the gun.

"You think I'm gonna sweat you, some fuck in a wheel-chair? Lemme tell yeh, fellah, I've had weapons aimed at me by the very best. I've had an Orange bastard, fueled on anti-Papal hysteria, believing the only good Catholic was a dead one, put a an AK-47 in me mouth and I survived that, so you think I give a shite's fuck about you and yer feckin' Glock?"

"I said I'll be asking the questions," Bobby said calmly, "and this is the last time I'm gonna tell you that."

Popeye didn't flinch—he barely even reacted. The guy must be a pro, Bobby thought. He was keeping his cool anyway, like he really didn't give a shit if he lived or died.

"Why'd you kill those two women?" Bobby asked.

"I didn't kill nobody."

"It's not exactly a big secret anymore. The police have that picture of you going around."

"You mean that snap in the *Post*? You telling me my nose looks like that?"

"Did Max Fisher hire you?"

"Ary Christ, what do you care, you're not a Guard."

"A what?"

"A cop, yah bollix."

"No, I'm not a cop," Bobby said. "I'm just the guy holding a gun on you. I'd think you'd want to answer my questions, but maybe you don't. Maybe you just want me to shoot you."

Popeye thought about this a second. Maybe he did want to live because he said, "Yeah, okay, he hired me."

"To knock off his wife?"

"Yeah."

"And what about the college kid—the girl?"

"T'was a bit of bad timing, as the tinkers say back home."

"And what about the cop?"

"Him I would've killed for a shot of Jameson."

"What?"

Popeye smiled out of the corner of his scarred mouth, said, "Where I come from, a Guard is a bonus." Then he pulled up his shirt to cover his face and said, "Jaysus, what the hell is that smell?"

Bobby couldn't smell anything unusual, but it was possible he had farted or shit in his pants. He was about to check when Popcye lowered his shirt and started sniffing some more.

"Me lady been here?"

"Who?"

"Colleen with a bust on her to die for. Name of Angela. Was she here?"

Bobby shook his head, smiling, thinking, *I should've fuckin' known*. All that bullshit, saying, *If you want to know the truth I think a wheelchair's kind of sexy*. She'd just been manipulating him, playing a game with the poor cripple, leading him around by the nose—or by the dick, more like it.

Still smiling, Bobby said, "Angela, huh?"

"Yeah, Angela, the hoor's ghost. Funny, smells like her scent mixing with the shite. Would you open a window? It's killing me, mate."

Bobby, not smiling anymore, didn't answer right away. Then he said, "Open a fuckin' window yourself, if you want to. I don't give a shit."

Popeye slid one of the panes open, letting the noise of traffic and blaring horns into the apartment along with the breeze.

"So how did you meet *Angela*?" Bobby asked.

"I met her in Ireland, at a pub."

"And you guys live together?"

"More than that, I gave her a Claddagh ring."

"So it was Angela's idea to knock off Fisher's wife?"

"Would love to take the credit me own self, but the idea was hers."

Bobby, thinking, *That bitch*, said, "And what were you planning to do then?"

"She was going to marry him."

"Then what?"

"The best part. I'd get to blast Fisher."

"And you thought this would work?

"Was working till you came along, fellah. Now, come on, why don't you put the gun down? If you shoot me what'll you do with me body? You have the doorman right downstairs. So how about you just let me go? When I get Fisher's money, I'll give you a nice cut, how's that?"

Bobby, keeping the gun aimed at Popeye, wheeled to the bookshelf and took down a folder with several pictures.

"Why don't you take a look through these?"

Popeye came over and snatched the envelope from Bobby. He looked through the pictures quickly, then handed the envelope back and said, "So?"

"So?" Bobby said. "That's your Angela, right? What do you think now?"

"I knew you had these. Angela told me all about them."

"Does she look like she's enjoying it?"

"Are you trying to get me riled?"

"You know why you thought you smelled her before, you fuckin' idiot? Because she was here."

"Why was she here?"

"To fuck my brains out, for one, and, I gotta admit she was pretty damn good at it."

"What do I care? She fucked Fisher too—lots of times. I don't do jealousy, mate."

Feeling stupid and sick, Bobby said, "She also came here to try to get me to kill you."

"Eh, that's bollix."

"She told me you were coming after me. She wanted me to get rid of you for her."

"Why would she want me dead?"

"Who the hell knows? Maybe her plan was to marry Fisher and then kiss your ass goodbye, man. Hell, maybe she was even planning to hire a hit man to knock you off."

"Ah, you're talking shite, that dosh was for us. I fooking earned that."

Bobby put the gun down in his lap, said, "That's just what she told you to get you to kill Fisher's wife. All along they were planning to fuck you over. If I hadn't come along they probably would've ratted you out already, but then they thought they still needed you, to get rid of me."

"I'll tell you what I think. I think you would have made a good Brit, cos you like fookin with me head."

"Jesus Christ, why the fuck would I lie to you? I have the pictures, I have the gun, I don't have to help you. I'm just telling you the way it is. They're gonna tell the cops you killed those two women, they'll say they had nothing to do with it. They'll say you were fucking Angela, you got jealous, you broke into Max's townhouse to kill him, but he wasn't there and the women were, so you did them instead. And who's the judge gonna believe? You know a guy like Max Fisher is gonna hire some hotshot lawyer. The judge won't give a shit about you. And once the press starts calling you a cop killer too, forget about it. Meanwhile, Angela and Max'll be living happily ever after."

There was no sound in the room other than the noise of the traffic in the street outside. "So what're you saying?" Popeye finally asked.

"It's up to you how you wanna handle this," Bobby said, "but I know what *I'd* do."

"What's that?"

"I'd go by Angela's tonight, teach the bitch a fuckin' lesson."

"Keep talkin."

"Then, I'm just gonna throw this out there—maybe after you take care of Angela we can work together."

"Doing what, changing your diapers?"

"What I did before I landed in this fucking chair, asshole. Hit banks, jewelry stores, anywhere where there's money."

"Why would I want to do that?"

"To make some money, Popeye. You like money? First we'll soak Fisher for all he's worth, then we'll move on to bigger and better things. See, this picture shit—it's just a sideline for me. I'm into armed robbery—pulled some of the biggest jobs on the east coast. I got a few jobs I'm lookin' to pull right now and you can be in my new crew."

"What do you need me for?"

"I can handle a gun, but I can't muscle people the way I used to. You ever do any muscle work, Popeye?"

"You're fooking codding me, muscle work is me middle

name, leaning on fookers, tis me birthright. I did some protection work for the Ra, the IRA to you."

"The IRA?" Bobby said, impressed. "That's great. So you already have some useful experience. So what do you say?"

Popeye thought about it, said, "What about the Guards? I can't be waiting around New York, you know."

"You ever hear of Willie Sutton?"

"Is he gonna be in our crew too?"

"No, he was a bank robber from the old days, the best who ever lived. Anyway, when the cops were coming after him he used to dress in disguises. One time he was living right next door to a police station and they never found him."

"Fookin A. My kind of fellah."

"So what we'll do," Bobby said, "is put you in some disguises. Or—I got a better idea—I know a guy out in Long Island City—you know, a plastic surgeon. He specializes in cons on the run."

"Any chance he can make me look like Colin Farrell?"

"Those guys can work fucking miracles."

Popeye smiled, stuck his hand out, said. "In that case, tis a deal, mate."

Twenty-One

I put on the suit and hey, I was Dillon Blair; same shit-eating
smile. You wear a suit like that, you get a hint of why the rich
are so smug. Later, in Bedford Hill, a hooker said
"Suit like that, you want to play busted?"
"Play what?"
"I sit on yer face and you guess my weight?"
Like I said, the suit was a winner.
KEN BRUEN, *The Hackman Blues*

Angela woke up when Dillon came home and turned on
the light. He was wearing his leather jacket and was
holding a big white shopping bag. He looked angry.
Angrier than usual. Without saying a word to Angela, he
went into the bathroom, still wearing his jacket and carrying the shopping bag.

Squinting, still half-asleep, Angela remembered what
was supposed to happen tonight and obviously hadn't
happened. Bobby was supposed to take care of Dillon for
her, but something had definitely gone wrong. Was
Bobby dead? He must be if Dillon was still alive. Angela
prayed that she was still sleeping, that this was a nightmare and that she'd wake up any second.

Dillon came out of the bathroom, still wearing his
leather jacket.

"So?" Angela asked. "How did it go tonight?"

Dillon stared at Angela for a couple of seconds then
said, "How did *what* go?" His tone had a combination of
sarcasm and amusement, but he wasn't smiling.

"You know what—with Bobby Rosa, the guy in the

wheelchair." She swallowed. "I mean did you kill him like you were supposed to?"

"Why the fook do you care?"

"I'm just asking. Jaysus, I have a right to ask, don't I?"

Again, Dillon stared at Angela for a few seconds. His mutilated lips seemed to be wet, like a pair of ugly snakes. Angela had no idea what was going on. The only thing she could think of was that he had found out about her and Bobby's plan. But this didn't make any sense. Bobby would never've told Dillon about that unless Dillon had tortured him. Imagining Dillon torturing a poor guy in a wheelchair and enjoying it—she *knew* he'd enjoy it, all right—pissed Angela off big time.

"What's wrong with you?" Angela said. "Why are you looking at me like that?"

"I can look at you any way I want to," Dillon said.

"Well, I don't like it when you wet your lips like that, so just stop it."

"You think there's something wrong with me mouth?"

"I don't think anything," Angela said. "I just don't like it when you do that. It gives me the creeps."

Dillon stuck his tongue out and slowly ran it along his upper lip, then his lower. Then he said, "I'm going to miss that shite you talk."

"What do you mean, *miss* it? Where are you going?"

"I'm not going anywhere," he said, still smiling.

"Look," Angela said. "I wish you'd just tell me what's going on here. It's late and I have to get up to go to work tomorrow."

He laughed out loud, said, "Missing work is not really something you'll have to be bothered about."

"Did you kill Bobby Rosa?" Angela asked. "Did you torture him first?"

"Why you care so much about Bobby Rosa?"

"I don't. I just want to know what's going on."

"Maybe I did have some fun with the bastard. What's it to you?"

Dillon's left hand came out of the jacket pocket holding the gun he had used to kill those women and the cop. He aimed it at Angela. There was glint in his eye, part sexual, part adrenalin. He was having the time of his life.

"What's that for?" Angela asked.

"It's for you acting like you're a tinker and you just stole me wallet."

"Stop pointing that thing at me."

"I never told anyone about the tinker, you know."

"I'm gonna scream my feckin' ass off," Angela said.

Dillon grinned, said, "Go on. Pretend you're trying to steal me money."

"I'm serious," Angela said.

"Try, go on, put yer hand in me jacket."

Dillon's right hand came out of the other pocket holding a switchblade. The blade sprang open and he lunged forward, slicing Angela across her right thigh. A deep gash opened and blood spread in a thick stream down Angela's leg. Dillon laughed. Again, Angela was struck by the thought that this had to be a nightmare. She didn't feel any pain yet, and everything was happening too fast, like it wasn't real. But then the pain kicked in, like a stick of dynamite exploding in her leg, and Angela knew that in dreams you weren't supposed to feel pain like this. She grabbed a pillow from the bed and put it over her leg to stop the bleeding. It didn't help. Her leg was wet and hot. She sat down.

Dillon sat next to her on the bed and held the switch-blade against her neck. He said, "Snatch me wallet yah tinker."

Angela's mouth was trembling. She couldn't speak. Dillon was grim-faced now, ordered, "Go for it, go for me cash."

"No," Angela said.

Dillon looked like he might slash Angela again. She started to scream as he pushed her down onto the bed. All she had on was a pair of panties; he got one hand in under the waistband, slid the switchblade roughly under the fabric, and sawed through it with two strokes. He yanked the tatters off her body. Holding her down with one hand, he took down his jeans and underwear with the other. Angela cast around desperately for a weapon. Dillon had the switchblade in the hand that was holding her down—she didn't know what had happened to the gun.

There was a glass on the night table where she'd left it after swallowing a couple of Midols before going to sleep. She grabbed the glass and smashed it against the side of Dillon's head. He let go of her, brought his hand to his head and brought it away bloody. Angela looked at her hand and saw she was still holding about half the shattered glass, a jagged, splintered wedge dripping water and blood. She slashed the edge across Dillon's throat.

Dillon tried to scream, but couldn't make a sound.

Angela freed the blade from Dillon's fist and managed to slide out from under him. He turned to reach for something, maybe the gun, and Angela lunged forward, sinking the blade in his back till it couldn't go any further. She tried to pull it out, but the blade was stuck. Angela stood back in horror as Dillon stood up. He stumbled a few steps, looking into her eyes, then he collapsed in the middle of the floor, where the circular throw rug beneath him promptly soaked through.

She couldn't believe it had been so easy to kill the fucker.

Angela turned on the stereo to some pop station. It was eighties night and Debbie Gibson was singing "Only In My Dreams."

The pain in Angela's thigh, which she'd forgotten in the moment, was back now in full force and blood covered her entire leg. Angela stepped over Dillon and went into the bathroom and rinsed her leg in the shower. She knew she should probably get to a hospital, but she also knew there was no way she could do that now. She didn't have any gauze, so she put some paper towel over the wound and wrapped it up with painting tape.

When she turned off the water, she thought she heard a noise in the other room. She waited, even held her breath, but there was nothing; the sound must've come from another apartment. She remembered what always happened in those horror movies, how whenever it seemed like the killer was dead, it turned out he was still alive. Angela wished she had taken the gun or something with her into the bathroom. She opened the bathroom door slowly and peeked her head out. She relaxed when she saw Dillon still lying on the floor in the same position she'd left him in, his wide-open eyes looking up at nothing. It annoyed her that the bastard looked so fucking relaxed, even Zen-like.

Angela had no idea what she was going to do now. With Bobby dead, she had no one left in the world to help her, except Max, and she knew Max would never get involved in something like this. He'd probably go to the police and say the whole thing had been her and Dillon's idea, that he'd had nothing to do with it. The police would probably believe him too.

Then Angela noticed the white shopping bag that Dillon had left in the bathroom. She looked inside and saw five containers of Drano. She could only think of one thing that Dillon could've been planning to do with them. Well, as her mother used to say, *waste not, want not.*

Holding him by the feet, she dragged Dillon's body into the bathroom, leaving behind a long streak of blood across the floor. Her arm ached, and it was hard to lift him up to put him into the bathtub. But she forced herself, lifting Dillon's legs up first then standing in the bathtub and pulling the rest of him up and over.

Next, she put the stopper over the drain and poured a container of Drano over Dillon's body, saying, "Who's the tinker now, huh, you prick? Who's the tinker now?" She added the other four containers and then she pulled the shower curtain closed.

Back in the main part of the apartment, it crossed her mind to throw his Zen book in after him. But she decided not to, thinking it wasn't worth having to see his face again. Besides, maybe Max might want the book. God knows the guy could use something to help him relax.

Only then did Angela realize how stupid she'd been. How was she supposed to wash up now with Dillon in the bathtub? She could use towels to clean her leg, but she hated washing her hair in the sink.

She had small cuts on her hands from the glass. She poured peroxide all over her wounds, wincing from the pain, and then wrapped the worst of them with more paper towel and painting tape.

Angela was exhausted. She just wanted to get some rest and worry about everything else in the morning. It wasn't as if she could solve all of her problems tonight anyway. She turned the dial on the stereo to an easy listening station and lowered the volume. There was still a huge bloodstain on the floor, in the middle of the room. She didn't feel like mopping now, but she felt uncomfortable sleeping next to a pool of blood all night, knowing it had come from Dillon. She pulled the bed out, away from the wall, to cover the blood—that was better. Then she shut off the light and lay back down, listening to the soft rock music. She decided she'd just have to go over to Max's tomorrow night and take a shower at his place.

Then, as she was falling asleep, she thought she heard faint laughter. It reminded her of a tinker she'd seen in the park when she was a little girl, one who had been laughing his mad head off. But one thing she was sure of—it wasn't Dillon. At least she had one less nightmare to worry about.

Twenty-Two

He might have tried to hide it by dressing in a smart, well-cut suit and putting an easy smile on his face as soon as he saw me, but I could tell this straight away: Roy Fowler was one of the world's guilty.
SIMON KERNICK, *The Murder Exchange*

In 1979, when Max needed a lawyer for his business, he had picked Sid Darrow out of the yellow pages, figuring that a guy with the last name Darrow must know something about the law. But it turned out Darrow wasn't nearly as good as his namesake, bungling a couple of simple contract negotiations that wound up costing Max thousands of dollars. Later, Max found out Darrow's name had been shortened from Darrowicz, but Max didn't fire Darrow for this misrepresentation or for his incompetence. Through the years, he had kept Darrow on the payroll, mainly because he was too lazy to look for someone else and because he figured that all lawyers were basically the same anyway.

When Max called Darrow for a reference to a good criminal lawyer Darrow asked Max what the problem was. Max explained how the police had questioned him last night about his wife's murder.

"If you want my opinion," Darrow said, "you shouldn't have answered any of those questions."

"I don't want your opinion," Max said.

Darrow gave Max the name of a criminal lawyer—Andrew McCullough. Max couldn't think of any famous lawyers named McCullough, but he didn't have time to be choosy. Once the police played back that security tape and saw him and Angela arriving at the hotel the situation would be way out of control. Max knew that Angela wasn't bright enough to keep her story straight and it was only a matter of time until she mentioned Popeye and the murders.

McCullough wasn't in. Max said to his secretary, "Well, can you tell him to call me as soon as he comes in?…Yeah, it's fucking urgent—the cops're trying to nail my ass!"

As Max slammed the phone down there was a knock at his door.

"What?" he yelled.

The door opened slowly. Harold Lipman entered.

"What the hell do you want?"

"I could come back later if…"

"No, come in," Max said. "Sit the hell down."

When Harold sat down across from him, Max could tell by the way Harold wouldn't make eye contact with him that he hadn't made any progress.

"Let me guess," Max said, "you lost the sale?"

Lipman nodded slowly, looking at his lap. Sweat glistened on his forehead.

"What happened?" Max asked.

"He went with someone else," Lipman said dejectedly. "I did the best I could, but our prices just weren't competitive enough. The guy's quote was twenty, thirty thousand dollars lower than ours."

Max was seriously pissed.

"I told you what you had to do to close that sale."

"I'm sorry," Lipman said, "but there was nothing I could do."

"I'm sorry too," Max said, "but your best obviously wasn't good enough. The company can't afford to keep you on, paying you the draw that you're making now, when you're not producing. I'm sorry, but I'm going to have to let you go."

"You're firing me?" Lipman said. "Just like that?"

"You have a half an hour to clean out your desk and leave the premises. And don't take any leads with you—all leads are property of NetWorld."

"Come on, Max—give me another chance. Please. I swear I'll do better."

Max was shaking his head.

"I gave you solid sales advice and you refused to take advantage of it. I'm sorry, but the decision is final—you're terminated."

Max had always loved firing people. In fact, when it came right down to it, it was probably his favorite part of running his own business. He loved controlling people's lives. It made him feel like…well, like God.

He knew he still had a lot of deep shit to climb out of, but tried to focus on the positives. Last night Popeye had killed Bobby Rosa. Now Max's only problem was Angela. He couldn't fire her right away. He'd just have to tell her he wanted to let things cool for a while and hope she kept her mouth shut. Then, after enough time passed, he'd terminate her Greek-Irish ass and hope he never saw her again. His only other problem would be that hotel video-tape, but it wouldn't be nearly as harmful as Bobby Rosa's pictures could have been. All the videotape would show was him and Angela checking into the hotel that night, but it wouldn't be real evidence of an affair. A hotshot criminal lawyer like McCullough would be able to get around it somehow and then he'd be home free.

He retrieved the bid that Harold hadn't been able to close from a file folder and called the guy up.

"Hello, Mr. Takahashi? Max Fisher calling—I'm the president of NetWorld, how are you today?…Good, I'm glad to hear that…I just had a conversation with Harold Lipman and he said you decided to go with someone else for your networking job, is this true?…Well, we try to

keep our costs as low as possible…Yes, I understand….
Oh, of course….No problem, Mr. Takahashi, but can I
just ask you one semi-personal question and then I'll let
you go?…Are you married?…The reason I ask is I'd like
an opportunity to re-explain this quote to you….I understand, but there's a place I'd think you'd love—I know I
love it. Have you ever been to Legz Diamond's?…That's
right, and I sort of get VIP service there. I know this one
stripper there—you don't have anything against black
people, do you?…I didn't think so. Anyway, this black girl
they got there is dynamite. She's a personal friend of mine
too and, I assume you like women with large breasts, Mr.
Takahashi…Well, wait till you see this girl. I'm talking 44
triple-Ds…I'm serious. You didn't sign that other quote
yet, did you?…Good. I'm gonna show you a time you'll
never forget. How's tonight at six sound?…Six-thirty's
terrific. I'll be outside your building in a cab. You won't be
disappointed, Mr. Takahashi."

Max hung up, shouted, "Baby!"

The quote was for $220,000 and Max knew that there
was no way Takahashi wasn't going to sign it after the
night he'd have tonight. And this was only the first job for
this client. Their network had over one hundred users
and there could be ongoing work there. Harold had been
working on this quote for weeks and hadn't gotten anywhere and now Max had practically closed it in less than
one minute. No one could sell computer networks the
way Max Fisher could—no one.

Max buzzed Angela—he was hungry and wanted her
to order him some breakfast—but there was no answer at
her desk. He thought this was strange, since it was after
nine o'clock and she was usually in by eight-thirty. He
buzzed the receptionist to ask if she had called in sick or
to say she was going to be late, but the receptionist said
that she hadn't called.

A few minutes later, Max was on the phone with a software vendor when there was a knock at his door.

He assumed it was Lipman, coming to beg for his job back, and Max put the vendor on hold and yelled, "Go away!"

But the knock came again, a little louder, then Max said, "Who the hell's there?"

The door opened and Bobby Rosa wheeled into the office. Seeing the bearded cripple again made Max's throat close up. He reached for a mug of day-old coffee on his desk and swallowed the murky crap as fast as he could. Bobby had closed the door and was smiling now, watching Max. Max looked at Bobby's black sweatshirt with the words *Average White Band* inscribed on it and thought, Jesus, what's this guy, in the KKK or something?

"Surprised?" Bobby asked.

"No," Max said, forcing a smile. "Why would I be surprised?"

"I don't know. I just thought it would be natural for a guy to be surprised when someone he sent a hit man to bump off shows up in his office the next morning alive. But hey, that's just me."

"I really don't have the foggiest idea what you're talking about," Max said. There it was again, *foggiest*.

"You want to keep playing games, be my guest," Bobby said. "It won't matter soon anyway."

"How the hell did you get in here?" Max said, his throat tightening again.

"Don't blame the girl at the desk," Bobby said. "I'm good at getting into places I'm not supposed to be. But I think you already know that."

"Look, if you're not out of here in two minutes I'm calling the cops."

Bobby laughed, then said, "You still don't realize what kind of trouble you're in, do you? You sent Dillon after me, but that was your last card—you shot your load."

"Dillon?" Max said. "Who the hell's Dillon?"

"You know him as Popeye, but his real name's Dillon. It doesn't matter now anyway because he's out of the picture."

"What do you mean, out of the picture?"

"Not what you think it means. He's working with me now."

Max couldn't believe this was happening, that this freakazoid in a wheelchair was really here again, trying to ruin his life.

"Oh, and your executive assistant," Bobby went on, "the one I got in that picture with you—Angela, I think her name is. I don't think she'll be coming into work any-more, so you might just want to clean out her desk."

"Why? Is she working with you too?"

"No, she's really out of the picture, and I think you know exactly what I mean."

Max picked up the phone and said, "That's it. I'm calling the cops."

"I'd think about that a second," Bobby said. "I mean what are you gonna tell them?"

Max paused, realizing Bobby was right, and replaced the receiver.

"Why are you doing this to me?" Max said, feeling like he might start to cry. "What did I ever do to you?"

"You were just in the right place at the wrong time," Bobby said. He took out a mini-cassette recorder from the pocket of his windbreaker and placed it on the desk. He said, "You want to do the honors or should I?"

Max didn't move so Bobby went ahead and pressed the PLAY button.

> *"Did Max Fisher hire you?"*
> *"Ary Christ, what do you care, you're not a Guard."*

Max looked at Bobby, but Bobby was looking down at the tape recorder, smiling. There was more conversation, something about Bobby holding a gun, then Popeye said:

> *"Yeah, okay, he hired me."*
> *"To knock off his wife?"*
> *"Yeah."*
> *"And what about the college kid—the girl?"*
> *"T'was a bit of bad timing, as the tinkers say back home."*
> *"And what about the cop?"*
> *"Him I would've killed for a shot of Jameson."*

Bobby pressed the STOP button and said, "Oh, one other thing. I don't want a quarter of a mill anymore."

"Yeah?" Max said weakly. "What do you want?"

Bobby leaned forward in his wheelchair, then said, "Everything."

Before Angela left for work, she checked to see how Dillon was doing in the bathtub. The Drano had burned through the top layer of skin on his face, turning it yellow and gooey, but at this rate it was going to take weeks until his whole body was dissolved, if it dissolved at all. Meanwhile, the room stank so bad she could hardly breathe. It figured that Dillon would come up with some stupid idea that had like zero chance of working.

Then she saw something glinting in the gooey yellow. For one awful moment, she thought maybe his gold tooth fell out and her stomach heaved. But it wasn't a tooth, she realized, it was the pin, and she muttered out loud, "What's with that feckin' pin?"

She picked it out, real careful not to touch any of Dillon, going under her breath, "Sweet Jesus, oh Sweet Mother of all Heaven."

She put the pin on the sink, figuring she'd stash it in her handbag later. The pin was tarnished from the Drano, but compared to Dillon himself it was in great shape.

Angela had already mopped up most of the blood off the floor and reluctantly she washed her hair in the kitchen sink. Even after she blew it out, it still looked flat. And, to make things worse, although the wound on her thigh had stopped bleeding, it still looked pretty bad and she couldn't wear a skirt to work.

She was running so late she decided to take a cab. It was a nice, cool day and it felt good to get out of that stuffy apartment. As the cab headed up Third Avenue, Angela decided that she would have to slowly get her life back together. First she was going to have to get the apartment clean and wash Dillon down the drain, then she could start worrying about a relationship again.

But now that Dillon and Bobby were both gone, she wondered if she should go back to her original plan and get married to Max. She still thought he was an asshole, but the whole experience with Dillon had taught her that she had no idea what she was doing when it came to judging men. At least Max was rich and, when it came right down to it, what was more important than money?

It was ten-fifteen when Angela arrived at NetWorld. The door to Max's office was closed and she didn't feel like bothering him. So she turned on her computer and started to catch up on some work. When Max came out of his office he stopped and stared at Angela for a second or two, like he was surprised to see her.

"What happened to you?" he asked.

At first, Angela thought Max was talking about her being an hour and a half late, but then she realized it had to do with the bruise on her face. Where Dillon had punched her she had a big black-and-blue mark that her makeup couldn't hide.

"Oh, *that*," Angela said. "My roommate swung another door into me again. She's a real ejit."

"You should get rid of those swinging doors," Max said seriously, "or that stupid roommate."

"Yeah, that's a good idea," Angela said, thinking about Dillon dissolving in the bathtub.

"Why don't you come into my office?" Max said. "I need to dictate a letter."

Angela followed him into his office and sat down on the couch. Max was already sitting at his desk.

"First of all," Max said, "I have to talk to your cousin."

"My cousin? What for?"

"Never mind what for, just give me the goddamn number."

"I don't have it."

"What do you mean, you don't have it? You had it yesterday."

"Why do you need to talk to him?"

"To find out if his friend Popeye—I'm sorry, *Dillon*, is still alive."

"Dillon?" Angela asked.

"That's Popeye's real name," Max said. "At least that's what Ironside told me."

Angela was confused.

"Mr. Average White Man in the wheelchair," Max continued. He was here about a half hour ago. He told me that you 'wouldn't be coming in anymore' and that Dillon was 'out of the picture.' But since you're here I'm starting to think he's full of shit about everything."

"Bobby Rosa was here?"

"Yes," Max said. "Don't you pay attention to a god-damn word I say?"

"But he's dead."

"Then I guess it was a ghost who was just in here, trying to blackmail me again. And my question is, Why? If this Popeye—*Dillon*—is supposed to be on our side, why isn't he killing the people he's supposed to kill? Why is he telling Rosa that I hired him? The only thing that makes sense is they're working together, and that they've been working together all along. Why else would Bobby go into that hotel room that night unless he knew we'd be there? So what I'm gonna do is call that little mick and say 'Tell the cripple to back off or I'm taking you down.' And I'm serious. I have the name of a top-notch lawyer now and I'll pin this whole thing on him. I don't need all this bull-shit in my life right now—I have a business to run."

Max's face had turned red during his long speech and he was breathing heavily. He looked like he might croak at any moment. But Angela had something bigger on her mind—Bobby was still alive. She had to talk to him, figure out some way to get him off their backs.

"Sorry, Max," Angela said standing up. "I have to go to the bathroom. Oh, but wait, I have something for you." She rummaged in her bag and took out the book. "It's a present. Sorry I didn't have time to wrap it."

It had crossed her mind to give him the pin too, but she kind of liked it.

Max took the book cautiously and Angela said, "Don't worry, it's not gonna blow up."

Max gave her a look as if he wasn't so sure. Then, squinting at the book, holding it at arm's length because he didn't have his reading glasses on, Max said, "*Wisdom of Zen*? What's this crap?"

"It'll bring you peace," Angela said, thinking about Dillon again, lying there in her bathtub, all yellow and Zen-like.

"I get enough of that Zen peace talk shit from my asshole chef," Max said. He flipped the book onto his desk then demanded, "What about your cousin's phone number?"

"I think I better call him," Angela said.

"Why can't I call?"

"He has a bad temper—you know how Greeks are. If you call and he thinks things got messed up he might start going crazy."

"I thought your cousin's Irish?"

"Half Greek, half Irish. Like me."

"I don't know what the fuck's going on anymore," Max said, shaking his head in frustration. "Just get me another meeting with Popeye today before five or I'm calling the cops. And close the door on your way out, will ya? I have to do my breathing exercises."

Diane Faustino from Accounting was talking to Sheila in Payroll near Angela's desk and Angela wanted to talk to Bobby in private. So she went to the back of the office, to the supply room. She called, but there was no answer. She went back to her desk, but it was impossible to concentrate. Max came out of his office every couple of minutes and asked if she had made "that call yet." Angela kept saying, "Yeah, but he's not home."

Max was getting to be a real pain in the ass. Angela couldn't believe that less than an hour ago she was seriously considering spending the rest of her life with that loser.

After waiting for about half an hour, Angela went back to the supply room and dialed Bobby's number again. This time he picked up.

Bobby was about to get into the bathtub when the phone rang. He lifted himself back into his wheelchair and went out to the living room. He answered the phone on its sixth ring.

"May I speak with Bobby Rosa please?"

It was an official-sounding older woman. Bobby figured it was another one of those asshole telemarketers. Even though he'd put himself on the national do-not-call list, those fucking cold callers kept hassling him twenty-four-seven. If she was a telemarketer, he was going to do what he always did when those pricks called his apartment—tell her Bobby Rosa had died. That usually got him off whatever list he was on.

"Why do you want to talk to him?" Bobby said.

"Is this Mr. Rosa?"

"Maybe, maybe not."

"It's very important that I speak with Mr. Rosa."

"Yeah? And why's that?"

"My name is Estelle Sternberg from the Jewish Home for the Aged. I'm afraid I have some bad news regarding his mother. Who am I speaking with please?"

"What happened to his mother?"

"I'm afraid she passed away last night," the woman said.

Bobby paused, letting the news sink in, then he said, "Yeah, well, this is Bobby so you can tell me what happened."

Ms. Sternberg explained that Mrs. Rosa had died in her sleep the night before. She asked Bobby if he wanted any assistance in making the funeral arrangements.

"No, I'll take care of it myself," Bobby said, thinking, Well, at least I didn't have to shoot her.

When he hung up, Bobby realized he was starving and he decided to take his bath later. He hadn't had pancakes in a long time so he cooked some up the way he liked them, with a lot of butter. Then, as he was eating, it hit him. He lost it, wheeling around his apartment, screaming and throwing things. It wasn't good enough—he needed to start shooting shit up. He was on his way to the closet to get a piece when he heard the phone ring.

He picked up, going, "What?"

"Bobby?"

Fuck, it sounded like Angela. How was that fucking possible? Was Dillon completely fucking incompetent?

"Yeah," he finally said.

"You know who this is?"

Straining for a Mr. Nice Guy tone, he said, " 'Course I do, sweetheart. How's it going?"

Why, why was that cunt still alive and his mother was dead? What kind of fucked up world was this?

"I can't talk much right now," Angela said. "I'm at work. You won't believe what's been going on. I can't even believe I'm talking to you."

"Yeah," Bobby said. "Me neither."

Angela lowered her voice to a whisper, said "We don't have to worry about Dillon, I mean Popeye, anymore...I got rid of him last night."

"What do you mean *got rid* of him?"

"I can't talk about that right now."

"Is he dead?"

"Yeah," Angela said.

"You killed him?"

"You know, Bobby, I really think we should talk about that somewhere private. Can you meet me somewhere or something?"

Bobby might have left Angela alone—forgotten about her—but it was too dangerous now. She knew about three murders and had committed one herself, meaning the cops would be after her soon, if they weren't already. If she was arrested she'd flip on Max Fisher, and after that the million-dollar photo of Max and Angela would be worth about as much as any of the other pictures he had taped to the walls.

Besides, he was in the mood to go kill somebody, let off some steam.

"Sure," Bobby said. "I can meet you. Let me think a sec."

"How about tonight?" Angela said. "I could stop by your place on my way home from work."

"Nah, I don't think we should wait that long," Bobby said. "I wanted to get out of the house anyway today. I know, let's meet in Riverside Park this afternoon. How's two o'clock work for you?"

Twenty-Three

I would extricate myself, I was sure, though I thought, too, of what I'd told the police, how the killer was still out there, and I felt a sense of danger beneath the veneer of the moment, everything about to break loose.
DOMENIC STANSBERRY, *The Confession*

When Angela told Max she was taking a late lunch, Max said, "What about that phone call?"

"I'll try again from the street," Angela said. "I have to go—I have a two o'clock appointment at my hairdresser."

Angela had just said this as an excuse to get out of the office, but on the way downstairs she decided that getting a haircut would be a good idea. Maybe she could get a blow out and a wash every day until she could start using her shower again.

Angela took the 1 train from Times Square and got off at Ninety-sixth Street. Bobby had said he wanted to meet on the Riverside Park promenade, between the Hudson River and the tennis courts.

Angela's bruises and cuts were still bothering her, especially the one on her thigh, but she knew she'd feel better once she figured out a way to get Bobby out of the way. Maybe she'd sleep with him again if she had to. He had B.O. and he wasn't the best-looking guy in the world but, she had to admit, there was something kind of hot about wheelchair sex.

She entered Riverside Park at Ninety-sixth Street and walked toward the river. She came to the underpass Bobby was talking about and went through to the promenade. It was a clear, sunny day, about seventy degrees. There were a few old men sitting on benches and other people out jogging and walking their dogs. Angela got to the spot Bobby had described and looked around. She didn't see him anywhere. She checked her watch—a few minutes after two.

She was tired and her thigh was hurting worse than before. She wanted to sit down, but all the benches nearby were either taken or covered with bird shit. She went back toward the water, leaned against the railing, and stared out toward New Jersey.

Bobby was waiting on a path on the wooded hill behind the tennis courts. The trees had blossomed a few weeks earlier so there was good cover. From his position, he had a nice, clear view of the promenade. Angela wasn't there yet, but when she showed up he'd be ready for her. In the big front pocket of his windbreaker he had a stainless steel .44 snub nose Mag Hunter. Yeah, fuckin hardware— it made the man.

Angela would be about sixty yards away—a tough shot for most people, but point-blank range for Bobby. He was already getting flashbacks of all the towelheads he'd taken down in Iraq, the sheer rush he'd get when he had those sand rats in his sight.

A few minutes later, Bobby saw Angela walking along the promenade. For some reason she was limping. She looked pale and drawn, not nearly as sexy as she had the other times Bobby had seen her. He remembered what she'd said, about the wheelchair being "kind of sexy." An old song began to play in his head, *Where was the love?*

When she got to the spot where they were supposed to meet Bobby took out the Mag and fitted on a silencer. Man, just holding a loaded gun again got Bobby juiced.

He looked around to make sure there was no one

nearby, watching him, then he raised the gun and aimed at Angela's chest.

Angela limped toward a bench and looked like she was about to sit down, then she turned and went back toward the railing of the promenade. She put her hands on the railing and looked out across the river. Bobby was locked in on a spot right between her shoulder blades, figuring he'd give it to her in the back. But when Bobby fired, the bullet tore through Angela's right thigh instead, his chair bucking from the recoil. Angela fell back against the railing, then her legs buckled and she coiled onto the cement. Bobby fired again, but the angle was shitty and this time he missed completely, the bullet whizzing by above Angela's head. Bobby cursed and fired again. The bullet hit the concrete on the promenade and ricocheted into the Hudson. Angela was on her knees now. He fired two more times—one bullet entered the left side of her stomach, the other, finally, ripped through her chest. Now Angela was on her side, covered in blood. Bobby twisted off the silencer, put it and the Mag back inside his windbreaker, and wheeled out of the park, thinking, Who sang that goddamn song?

Twenty-Four

*Everyone knows what he has to do next and sticks to it. It's a
simple way of life, and one that allows a man to get the most
out of his simple pleasures, without cluttering up his swede
with plans stretching too far hence.*
CHARLIE WILLIAMS, *Deadfolk*

Sherry, today's temp receptionist, buzzed Max's office
and told him there were two police officers here to see
him. Was there a tiny smug tone in her voice?

"Shit," Max said. "Tell them I'll be right out."

Max had been calling Andrew McCullough all afternoon and the bastard wasn't returning his calls. And
Angela still wasn't back from lunch so Max didn't know
what was going on with her cousin and Popeye. As he
opened his office door Max promised himself that this
time he wouldn't say anything without some kind of
lawyer present, even if he had to use fucking Darrow.

Louis Ortiz, the detective who had questioned him
the other night, was standing next to the reception desk,
next to a tall, older man with a mustache whom Max had
never seen before. Ortiz and the older guy were both
wearing plain gray suits and they both had serious, angry
expressions.

Max thought, *Uh oh*, and wished he'd taken a look at
that freaking Zen book. Maybe if he had he'd be relaxed,
he wouldn't be shitting fucking bricks right now.

"Hello, gentlemen," Max said, trying to stay as calm as
possible. "Can I help you with something?"

"You can get your coat," Ortiz said.

"Am I under arrest?" Max asked, trying to make it into a joke.

"We're taking you in for questioning," Ortiz said.

"What if I don't want to go?"

"You don't have a choice," Ortiz said.

"I don't understand," Max said. "What's going on?"

"Angela Petrakos was shot earlier today," the tall man explained, "in Riverside Park."

The words took a few seconds to register.

"Angela Petrakos?" he said. "You mean the Angela Petrakos who works for me?"

Several people in the office had been eavesdropping. Now people were talking at once, asking the detectives what was going on. Finally, Ortiz, talking above everyone, said, "This is police business. You'll all be briefed as soon as it's appropriate. Right now we need to talk to Mr. Fisher. Mr. Fisher, are you gonna come with us or am I gonna have to cuff you?"

Ortiz had a malicious grin, looking like he wanted to cuff Max more than he wanted his next meal.

Suddenly, the office was quiet. Although he was still looking at Ortiz and at the other detective, Max could sense that everyone else was staring at him. He remembered watching *Law and Order,* the ones with Jerry Orbach, and he was tempted to say, *I think I need to get lawyered up*. But instead he said, "Let me just get my coat," and he went back into his office. When he came out, wearing his sport jacket, a larger crowd had formed.

"This isn't a vacation day," Max said, above all the other voices, using a tone of authority, of steel. "Come on everybody, let's get back to work."

A few people went back to their desks, but a large group remained near the front of the office. No one seemed to feel sorry for Max. Actually, the bastards seemed happy to watch him being taken away. Max couldn't understand this. He'd always been a good boss. He only fired people when they deserved to be fired and hadn't he just announced a ten-percent raise?

On the way to the precinct, Max remembered the appointment he had made with Mr. Takahashi for this evening at six-thirty. Sitting in the back of the car, Max asked the detectives up front how long this questioning was going to take.

"As long as it needs to," Ortiz said.

"Seriously," Max said. "I have an important appointment with a client in less than two hours. Am I gonna have to reschedule it or not?"

The detectives looked at each other as Max reached into his jacket for his Blackberry. The car stopped short. Ortiz got out and opened the back door.

"Give me that fucking thing."

"What's the big deal?" Max said. "I'm just making one call."

Ortiz reached for the Blackberry. Max wouldn't let go and, turning away, he elbowed Ortiz in the face.

"You fucked up big-time now," Ortiz said. "I'm gonna book you for disorderly conduct and assaulting a police officer."

Max thought Ortiz was kidding until he pulled him out of the car and cuffed him.

At the precinct, after he was booked, Max used his one phone call to call McCullough. McCullough was still in the office, thank God, but he was in a meeting and couldn't be disturbed. Max screamed at the secretary, demanding to speak with him. The secretary said, "I don't enjoy being spoken to this way" and was about to hang up. Max begged her to stay on the line and then he left a message that he had been taken into police custody and to please come to the precinct as soon as possible.

Max was put in a holding cell with two other men who

looked homeless. One of them was lying on the bench, passed out, handcuffed to the bars. The other guy was squatting in the back of the cell, his hands crossed in front of his knees, mumbling to himself. They were both wearing ripped, dirty clothes. The whole place smelled like piss.

Max had been waiting in the cell for nearly two hours when McCullough finally showed up. Max was disappointed by how he looked. He was expecting an older, seasoned guy, but McCullough looked like he was right out of law school. He had short blond hair and light blue eyes and he didn't look a day over thirty. He pulled a chair up outside the cell and spoke to Max through the bars.

"Sorry I couldn't get here any sooner," McCullough explained, "but I've had a chance to speak with a couple of detectives, so hopefully I can give you an idea what's going on."

"Just get me the hell out of here," Max said.

"I'm working on that, but legally they can hold you overnight, or until a judge can see you downtown."

"If you think I'm spending a night in jail—"

"Let's not worry about that right now. The important thing right now is *why* you're here. I understand you assaulted Detective Ortiz."

"I didn't assault anybody," Max said. "I was just trying to use my Blackberry and I accidentally elbowed the guy in the face."

"Yeah, well, you've got bigger problems anyway," McCullough said. "The detectives seem to think you had something to do with the murders of your wife and your niece and Detective Kenneth Simmons, as well as the attempted murder of Angela Petrakos. Now before I can agree to represent you I need to know the truth—did you have anything to do with any of those crimes?"

Max remembered *The Godfather*, Diane Keaton asking Al Pacino if he was in the Mob. Max stared into McCullough's eyes for a few seconds, trying to get his face to look like Pacino's, then said, "Absolutely not."

"Alrighty," McCullough said, opening a small notepad, "so now we can get down to business. Let's talk about Angela Petrakos first—she's your executive assistant, I understand?"

Max nodded.

"She was shot this afternoon in Riverside Park, a little after two o'clock." Max thought there was a prissy tone in McCullough's voice and he noticed that the man's teeth were capped. The caps were bad news. They were a sign of self-absorption, the last quality in the world you wanted from your lawyer.

"Who shot her?" Max asked

"They don't know yet. They haven't had a chance to speak with her. She's still in critical condition at Columbia Presbyterian."

Fuck, Max had been hoping she was dead. If she lived, it would be a freakin' disaster. The police would grill her and, in her condition, she'd probably spill everything. Wasn't he ever gonna catch a break?

"So, do they think she's gonna make it?" Max asked, praying the answer would be no.

"It's hard to say," McCullough said. "Her injuries are quite severe."

"Shit," Max said, hoping "severe" meant brain damage or something like that.

"Unfortunately, that's not all the bad news," McCullough continued, reading from his pad. "About an hour ago, the police entered Angela's apartment on East Twenty-fifth Street and discovered a body decomposing in her bathtub."

Max blinked. "A body?"

"Apparently the neighbors had complained about the smell. According to the police, she or someone else had poured Drano all over the corpse."

Jesus Fucking Christ. She was a psycho. It was as simple as that. Max couldn't believe he'd fallen for her. If he'd just had a thing for flat-chested women none of this would have happened.

"The police haven't been able to get a positive ID on the body yet," McCullough said, "but going by some other evidence they found in the apartment, they're almost certain the dead guy is Thomas Dillon. Does that name mean anything to you?"

Max tried not to have a reaction. If he'd learnt one lesson in business, it was never show the person sitting across the table from you what you were thinking. He shook his head slowly.

"They've talked to some people who'd seen Dillon around the neighborhood, and they said he used to carry a book around with him, a book about Zen. They think it's the same book they found on your desk in your office."

"Wait a minute!" Max said. "Angela gave me that! This morning, she said it was a fucking gift."

"Unfortunately, she's not in a position to corroborate that right now. In the eyes of the police, it's a connection between you and Dillon."

Max shook his head miserably, thinking, What next?

"The police also found a gun in the apartment," McCullough said. "A Colt Lady .38. They think this was the gun that was used in the three murders."

"So Angela killed my wife?"

"Or Dillon," McCullough said, "or both of them. The police definitely don't think it was just a coincidence that Angela works for you. They think you were having an affair with her and conspired with her, or with her and Dillon, to kill your wife."

"That's ridiculous," Max said.

"Well, we'll have to convince a judge of that," McCullough said. "Which means we need a better explanation for what happened. For instance, maybe Angela had the idea to rob your house, talked Dillon into doing it, and gave him the code to your alarm, but then your wife and niece came home during the robbery and everything went to hell. I don't know how that cop got killed, but I'm sure he'll fit into the picture somehow."

Max hesitated for a second, then said, "There's one problem you need to know about. A big one."

McCullough looked at him, waiting. Max wasn't sure he could trust the guy, but what choice did he have? He had to figure out some way to take care of Rosa and he couldn't do it if he was spending the rest of his life in jail.

Max leaned close to McCullough and whispered through the bars, "The problem is, it's true, I *was* having an affair with Angela. And there's this guy—his name's Bobby Rosa—he has these pictures of Angela and me…"

"What kind of pictures?"

"He got into our hotel room the other night," Max said, "while Angela and I were…well. We were in bed, and he took photos. Then he came to me and asked for a quarter million dollars. I said no, of course. What am I gonna do, start paying off a blackmailer, right? But if those photos get out, it would be bad. I mean, wouldn't it?"

"The detectives told me about that hotel room. They say they have surveillance video from the hotel showing the two of you going into the room. I don't know that having photos of you actually in the room would make things a lot worse."

Max didn't have an answer to that. He wanted to tell McCullough the rest, wanted to tell him about the cassette Rosa had played for him, about Dillon admitting to

Rosa on the tape that Max had hired him to kill his wife. But he couldn't.

"I agree the affair makes things a little more complicated," McCullough continued, "but your case isn't impossible. If it turns out Angela's the one who killed Thomas Dillon and poured Drano on him, it'll be easy to show she's unstable. As long as you're telling me the truth, I think we'll be able to build up a solid defense."

As long as you're telling the truth. Always a goddamn catch.

"What about Bobby Rosa?" Max said, trying again.

"So he has some pictures of you having sex. So what? It's not like he has pictures of you killing somebody."

This was hopeless. He'd have to find a way to handle Rosa himself.

Max shot a glance at the homeless guy on the floor and lowered his voice further. "Do me a favor, don't tell anybody about Rosa, all right?" He hated that he was almost pleading with this teenager, this freaking child. "Forget I ever mentioned his name."

"Mr. Fisher, if it's going to come out, it's better if we're the ones who disclose it—"

"Don't. Just don't."

"But—"

"No." Max wanted to grab him and bang his head against the bars, get him to fucking pay attention for Chrissakes.

"What if Rosa had something to do with the shooting? What if he was working with Thomas Dillon—"

"Look," Max said, "we didn't discuss your fee yet, but you came highly recommended and I'm willing to pay top dollar for you to take me on as a client. But if I'm your client that means you work for me. Those pictures Rosa has could be a big embarrassment, especially if turns out Angela is involved with the murders. I don't want the police finding the pictures and the whole story going public. Do you get it?"

Reluctantly, McCullough agreed not to bring up Bobby Rosa's name to the police. He stayed with Max for a while longer, discussing strategy, then an officer came and led them into a small interrogation room with a square table. Ortiz and the tall detective sat on one side of the table, and Max and McCullough sat across from them on the other. In the middle of the table a little recorder was going. Ortiz began grilling Max, asking many of the same questions he'd asked the other night. Before answering each question, Max looked at McCullough, but McCullough had a blank expression, like a kid in the back of the class who didn't do his homework assignment, and didn't interrupt one time. These days it seemed like they handed out law degrees on street corners—you can probably get one online; answer a few questions and, boom, you're a lawyer. Max just hoped this McCullough knew what the hell he was doing. But Max had to take it easy. He knew the cops would love it if he started chewing out his own goddamn lawyer in front of them. His lawyer was his ace, his only good card in a shitty hand. His father, a poker addict, used to say, *Doesn't matter about a bad hand, it's playing it badly that matters*. Max finally understood what the hell the bastard had been talking about.

Then Granger, the tall detective, asked Max if he was "involved" with Angela Petrakos.

"Yes," Max said. "We'd been having an affair for the past few months."

"How come you didn't tell me that the other night?" Ortiz asked.

"I didn't want it coming out," Max said, "out of respect for my dead wife and her relatives." He made sure he hit the right somber note. He didn't go overboard, wiping at his eyes and sniffling, but he let the words hang there.

Max looked at McCullough who blinked once as a sign of approval, or maybe just to show he was actually alive.

"We might as well tell you, then," Ortiz said, "we talked to some people at the Hotel Pennsylvania and they ID'd you and Angela Petrakos. So it's just as well you admitted it. Now, you want to tell us where you went after you left the hotel that night?"

"I went home," Max said. It was nice to tell the truth for a change. Being honest was so foreign to him it gave him a rush. He'd have to try more of it.

"You never saw Detective Simmons that night?"

"Absolutely not."

"Did you ever meet a man named Thomas Dillon?" Granger asked.

"No," Max said, hoping the British accent wasn't coming out again.

"Were you aware that Angela Petrakos had been living with Dillon?"

Now Max felt feverish, realizing what an idiot he'd been for believing all those stories about Angela's roommate. He would've killed for a half bottle of Stoli.

"Angela led me to believe that she lived with a woman."

"So you never went to her apartment?" Ortiz asked skeptically.

Max shook his head.

Ortiz and Granger continued to grill Max for about another half an hour. Max continued to deny knowing anything about Angela and Dillon's relationship or any murder plot to kill his wife. When Ortiz suggested the possibility that there might be "a fourth person," someone Max had hired to try to kill Angela this afternoon, Max could tell McCullough wanted him to bring up Bobby Rosa, but Max told the detectives he had absolutely no idea what had happened in the park today. He was going to add, *What the hell's happening to our city?* but was scared it would come out in that fucking accent.

Finally Max was taken back to the holding cell. About a half an hour later, McCullough came to the cell and said, "I have some good news for you—they're dropping the assault charges."

"That's very nice of them since I didn't assault anybody."

"And they're going to let you go on your own recognizance."

"For good?"

"No, just for now. They want to see what happens with Angela and get her side of the story. If they get a confession out of her you might be off the hook, so let's just hope, for your sake, she pulls through."

Twenty-Five

Little Girl Lost
RICHARD ALEAS

Bobby couldn't stand lying in bed anymore, staring at the fucking cracks in the ceiling, so he went into the living room and lifted himself out of his wheelchair onto the couch and turned on NY1, the local twenty-four-hour-a-day TV news station. He watched the same bit on Angela's shooting three times, wondering each time, How the fuck could she not be dead? What the fuck was with that?

Finally, he fell asleep. When he woke up, at a little after six, the news was running a different segment about the shooting with a different reporter live on the scene. The reporter said that Angela was in critical but stable condition. He also said something about the cops finding a body in her bathtub soaking in Drano, which he figured answered the question of what she'd meant by "got rid of." Bobby still didn't know how the hell she'd survived those shots. He'd thought the one in her chest had gotten her for sure, but the bullet must've just missed her heart. He didn't get this because Bobby Rosa never, *never* missed a fucking target. Was he losing his touch? It was bad enough that he couldn't walk and that it took the stars aligning just to be able to bang a chick, but now was being in a wheelchair affecting his ability to kill people?

Bobby knew there was no way he would be able to fall back asleep now. He put on some clothes and went down to the deli and bought a couple ham and egg sandwiches on rolls, a large black coffee, and a copy of the *Daily News*.

Back in his apartment, he wolfed down the sandwiches and read the newspaper articles about the Riverside Park shooting. Like on TV, there was no mention of Max Fisher and no mention of any possible suspects. He didn't know if this was good or bad. Fuck, he didn't know shit about anything anymore.

Later, Bobby was finishing his bladder routine when he noticed something funny and muttered, "The hell is that?"

It looked like a blister down there, then he looked closer and noticed that there were others clustered around. Bobby laughed. If he'd caught herpes a few years ago he might have been upset, but now he couldn't feel any pain down there so what the hell difference did it make?

Bobby started to plan his mother's funeral. He got hold of a funeral home on Amsterdam Avenue and arranged for them to pick up the body from the morgue at the nursing home. Then he called Information in Brooklyn and got the phone numbers of a few of his mother's oldest friends. One of them, Carlita Borazon, had died a couple of years ago, her husband told Bobby, but her two other close friends—Anna Gagliardi and Rose-Marie Santos—were alive and well. They both seemed very upset when Bobby broke the news.

After he got off the phone with Rose-Marie, Bobby turned on the TV. There was an update on the Riverside Park shooting. A spokesman from the hospital said that Angela was out of her coma. She was awake and alert, but still in critical condition.

"Fuck!" Bobby shouted and threw the remote at the TV.

He got the address of Columbia Presbyterian Hospital from the phone book, then went down to the street and took the Broadway bus uptown to 168th Street. The hospital lobby was crammed with reporters and camera crews, but no one paid much attention to him, some guy in a wheelchair. It took a long time, but Bobby finally made his way through the halls to the nursing station and found a clipboard that showed what room Angela was in. He half expected to see a pair of cops stationed outside the door and was prepared to just keep rolling if there were, but the door was open and there was no one outside it, so he just went in.

Angela looked like shit. Her face was white and there were tubes coming in and out of her body. How the hell had she survived? The luck of the Irish, that's how. Ask any Brit—it's friggin' impossible to kill those mothers. No wonder the Irish made such a big deal about funerals. It was so hard to put a mick in a box, they actually celebrated when they got one there.

Bobby wheeled close to the bed. The easiest thing would have been to smother her with a pillow, like what that Indian did to Jack Nicholson in that *Cuckoo's Nest* movie. But that would be crazy with the door open and cops in the building.

Angela was sleeping or resting, but when Bobby touched her wrist her eyes opened. She turned her head slowly in his direction.

"Don't try to talk," Bobby said. "I just came by to see how you were doing."

"I'm doing okay," Angela said weakly.

She squeezed Bobby's hand. Bobby felt uncomfortable, but he left his hand there anyway.

"Did the cops talk to you yet?" Bobby was trying not to sound too anxious.

Angela shook her head.

"That's good," Bobby said. "That's real good. What about what happened in the park? Did you see who shot you?"

Again Angela shook her head, then said, "All I remember is lying on the ground bleeding."

"Some kid with a gun probably took a pot shot at you," Bobby said. "Fucking kids these days—running around, shooting people for kicks. I ever get my hands on them…"

He let the threat hang there, to show how much he cared about her. Man, he was a great actor.

Now Angela was squeezing Bobby's hand tighter. She was trying to say something, but Bobby couldn't hear her.

Then Bobby said, "Don't worry, everything's gonna be all right. I just talked to your doctor and he said you'll be walking out of here in no time, so you don't gotta worry about that. Understand?"

Angela nodded.

"But listen," Bobby whispered, "the police are gonna want to talk to you and it's very important what you say to them. You listening? They found Dillon in your bathtub, but you don't have to worry about it. He came after you and you killed him in self-defense—it's as simple as that. But here's the important thing—when the police ask you about Fisher hiring Dillon to kill his wife you have to say you know nothing about that. Remember—you knew nothing about that. Whatever you do, don't finger Max. I don't wanna see you get in trouble and this is your only way out of this mess. So just tell the police you know nothing about Max—tell them the robbery was all Dillon's idea. Max had nothing to do with it, got it?"

She managed to smile, then said weakly, "Oh, I understand, Bobby. It's really sweet of you to try to protect me. But there's one thing you've got to understand, too." Her voice was fading and she had to pause to take a breath. Bobby had to lean close to hear her say, "I get half the money."

○

That night Angela was the top story on all the newscasts. She claimed that her live-in boyfriend, Thomas Dillon, had killed Deirdre Fisher and Stacy Goldenberg and that Fisher's husband Max had nothing to do with it. She also said that Dillon killed that cop, Kenneth something.

Bobby knew he could do it now. He could show up at Fisher's office Monday morning and go for his full bank account, his stocks, his cars, get him to sell that fucking townhouse. It was all there for him to take. Even half the take would be a nice score. But, for some reason, he couldn't get psyched up about it. Part of it was the idea that he'd have to split the money with that lying bitch, but that wasn't all of it. He needed to *do* something, to show that he still had what it took to get the job done. The business in the park had really gotten to him, shaken his confidence. He had to prove to himself that he hadn't lost the touch.

He called Victor. He got his voicemail, said, "I'm gonna leave an envelope at the desk for you. Don't say I never gave you nothin' you dumb fuck." Then he hung up, feeling nice and pumped.

Yeah, he knew exactly what he had to do next.

Twenty-Six

I love storms.
GANDHI

Monday morning, Max wasn't expecting a party in his office, but he thought there would at least be a few smiling faces. Instead, no one even said hello to him. Max didn't understand it. Didn't anyone read the papers or watch the news on TV? Didn't they know that Angela had cleared his name? He'd fire all these bastards, see what they thought then. Christ, couldn't an innocent guy get a break?

Max went to Diane Faustino's desk and asked her to please come into his office. He had steel in his voice, thinking, *You wanna play hardball, baby? All right, then come to Daddy, sweetie. Come to Daddy.*

"What for?"

"I'm your boss—I don't need a reason." He let his eyes turn to stone. He'd seen Eastwood do that.

Diane breathed deeply, then followed Max.

In his office, Max asked her to shut the door then he said, "All right, now what the hell's going on here?"

"Going on with what?" Diane said coldly. She was still standing near the door, looking like she was staring down a man who'd raped and killed her family.

"The silent treatment," Max said. "You'd think I was Charles Manson or something."

"The police came back here Friday afternoon, after they took you away."

"So?" Max said.

"They were talking to everyone, asking a lot of questions."

"That's what police do," Max said, trying to seem patient. "When somebody gets shot they go to their office and ask a lot of questions."

"You don't care, do you?"

The question confused Max. He wasn't sure whether Diane was trying to change the subject or not. "Care about what?"

"You really don't know, do you?" Diane said. "You're pathetic."

"That's out of line," Max said. "If you don't—"

"Everybody thinks you did it."

Max stared at Diane. He couldn't believe she had the balls to talk to her boss this way. What the hell was happening to the world?

"Did what?" he said.

"Hired that guy to kill your wife," Diane said, "hired somebody else to shoot Angela."

"I didn't hire anybody to shoot Angela."

"But you hired somebody to kill your wife?"

"I didn't hire anybody to do anything."

"I don't believe you. Nobody believes you. We knew you were an asshole, I just can't believe I've been working all this time for a murderer. And no, don't bother firing me—I quit."

"Will you just calm down?" Max said. "Jesus, I hate it when you get hysterical." He wondered if she had any valium. Women always had that stuff and God knew he could use some too. He'd been having chest pains again lately and needed something to ward off a heart attack. How much could one decent man take?

Diane stormed out of the office, letting the door slam behind her. To hell with her, Max thought. If an employee wasn't loyal to her boss, what use was she? Besides, accounting people were a dime a dozen and it was a known fact that the Chinese were better than Italians anyway. He'd make a call to a headhunter and tomorrow morning there'd be ten Chinese guys lined up for Diane's job. His heart pounding, he looked at his Rolex, went to the drawer, poured a large glass of vodka, and gulped it down, spilling some on his tie, thinking, *Aw, c'mon, gimme a break.*

There was a knock on Max's door. Diane begging for her job back? That was fast. But instead it was Thomas Henderson, NetWorld's CFO. He told Max that he was resigning, that he just couldn't work here anymore. Max said this was fine with him. A CFO would be harder to replace than an ordinary accountant, but fuck it, Max didn't want anyone working for him who didn't have loyalty to the company.

Eleven more people resigned during the next half hour, including four of his Senior Network Technicians, a few cable installers, and two of his best PC technicians. Goddamn it, his whole company was hemorrhaging. Now Max was starting to get frightened and more than a little drunk. As they filed in and out of his office, he said to one guy, "When the going gets tough, the tough get fucked." He knew that wasn't right, was it? What-the-fuck ever. He said to some woman, "Easy go, easy come for me, baby." Like he didn't give a goddamn, but he did, oh yeah. After another glass of Stoli he screamed at another woman, "Get out of my fucking face!" Max realized he was losing it. It was one thing to lose a couple of people, but all of a sudden his entire company was falling apart in front of him.

Max ordered the temp who was answering phones today to call all the headhunters NetWorld dealt with and to transfer them to his line as soon as she got through. Later, when the headhunters returned his calls, Max told them to set up appointments to interview people for the vacant positions. This made Max feel a little more at ease, until clients started calling. He realized he was slurring and the damn vodka was empty, *How the hell'd that happen?*

At first, there were just a few smaller clients, calling to cancel their service and consulting agreements. They were five- to ten-thousand-dollar-a-year clients that Max wouldn't miss, but then a few bigger clients, where Max had placed full-time consultants and did steady business, called to say they were planning to look for a new company for network support. All of the clients had the same story—they didn't like the bad publicity that Max and NetWorld were getting so they had decided it was best to take their business elsewhere. Max tried desperately to save the clients, but nothing he could say worked. It was like he was shouting and the world was, what, deaf? He hated how he sounded, like he was fucking *pleading.* Then, craving another drink, he went to the stash of Chivas Regal he kept for special clients. He poured a glass, some going on his tie, thought, *Fuck it*, and started guzzling. Vaguely, he remembered the hangover from hell the last time he mixed vodka and whiskey, but he didn't let that slow him down. He hit the intercom button and ordered his temp to go out to get some pistachios, figuring they'd soak up the booze.

Ten minutes later, clutching the bottle of Chivas, Max wobbled out to the temp's desk and said, "Where the fuck are my nuts?" Then he said, "Wait I know where they are, they're right here," and grabbed his balls.

The girl mumbled something with the word "disgusting" in it and Max interrupted, "Hey, you talking back to me? Don't you know, I own your arse!" He smiled, realizing he'd channeled Thomas Dillon, old Popeye himself.

Now the girl was saying something about quitting and

Max said, "You know, you're getting just a tad on my nerves." Then he thought, *Tad?* How fucking British was he gonna get? And where the hell was that Zen book? Hadn't the police returned it? How was he gonna mellow out if he couldn't find the goddamn thing?

The girl got up to leave. No big loss—she was thin, had no shape.

"And Zen there were none!" Max yelled at her as she ran out of the office.

He opened the Chivas for another dose and then shouted, "Fuck!" as the cap cut into his index finger, blood leaking out. In the bathroom, full-blown panic set in as he rinsed his finger, watching what he was convinced were pints of blood go down the drain. He was gonna bleed to death from a Chivas bottle cap—how pathetic was that?

The bleeding finally stopped but, but he was convinced he'd lost vital amounts of blood and back at his desk, he drank from the bottle, trying to replace the fluid, thinking, *Yeah, like that was gonna work.* Then, thinking out loud, he said, "Did I just think out loud?" Fook on a bike, as that Irish cow always said. Why wouldn't the bitch do the decent thing and fuckin' die? Was it so much to ask?

Max stood straight up, muttered about getting focused, even though he was seeing double. He was determined to save his business. Then, the whiskey pumping him up, he thought, The office? Why stop there? He could save the world, maybe give Angela's buddy Bono a run for his money.

Then Jack Haywood from Segal, Russell & Ross called to tell Max that his company wanted to sever ties with NetWorld. Max nearly cried, *No, not fucking Jack.*

"Come on, Jackie baby," Max pleaded, "after all we've been through, all the lap dances and hookers? Come on, buddy, you know what kind of guy I am? You know I'd never get involved with any of those sleazeballs you're hearing about in the news, I thought we were tight, man?"

There was silence on the other end of the line. Max thought Jack might have hung up, then he was saying, "I want to believe you, Max, but I saw you with that stripper the other night and I've seen you with strippers before and I know how you were always putting down your wife, talking about how you sleep around—"

"Jack," Max shouted, "that was just bullshit I say when I'm selling. You don't really think I…whatever you do, Jack, please, don't tell the police that!"

"It's not my decision anyway," Jack said. "If it was up to me, I'd keep you on, but the partners don't like it. But hey, listen, I'll keep your number in my rolodex. If I ever move to another company, I'll give you a call. Maybe we can do something." There was a long pause then Jack asked, "Are you drinking?" Then, "I mean, it's none of my business, pal, but you need to stay sober if you want to regain any credibility."

Max squinted hard, said, "Regain?"

Wasn't that the shit to save your hair? Hell, maybe it could save his firm.

By the end of the day, half his client list was gone, kaput, *finito*. And the other half would've been gone too if, at some point, he hadn't stopped answering the phone.

Twenty-Seven

*You have a saying "to kill two birds with one stone." But our
way is to kill just one bird with one stone.*
SUZUKI ROSHI

With a gym bag resting on his lap, Bobby wheeled into
the liquor store on the corner of Amsterdam and Ninety-
first. The same old Pakistani guy Bobby always saw there,
morning or night, was working the counter. What was
with that? Did they sleep, like, standing up?

There were two customers in the store—a Chinese
woman and a black man. Bobby wheeled to the back of
the store and started browsing in the Merlot section.
Meanwhile, in one of the overhead mirrors, he was
watching the activity at the checkout counter up front.
The Chinese woman paid for her purchase in small
bills, even counting out coins to give exact change, for
Chrissakes. But eventually she finished, took her bag,
and left. Now it was only Bobby and the black guy in
the store. Bobby felt like he could get out of his chair
and walk.

The black guy moved to the checkout counter. Bobby
thought he saw the Pakistani guy looking in the mirror,
watching him, maybe suspiciously, but Bobby wasn't worried. He was in the groove—nothing could get to
him now.

"Thanks," the black guy said.

When the door closed and the little bell above it rang,
Bobby moved—not fast, casually, toward the front of the
store. The Pakistani guy was looking down, writing some-

thing in a pad. Bobby opened his gym bag and took out an Uzi. The rush he felt when he had the weapon in his hand—yeah, this was the old Bobby.

"This is a stick-up," he announced. "Don't try to be a hero. Just fill up this bag up with money and you won't get shot."

He had just the right amount of hard-ass and vicious-ness in his tone, just like the good ol' days, just like Isabella had taught him.

Everything the Pakistani guy did was magnified. Bobby could hear his breath, see the sweat spreading out of his pores. Was he imagining it, or did the guy smell like the back seat of a cab?

Then he saw the guy's right arm start to move. Bobby imagined that a lot of guys might have missed this, guys who weren't as sharp and quick as he was. This was what he had learned from twenty-plus years in the life—to notice the little things. Maybe the guy was going for an alarm or maybe he was going for a gun, but Bobby wasn't going to wait and find out. He started firing, unloading half a round in an instant. He had a flashback to Desert Storm, the time a sniper was running across the sand and Bobby shot him in the neck so many times his head fell off, but his body kept running a few feet before it dropped. Then he saw flashes of himself on jobs—running out of jewelry stores and banks. This was where he belonged—in the action, on the front line. Bobby was smiling now, watching the little towelhead store owner flying back against the back wall in slow motion. The bullets shredded the little fucker to bits.

Then Bobby heard footsteps behind him. When he turned around he didn't see another towelhead, but an old woman, probably the owner's wife. She had a gun, a little revolver, in her right hand and she was screaming in a language Bobby didn't understand. Bobby didn't want to fire, but when he saw her trigger finger starting to move he had no choice. What, he survived Desert Storm to let some old broad get the drop on him? *Getoutta here.* He sent the screaming old woman into a wine rack, shattering glass and spilling red liquid everywhere. Red with meat, right?

The store was quiet again. Moving quickly, Bobby hoisted himself up onto the counter so he was sitting next to the register and reached into the open cash tray. Then he wheeled himself to the back room and found some more money in the old woman's pocketbook. The whole score only came to a thousand bucks and change. It wasn't as much as if he'd gotten them to open the safe, but what could you do? He'd just have to make it up on the next job and the job after that. He put the money and the Uzi into his gym bag, closed the zipper all the way, and, with the smell of cordite rocking his brain, wheeled out into the twilight.

Heading across the street, Bobby saw the cops get out of the squad car before the cops saw him. He went for the Uzi again when he saw another cop across the street aiming a gun at him, yelling "Stop, police!" Shit, why'd he put the Uzi away? He had his hand in the gym bag when the first bullet went into his leg. He laughed, didn't even feel it, but the bullet sent his wheelchair out of control. The laundry truck, shit, it was coming right at him.

Twenty-Eight

He was one of those "There but for the Grace of God" guys; one of those guys that thought if you went out of your way to ignore someone else's bad shit then the same bad shit was liable to boomerang and smack you in the head.
JOHN RIDLEY, *Everybody Smokes in Hell*

Max was on line at the checkout counter at Grace's Marketplace on Third Avenue, buying some vegetables to steam for dinner, when he heard these two young guys talking.

The bigger guy said, "Did you hear what happened on the West Side?"

Max's hangover had kicked in big time and, although the guy was talking in a normal tone, it sounded like he was screaming directly into Max's ear with a bullhorn.

"No," the other guy said, sounding just as loud. Max had taken two Advils, but they were doing shit.

"This afternoon," the big guy said, "couple hours ago. This guy in a wheelchair robs this liquor store on Amsterdam Avenue and loses it. He goes in with an Uzi and starts shooting up the place—kills the owner and his wife."

Now Max was straining, listening closely, as the guy went on, explaining how the guy was run over and crushed to death by a laundry truck.

"That's it," the other guy said, shaking his head. "I'm moving to fuckin' Jersey."

As the guy went on, talking about something else, Max said, "Excuse me," then more softly because of his aching brain, "excuse me, I just overheard what you were saying—about this guy in a wheelchair."

"Yeah," the guy said. "Pretty fucked up, huh?"

"You didn't, by any chance, hear what his name was, did you?"

"Yeah, it was, I don't know—something Spanish. Ramirez, Rojas…"

"Could it have been Rosa?"

"Maybe," the guy said. "I wasn't really paying attention too much to that part."

He was staring at Max like Max was some wino or something. Max didn't get it. Before he left the office, didn't he have all those Altoids? There was a goddamn guarantee on the packet, wasn't there?

Max left the vegetables in the shopping cart, and jogged back to his townhouse, nearly out of breath when he got there. His heart, fuck, it felt like it was about to explode.

He turned on the TV, expecting to find out that it was all a big mistake, that there were two crazy cripples with Spanish names in this city. But, sure enough, the reporter, live at the scene, said, "…police are releasing no other information about the gunman right now, but we have learned that Robert Rosa was an ex-convict who had been arrested several times for gun possession, armed robbery, and related charges. He was not married and it is not known whether he has any relatives."

At first, Max was elated, but then he realized that his troubles were far from over. The police were probably searching Bobby's apartment at this very moment. It was only a matter of time until they found that cassette.

Max turned off the TV and sat on his living room sofa in silence, the only noise coming from the refrigerator buzzing in the kitchen. At any moment, the police would come to the door, demanding to be let in.

He had to see Angela. He'd been thinking about her all last night, and most of the day today, wondering what was going on in her head. He knew she still loved him or why would she have lied to the police to protect him? Sure, she was covering her own ass as well, but she could have done that just as easily by letting him burn. Unless she figured he'd turn on her if she turned on him. Which he would have.

He needed another drink. He chugged a quarter bottle of Stoli then, thinking *That was the problem, never should've switched to whiskey*, left the townhouse and headed toward Third Avenue to hail a cab. Was he staggering a little? Nah, just nerves, that's all. It was all perspective, how you looked at the picture. He muttered, *"So you had a wee dram."* Then, horrified, he thought, What was that? Scottish? Jesus. "Coulda been a contender." Fuck, get a grip.

"Columbia Presbyterian Hospital!" he shouted at the driver.

The twenty-minute cab ride sobered Max up a little, but at the hospital he was still half-drunk and it took him a while to find Angela's room.

A cop on duty recognized Max immediately.

"Hold it right there, Mr. Fisher."

The cop was short, heavyset, with curly hair. He stood up with his hands on his hips, sticking out his chest.

"I wanna see Angela Petrakos," Max said.

"Yeah, I bet you do, but I can't let you in there."

"Why not? I'm not charged with anything."

"I still can't let you in there."

"Did someone tell you I couldn't see her?"

The officer thought this over for a second then said, "No. But I still think it's best."

Max was in that weird zone of half hung over and feeling like he was seeing everything through glass, very dirty glass. For a mad moment, he was ready to take a swing at the guy.

He said, "Unless you want to embarrass yourself when I start making phone calls to your boss, I would suggest you let me inside there. The woman works for me, for Christ's sake."

Max was trying to summon up the old powerbroker Max, before his life went in the toilet, and maybe it was working. He thought the cop looked a little worried. Nothing like sticking it to the boys in blue to restore the old Max Fisher confidence.

The cop said, "All right, you can talk to her, but just for a couple of minutes, and I'm comin' in there with you."

Max was expecting Angela to look like hell, but it was just the opposite. She was sitting up in bed, watching TV, and she looked almost normal. She wasn't wearing as much makeup as usual, but she was wearing bright red lipstick and her hair was nice. Her breasts looked great too. Who said hospital gowns weren't sexy? He looked over at the cop and had a feeling the guy was thinking the same thing.

Looking back at Angela's face, Max couldn't tell if she was happy to see him or not. He had to be very careful now.

"Surprise," Max said.

Angela continued to stare at Max with a blank expression, then she smiled slowly. But Max still couldn't tell what she was thinking.

"What are you doing here?" she said.

"I just thought I'd stop by and pay a little visit," Max said, "see how you were doing."

The cop was standing in the corner of the room, watching them.

"I'm doing okay," Angela said.

"Yeah, I can tell that," Max said. "I mean it. You look

dynamite." He nodded toward the TV. "I see you're watching the news. So I guess you saw about the robbery. That guy in the wheelchair. Crazy, huh?"

Angela nodded slowly.

"So…you should be feeling a little better, I'd think. Not out of the woods yet, but things are looking better."

"The doctors said I was really lucky," Angela said. "If the bullet in my chest had been an inch over to the right I'd probably be dead. They still think it's a miracle I made it with all the blood I lost."

Max's vision was still blurry and it was hard to concentrate. He knew there were things he wanted to say to Angela, important things, but he couldn't think of what the hell they were.

"So is that why you came here, just to see how I was?"

"No," Max said, "I also came here to tell you that I miss you—at the office I mean. I miss having you around, and I miss…I miss a lot of things about you."

"The doctors told me if I keep improving I might be out of here by next week."

"That's terrific," Max said. Out of the corner of his eye he saw the cop raise his arm and point at the watch on his wrist. "Look, I just want you to know that I appreciate your sticking up for me. It showed me that deep down you really do care. It meant a lot. Everyone else at the company walked out on me, pretty much. First sign of trouble and it was adios, amigo, sayonara, nice knowing you. But you were loyal, and…" He felt something swelling up inside him, the same feeling that had hit him that night years ago in the bar of the Mansfield Hotel. And look how well that had worked out for him. But, hey, sometimes, you just feel what you feel, and you've got to go with it, or whatever.

"I know none of this was your fault," he said, some of the words slurring, "and I just want you to know that I don't blame you for anything. The thing is I can't stand living in that big house all by myself. What I'm trying to say is, when you get out of here, I think we should get married."

Angela looked shocked. Her mouth sagged open. "Are you serious?"

"Oh, I know it'll be hard for a while," Max said. "I mean, getting over everything and everything. But eventually we'll get used to it."

"But the police are still—"

Max waved his hand dismissively, knocking into some big tube. "I have a good lawyer, and I'll have him handle your case. And then when it's all behind us, we can do everything we talked about doing— travel, go places, see things. What do you say?"

"I can't believe you'd propose to me after...after everything," Angela said, and he thought she looked like she was about to start crying.

"Say yes," Max said. "I hope I didn't have to schlep all the way up to Harlem for nothing."

She still wasn't answering. He was about to get on his knees, do the proposal in style, when she closed her eyes, maybe to squeeze back tears, and said, "Of course I'll marry you. Why wouldn't I?"

That night Max made a decision. If he somehow got through all of this, he was going to change his life—make up for everything he'd done. Innocent people had died and, while he knew it wasn't all his fault, he also knew he was at least partly responsible. He was a stand-up guy, could take some blame. He was going to quit booze and start going to a synagogue. Better yet, he'd read that damn Zen book, if he could ever find it. Yeah, that's right, to hell with Judaism, he was going to finally see what this Buddhism shit was all about. Maybe there was something to meditating—maybe sitting Indian-style, thinking about nothing, was the answer to all his problems. He didn't care what he had to do, he was going to make big changes in his life and things were going to be different.

Max woke up feeling refreshed. His memories of the previous day were a little foggy, but he remembered proposing to Angela. Eh, what the hell? Maybe it wasn't something he would have done sober, but that didn't make it a mistake. After all, what were the odds of him having two fucked up marriages in a row? Maybe marrying Angela would be the best thing that had ever happened to him.

After he showered and shaved, he took a walk over to the newsstand around the corner and bought a copy of the Sunday *Post*. He felt great, whistling the song from *The Bridge on the River Kwai*, then he looked at the paper and the screaming headline PERVERT! Under the headline was a big picture of Bobby Rosa. He read the article standing in front of the newsstand. There were two full pages, all about Rosa. The police had discovered hundreds of pictures in his apartment of women— women in bikinis, women in their underwear, peeping tom shots taken through windows, upskirt shots, down-blouse shots. Many of the pictures were hung up on the walls in his bedroom and bathroom, but the police had found boxes of additional pictures in his closet, including the ones of Max and Angela having sex. But the most shocking news was that the police had found a gun in Bobby's apartment that had been used in the Riverside Park shooting. Max couldn't understand this at all. He knew Bobby had some screws loose, but the maniac had gone biblical. Max definitely didn't feel like whistling anymore.

The whole thing was so confusing now, Max had a throbbing headache. He bought copies of the *Times* and the *Daily News*, but their stories basically repeated the same information as the articles in the *Post*. The only good news, as far as Max was concerned, was that there was no mention in any of the papers of the police finding the incriminating cassette tape in Rosa's apartment. But how long would it be before they did?

He had a feeling that his life was about to go down the shitter again.

At a deli on Lexington Avenue, he bought a bouquet of red and pink roses, then he took a cab up to the hospital. A different cop was on duty in front of Angela's room. This one let him into the room without a hassle. Angela was sleeping. Max tiptoed up to the bed and woke her up with a soft kiss on the lips. Not his special, the hot one that never failed, but one with concern, damn it, plenty of real compassion in there. Angela's eyes opened suddenly, like she didn't know where she was, but then she saw Max's face. There was a moment of horror at first and then her expression softened into a smile though her eyes still looked strained and unhappy. He figured he must've woken her out of a bad dream or something.

At work the next morning, Max had his receptionist get Andrew McCullough on the phone.

"I have another job for you," Max said. "I want you to represent Angela Petrakos."

"Angela Petrakos?" McCullough said. "You're kidding, right?"

He hated the prick's tone, like he thought he was so high and mighty because he was the lawyer and not the guy who constantly needed one. "Why would I kid about that?"

"Since when do you care what happens to Angela Petrakos?" the dick asked.

"Since I asked her to marry me," Max said.

°

Max spent most of the day on the phone with his remaining clients, trying to shore up relationships. He also called some of the clients who had canceled their service agreements last week and asked for second chances. Most said they were sorry, that they were still going to take their business elsewhere, but he was able to sweet talk some into saying yes.

For the first time since before Deirdre was murdered, Max felt like his life was getting back on track. He was the kind of guy who worked best under pressure; it showed what he was made of.

He went to the gym in the morning, worked hard all day, then went to visit Angela at night. He was feeling healthier than he had in years. He felt a little bad about some of the things he'd done, but he also knew that somewhere inside him there was another Max Fisher, a better Max Fisher, and somehow he was going to let that Max Fisher out. He couldn't wait to let the world see the new model. Hell, he might even start leaving tips.

Nah, no need to get stupid.

In the mirror that morning, he said to himself. "You're a good person. Sure, you've had some tough luck, but suffering makes the man."

He was pretty sure the Zen book would have this type of crap in it.

A minor hitch developed in McCullough's case when the doorman at Bobby Rosa's building came forward, claiming that Angela and Dillon had visited Bobby's apartment on successive days. McCullough claimed that his client had been blackmailed by Bobby, and that she was at the building that night to ask for the sex pictures back. McCullough also speculated that Dillon was "the jealous type" and that he may have gone to confront Bobby, suspecting that Bobby and Angela were having an affair. As for the body in the bathtub, McCullough claimed that Angela was trapped in an abusive relationship and had killed Dillon in self-defense. The Drano was evidence of how desperate and illogical she had become. Angela's cuts and bruises backed up the self-defense claim and several people at the office came forward and vouched that they'd seen Angela arrive at work with a nasty black eye prior to the murder. Regarding the other sticking point, the code to the alarm, McCullough suggested that Dillon had forced Deirdre Fisher to give him the code to the alarm the evening of the murders, which was why he was able to reset the alarm before he left.

Max didn't think there was any way in hell the police would buy McCullough's bullshit. They were going to indict Angela and then, under pressure, she'd break down and implicate him. But then McCullough called him at work with the incredible news. The police had held a press conference announcing that the investigation was officially closed—Thomas Dillon and Thomas Dillon alone had committed the murders of Deirdre Fisher, Stacy Goldenberg, and Kenneth Simmons. Apparently, although it was clear that Max and Angela were having an affair, the DA's office didn't think they had enough evidence against Max to pursue a case against him. They also felt that Angela, as a battered woman, would be viewed as sympathetic by a jury, especially after it was announced that Dillon was also linked to the vicious slaying of a Japanese tourist. According to an Op Ed piece in the *Post*, the Mayor may have urged a quick resolution to the case as well, the start of the summer tourist season being a bad time for stories about a tourist having his throat cut to be in the news.

Two days after the case was closed, Angela was discharged from the hospital. She was transported out of the premises in a wheelchair and then she stood up and limped into Max's arms. Thanks to his Viagra he had a powerful hard-on, wanted to bang the living crap out of her right there. That night, he took her out to a romantic candlelight dinner at Demi on Madison Avenue and surprised her with a two-carat diamond engagement ring from Tiffany's. It was worth every penny it had cost to see the way her eyes lit up when she held it. Who said money couldn't buy happiness? Some dumb bastard who bought discount, probably.

Max started to go to the ashram a few times a week with Kamal. He listened closely as the swami talked about "the universal unconscious" and "the inner self." He started to read books on Buddhism and Eastern philosophy and he did relaxation exercises and meditated two or three times a day. Hell, he was born for this shit. Even the itching had eased and the blisters were fading. That Buddha, he delivered, no question about it.

One weekend, Max took Angela to a yoga retreat in the Berkshires. They had a great time meditating, chanting, going to yoga and exercise classes, eating macrobiotic food, and taking long walks in the woods. When they came back to the city, Max felt completely cleansed. He felt as if he had been asleep his whole life and had finally awakened. The new Max Fisher was a kinder, more relaxed person who treated his newly hired employees with respect. He realized that for most of his life he'd been on the wrong path. His ego and desires had been controlling his actions while his true self was trapped underneath. Though he knew this didn't justify or make up for anything he had done, he also knew the things he'd done weren't his fault either. His ego had decided to kill Deirdre, and now that his ego was gone, the killer was gone too. He also felt a new sense of humility about himself and sensed that people understood he was a man who'd risen above great suffering to become even more compassionate. He knew it wasn't just his imagination, people were looking at him differently. There was no use for false modesty now—he might as well display it for the goddamn world to see. He couldn't wait to talk about his entire journey someday on *Oprah*.

Then, one afternoon, his new executive assistant—a petite Indian girl whom Max had hired because she was a Buddhist; her breasts weren't even B-cups—came into his office and said there was a man waiting to see him.

"Who?" Max asked.

"He wouldn't say, but he said it was important."

"All right," Max said. "Send him in."

Max shut off the CD of Tibetan chants he was listening to on his PC and then a short, very thin man, completely bald, with a big crooked nose entered his office. He was wearing jeans, sneakers, and a hooded sweatshirt, so he definitely wasn't a salesman.

"Can I help you with something?" Max asked, smiling.

"Yeah, I think you can," the man said. His voice sounded very hoarse, like a chain-smoker's, or maybe even one of those people you saw sometimes who'd had throat cancer and talked through a machine.

"Why don't you take a seat?" Max said. "Make yourself at home."

"That's all right," the man said weakly. "I don't mind standing. I've been standing all my life, you know what I mean?"

Max thought, *Yeah, standing, waiting for a bus*, because he wasn't the type who'd ever have a car. Max had a message for him, *The bus wasn't coming, pal*, but with his new spirituality, he decided to treat the poor loser like one of the Buddha's own. Yeah, he was a loser, shit on the bottom of his heel, but Max wouldn't be the one to tell him.

Max assumed the man was looking for work, maybe as an installer, doing punchdown for machine rooms, something like that. Max decided that because the man looked like he was in need he would hire him no matter what his skills were. The Buddha would be pleased as hell about that, right?

Max noticed that the man was looking above him, at the framed picture of the Dalai Lama he had hung above his desk.

"You meditate?" Max asked.

"No," the man said in that scratchy voice.

"You really should try it. If you want, you can come down to my ashram some time. I'll introduce you to some people."

"Nah, that's okay," the man said. "I don't believe in that religious shit."

Feeling sorry for the man for being un-enlightened, Max said, "Well, you just call me if you change your mind. So do you have a resume?"

"What?"

"Do you have a resume with you?"

"Why would I give you a resume?"

"To get a job. That's why you're here, isn't it?"

The man smiled. It wasn't a pleasant smile.

"I didn't come here for a job. I just came to talk to you, Mr. Brown."

Max glared at the man, suddenly dizzy. He had quit drinking, but he suddenly craved vodka. Fucking Buddhism, where was it when your nuts were in the blender?

"Sorry," Max said. "What did you just call me?"

"Mr. Brown."

"I think you're in the wrong office," Max said. "My name's Fisher—Max Fisher." He wanted to rip the Dalai Lama to bits.

"I know your name," the man said.

"I get it," Max said. "This is some kind of joke, right? Angela put you up to this."

"Nobody put me up to anything," the man said.

Max hoped that this wasn't happening, that there was some explanation he couldn't imagine.

"Then why are you here?" Max's voice was almost as weak as the man's.

"I want one million dollars in cash by tomorrow at five P.M.," the man said. "I'll come back here to pick it up."

"Whoa, whoa," Max said, standing up. "Who the hell do you think you are, barging into my office like this? You know what I think I'm gonna do? I think I'm gonna call the cops."

Max reached for the phone.

"I don't think that would be a smart idea."

"Really? Why not?"

The man took a mini-cassette player out of his sweat-shirt pocket and held it up for Max to see. Max stared at the little machine, as if in a trance. He barely heard Dillon with that death-knell accent say, *"Yeah, he hired me,"* before his left arm went numb.

Later, sitting in the bar of the Mansfield, Max was getting shitfaced on Gimlet, whatever the hell that was. He wasn't even sure how he'd gotten to the bar. He remembered realizing, finally, that he wasn't dying of a heart attack—no, the fucking Buddha wouldn't put him out of his misery that easily; that Buddha, his ass was so fired—and running out of the office. At first, Max was planning to head to the ashram to center himself, but then he thought, Fuck it, and went to a bar. He started on Stoli, and worked his way up to liqueurs and other shit. He'd hit one or two or maybe three other bars on his way to the Mansfield—*hey, who was counting, right?*—and was still wearing his business suit, although it was wrinkled and stained and where the hell was his tie?

He finished his third Gimlet, screamed for another, then fumbled for his Blackberry. Muttering, "Where the hell...goddamnit...shit," he checked his two jacket pockets at least five times each before finding the thing in one of them. He thought he'd called Angela something like four hours ago to tell her how fucked they were, how they were gonna have to give the man everything, and to come meet him at the Mansfield. He called her again and was leaving another goddamn message when the next Gimlet arrived and he screamed, "Just get your ass over here, woman!" and he clicked off, knocking over the Gimlet in the same motion. The liquid stained his pants, making it look like he'd wet himself.

After Angela passed through Homeland Security—the guy had given her a nice little squeeze—she headed for the bar. The bartender smiled and asked her what she was having.

"A large Jameson, please."

"Are you Irish?"

"I am."

"Going on vacation?"

"I'm going home." Her engagement ring sparkled in the light for a moment and she added, "Home is where the heart is."

"Yeah, like that book I read in high school," the guy said smiling, *The Heart is a Lonely Hunter*."

Angela didn't get it, said, "I don't get it."

Then she noticed the guy staring at her chest.

"I like that pin," he said, although she knew it wasn't the pin that interested him.

She took a breath, expanding her bust for a couple of moments—why not make the poor guy's day?—then she let the breath out slowly and said, "Thanks, it belonged to me mother, the only legacy she left. It represents our hands reaching out to each other. It's my new good luck charm, I think."

"Wow, that's so cool," the guy said. He must've polished that same glass, what, five times?

Angela finished the Jameson in one long gulp, said, "Ta," and walked away, swinging her hips, her chest fully expanded.

Hey, you got it, you gotta strut it, right?